I0617811

Death Trap

S.R.Claridge

Global Publishing Group

Global Publishing Group

Printed in the United States of America

First trade edition: June 2012

10 9 8 7 6 5 4 3 2 1

ISBN 978-0-9898467-3-8

The author dedicates this book to her team of editors, namely Cash, Jerrye, Gary, Beth and Matt, for helping to bring the Just Call Me Angel series to life.

She would like to thank God for every blessing in her life, and her family and friends for their love, support and ongoing encouragement.

Special thanks to her husband and children for their patience and for always making her smile.

~

A complete list of books by S.R.Claridge is located at the back of this book.

For previews, reviews and information about the author, visit AuthorSRClaridge.com or find her on Facebook.

CHAPTER 1

Angel stared out the window of her grandfather, Giovanni's, private Gulfstream4 jet. A G4 was just one of the many luxuries that came with the title of Capo di Tutti Capi, the Boss of all Bosses. In typical Giovanni fashion, the G4 had been upgraded both in exterior fabrication and interior design. He added a cockpit security door and a rear access door which opened by sliding slightly inward into a hollow side panel, to facilitate emergency evacuations, or easy escapes from law enforcement. Tinted windows lined with multiple layers of polycarbonate material, were both bullet-proof and shatter proof. Likewise, the walls of anti-ballistic, polycarbonate layers allowed a gun to be fired inside the cabin with no fear of exterior penetration and loss of cabin pressure. Glancing around, Angel couldn't help wondering if Giovanni had ever ordered a hit inside the jet, and then she shuddered and forced the thought from her head.

Two tan, leather reclining chairs were adjacent to one another near the front of the aircraft. Matching brown leather couches faced one another in the middle of the jet and four Italian leather chairs were perfectly positioned around a square, embossed leather table near the back. The jet was alabaster white on the outside, but the classy interior was adorned in earth tone colors of cream, tan and brown. Typical of everything Giovanni designed, it was perfection right down to the smallest detail.

Angel mentally replayed memories of the last three weeks which she had spent on vacation in Italy with her mother, Sophia, and her Great Aunt, Olga. Beyond a doubt, the trip had been good for her soul, though she couldn't say the

5

same for her waistline. Twenty-one days of the richest Italian food she'd ever tasted made her blue jeans now fit like sausage casings. She took a deep breath, sucking in her stomach, and then sighed as she exhaled and shifted in her seat. Sophia and Olga had decided to extend their vacation and stop in New York for a few more days, but Angel was ready to head home to Chicago. Giovanni informed her that the repairs to her penthouse suite at the Towers had been completed and she missed her two furry felines, Midnight and Mo.

We should be landing in Chicago soon, she thought, gazing out the window. As eager as she was to return home, the mere thought of it caused an uneasiness to swell in her gut.   She knew exactly why. Tony Andriachini and Andrew Venturini. What was she going to do with them? Before leaving for Italy she had professed feelings for both of them, albeit in the midst of a bloody battle against the Russian Mob. *A girl shouldn't be held accountable for what she says or texts during duress,* she told herself, knowing full well that duress had nothing to do with her proclamations of affection. The problem wasn't that she regretted what she had said, but that she meant it; for both of them. Angel loved them both, differently but equally. She had hoped that the time spent away from them would bring clarity to her heart, that she would perhaps miss one of them more than the other, and then the answer would manifest itself in her longing; but that didn't happen. In fact, now she felt more confused and torn than ever. Knowing that they would both be awaiting her return with baited breath made her want to order the pilot to turn the plane around and head back to New York.

As overwhelming as her emotions were, Angel had to admit that Tony and Andrew weren't responsible for all the anxiety she felt. A greater part of the pressure building inside her came from the knowledge and fear of everything else awaiting her in Chicago. The Russian Bratva was defeated for now, but Angel wasn't entirely sure how deeply they had infiltrated the five Chicago families. The Galante Boss and Under Boss had been murdered and there was an internal battle waging for new leadership of the family. The loyalty of all members was in question and there was no room for mistakes in judgment. If dealing with the Bratva had taught her anything, it was that misguided sympathy and unearned trust could prove disastrous for her family. There had already been too many innocent lives lost.

"Ms. Maratinzano," Sean Shepherd's voice pulled her from her thoughts and she looked up in time to see him motion her toward the back of the plane. Sean, aka the Snake, was ex-Air force and had worked for Giovanni in New York for the past several years. He earned Angel's trust in Chicago less than a month earlier when he helped to stop a Russian uprising led by a vigilante group called the Vamloskaya. Though she hadn't known him for very long, his loyalty, tactical skill and military training had been proven during an attack at the Towers by The Shark, followed by a massive shoot out with the Vamloskaya on a vacant airstrip. In both instances The Snake had been influential in saving Angel's life. It was because she trusted his instincts that she requested he escort her from New York to Chicago. She also had secret hopes of convincing him to work for the Maratinzano family in Chicago instead of for her grandfather in New York. She needed to re-build her family presence in

7

the city and he was already well-acquainted with her men.

She rose from the tan reclining chair and joined the Snake on one of the couches. "What's up?" She asked, and then suddenly saw the concern in his dark brown eyes and deep lines that were formed across his forehead.

"Something's not right," he said in a hushed tone, and Angel's pulse quickened.

"What's not right?" She asked.

"We've slowed down and lowered in altitude, but we're not on course for Chicago." He checked the watch on his left wrist. "We've been hanging at 18,000 feet for the past ten minutes."

"How do you know?" Angel asked, peering out the left side of the jet and then crossing to the other couch and looking out the right side. It appeared that the Snake was right. The plane was low enough for them to see land but it looked rural, like it was divided up into perfect brown squares. There was no city in sight. "Did you ask the pilot?"

"The cockpit door is locked and when I knocked, no one answered."

"We can call the cockpit," Angel said and reached for the receiver, which hung on the wall next to the couch.

"I already tried that," the Snake mumbled. "No one's answering."

"Are you saying you think something has happened to the pilot?" Angel's eyes widened.

"No. I'm saying I have a feeling he knows exactly what he's doing and whatever he's doing isn't good." The Snake grunted, then rose from the couch and walked toward the back of the jet.

"Where are you going? What do you mean he knows exactly what he's doing?" She called after him but he didn't answer. Angel felt a pit forming in the depths of her stomach. It was that all-too-familiar intuitive pit of looming danger that made her heart beat wildly in her chest. She stared out the window desperately hoping to see the Chicago skyline and prove the Snake wrong.

When he returned to the couch he was wearing a harness that looped around his legs, his shoulders and fastened on his chest. He carried another harness and handed it to Angel. "Put this on."

She didn't need to exclaim *What!,* as she felt certain her eyeballs popping out of her head had sent the message.

"Hurry," the Snake ordered. "Slide your legs into the holes and put the straps over your shoulders." He helped her put on the harness and tightened the straps as he spoke, which was a good thing because Angel suddenly felt as if both time and her ability to move had slipped into slow motion.

"Is this a parachute?" She uttered breathlessly.

"Yours is just a harness. Mine has the chute," he answered briskly as he finished tightening her straps.

"We're not jumping!" Angel exclaimed with panic rising in her voice.

The Snake grabbed her shoulders and stared directly into her eyes with a look that told her this wasn't a joke. "It's just a precaution, but if something bad goes down, we go out." He pulled a .45 from the back of his black pants and Angel followed suit, grabbing her 9mm from the back of her jeans and holding it steadily in front.

"What's the plan?" She asked.

"I'm gonna bang on the cockpit door one more time and then I'm shooting through it."

"What if you shoot the pilot?" Angel stared at him, as if to say *are you crazy?* It was a good question, as shooting the pilot was certainly a valid concern.

"Then I fly the plane," he shrugged.

"I know you can fly a helicopter, but have you ever flown a jet?"

"Ms. Maratinzano," he cocked his head to the right, "I was a pilot in the Air force. I can fly this baby in my sleep." That should have made Angel feel better, but it didn't.

The Snake banged on the door. "Open up," he hollered. There was no response. He banged again and yelled, "Either open the door or I shoot it open." There was still no response. The Snake nudged Angel back a few steps and took aim at the door. Before he could fire off a shot the cockpit door forcefully flew open, knocking the .45 from his grip and pushing him toward the left of the door. Angel gasped as she stood face to face, staring into the cold dead eyes of the co-pilot. His body was thrust forward into her arms, knocking her to the floor beneath him. Angel shrieked and pushed at his body until she could slide out from under him and scramble to her feet. The Snake regained his balance but couldn't get to the cockpit door before the pilot pulled it shut and locked it. He fired off several rounds into the door, but they didn't penetrate the polycarbonate protective layers.

The Snake backed up and cursed aloud.

Angel pointed to the co-pilot. "He's dead," she muttered as a statement of the obvious.

"Holy Mary Mother of..." the Snake blurted but stopped before finishing his sentence. He bent down and without touching the body, he analyzed the knife handle sticking out of the co-pilot's chest.

"We got a problem," the Snake said.

Ya think! Her mind screamed. "What?" Angel asked.

The Snake rose to his feet, pulled a cell phone from his pant pocket and took a picture of the knife. "We've got to get off the plane." He headed for the back of the plane with Angel in tow. "We've got to get off the plane now."

She felt as if she might vomit from the pure, unadulterated fear that was surging through her body. "I hate to point out the obvious, but I don't have a parachute and I really don't like heights and I think we'll have a better chance if we wait until we land."

The Snake grabbed Angel by her harness, spun her around to face the door of the plane, and pulled her in so close she could feel the harness on his chest digging into her back. "You don't need a chute because you'll be strapped to me." He connected her harness to his at the shoulders and hips and pulled it so tight she felt as if she could barely breathe. "And if we stay until it lands there will be no chance of escape."

"How do you know?" Angel uttered.

"Because we're in a hostage situation and one of two things is gonna go down. Either the pilot has been paid to blow this plane to smithereens before landing it, or he's going to land it and we'll be escorted off by men who don't negotiate and place no value for on our life."

"How can you be sure? If he blows up the plane, he'll kill himself too," Angel's voice shook with fear.

"That's what terrorists do."

"Terrorists?" Angel gasped.

"I don't have time to prove it to you now. You're just gonna have to trust me."

She shook her head back and forth. "No, Sean!" She pleaded. "I can't jump!"

"With all due respect Ms. Maratinzano, it's really not up to you anymore." He was right. With his six feet, two-inch muscular frame, he pressed her toward the door, twisted the release handle and slid it open. She was harnessed so tightly to him that it rendered her powerless to struggle. The sound of the air and the engine overtook her senses.

Warm tears rushed down her cheeks. "I can't jump," she cried as he lowered them both to a squatting position. "I can't do it!"

"You don't have to jump. Just keep your arms to your chest and your legs bent back at the knees. I'll do all the work." He grabbed her hands which now trembled uncontrollably. "Don't panic and don't flail." She felt the Snake's breath against her ear as he spoke with his lips almost touching her. "I won't let you die, Angel. I took an oath to your grandfather that I would protect you even to the death. I never break an oath."

"I can't do this," she said, breaking into sobs.

The Snake released her hands, rocked back on his heels, gripped both sides of the doorway and thrust himself and Angel from the back of the jet. They flipped upside down and for a brief second Angel saw the plane above her before they rotated back around and she found herself facing the ground. Panic filled her and she drew her arms into her chest and tried to force herself not to flail. The air was ice cold and beat against her skin with a force unlike anything she had ever experienced. Trapped between the air pressure, the tightened harness on her chest and the weight of The Snake on her back, Angel felt like she couldn't breathe. Every time she opened her mouth to gasp for air, it felt like her lips and skin were being blown right off her face. Her hair whipped around wildly and stung as it smacked against her cheeks and stabbed into her eyes. She was certain it was also striking the Snake and hoped it wouldn't distract him from pulling the ripcord.

There was no way of knowing how far they had fallen when the jet exploded, but it couldn't have been very far because the explosion sent a wave of heat over them. The Snake yelled something in her ear, but she couldn't understand what he said; and then they spun out of control. Every muscle in her body was rigid as they plummeted toward the earth.

It seemed like it took forever for the chute to open. When it finally did, Angel's legs flew forward with such force that she felt an upward sensation in her stomach. In a matter of seconds, they went from falling to floating and it took Angel a few seconds to adjust to this new sensation. The Snake reached around to the front of her harness and loosened the straps. "Breathe," he said. "The hard part's over."

She filled her lungs and exhaled several times, trying to calm herself. "Are we falling too fast?" She asked, nervously watching the ground approach.

The Snake used all his strength to hold the chute steady. "We're on the back-up. The main chute didn't open."

Angel fought against rising panic. "What happened to the main chute?"

"I don't know. I felt an impact with the explosion. Something hit us and must have damaged it."

Angel wasn't sure exactly what that meant. "Are we going to crash?" She wailed.

"We'll be fine, but on landing I want you to lift your legs waist high and stick them out in front of you," he instructed.

13

Angel wasn't up for arguing. She leaned her head back against his chest and tried to focus on the horizon and not the ground. "Where are we?"

"I dunno," he answered, berating himself. "When we took off I knew we were on course for Chicago, but after that I didn't pay attention until it was too late." He cursed aloud. "It was Giovanni's regular flight crew. I talked with them at the hanger before we boarded. I had no reason to suspect danger."

"It's not your fault," Angel exhaled. They fell steadily for a few more minutes and Angel searched the horizon for any sign of a city or a town. It was farm land for as far as the eye could see.

"We're coming in fast," the Snake blurted. "Get your legs up as far as you can and hold them there." That was easier said than done while wearing a harness, but Angel pulled them up and held tightly, as her muscles trembled.

"We're gonna crash!" She shrieked as the ground grew rapidly closer.

"Calm down!" He ordered. "I've done this a thousand times."

"You've landed before with another person strapped to you, right?" When he hesitated to answer, she was sorry she had asked.

A few seconds later the Snake's feet touched the ground and they slid into a corn field, with Angel lying atop him. She had heard the loud snap when they first touched down and assumed it was the brittle corn stalks breaking beneath their weight; but now, hearing deep moans from the Snake, Angel knew he was injured.

"Are you okay?" She asked.

He unhooked her shoulders from his and then her hips. She climbed off of him, rolled to the side and immediately scanned his body for blood. "It's my right leg," he winced. "Something snapped in my right leg."

"I heard it," Angel grimaced. She unbuckled the harness from around his chest, slid it off each shoulder and carefully down each leg. She removed her harness as well. "Do you think you can walk if you lean on me?" She tried to pull him up, but even a sitting position was so painful, that he yelped in agony and flopped back down. "How did this happen? I thought you said you've parachuted a thousand times?"

"I have, but we were coming in too fast. Whatever hit us must have damaged both chutes." He winced from the pain. "We're lucky it didn't do more damage."

Angel gripped his fingers and gave them a squeeze. "Thank you," she said, aware that the mere phrase didn't come remotely close to expressing the gratitude she felt. "You have a bad habit of saving my life," she teased.

His dimple indented as he smiled. "Just doing my job, ma'am."

Angel stood up and looked around. She saw nothing but corn fields. "What do we do now?"

"Call Chase. He can track you with your phone. Have him bring the chopper."

"My phone blew up with the jet." Angel deflated. "It was in my purse."

"Get mine from my right front pocket. Maybe he can use the signal to locate us." The Snake's phone was not outfitted with the same tracking device Chase had placed in Angel's, Tony's and Andrew's, but there was still a chance he could locate them using a GPS signal.

Angel carefully slid her fingers into his pant pocket and pulled out the cell phone. She dialed Chase but nothing happened. "It's not working," she exhaled. "There's no signal here. Not even one bar."

"Then you've got to go for help," the Snake mumbled.

"I can't just leave you here. It's almost dark and we're in the middle of nowhere." Angel was beginning to have that intuitive feeling of looming danger again. "I don't even know what state we're in. What if there are wild animals and they attack you? What if the temperature drops to below zero and you freeze to death?"

The Snake cracked a smile. He started to chuckle and then grabbed his leg and moaned, "Don't make me laugh. It hurts to laugh."

"I'm serious!" She demanded, with her arms crossed and a stomp of her foot.

"We're somewhere close to Chicago. Maybe even in Illinois, Wisconsin or Iowa." Angel could tell he was guessing. "There are no wild animals that are going to come eat me and I doubt a severe cold front will suddenly move in." He couldn't say it without his lips curling into a grin and his dimple sinking in.

"Okay, say I go and get help. How will I find you again in the dark?"

He slid the wristwatch from his left arm and handed it to her. "Use the compass and walk east. I think I saw a barn or some type of structure off in the distance to the east when we were falling. When you come back just walk straight west until you run into me."

Angel swallowed hard. *I'm a city girl,* she thought. *I don't know how to use a compass and traverse corn fields in the dark."*

"Look around, do you see any kind of landmark?" He asked.

Angel looked in every direction. "There's a clump of trees over that way," she pointed over the Snake's head.

"That's west. How far do you think we are from the trees?"

Angel threw her hands up. "I don't know. Far."

"Is it like a football field away or farther?"

Angel put her hands on her hips. *Seriously? I've never stood on a football field to know how big it is.* "I guess it's like a football field."

She could tell the Snake was getting frustrated. "Okay, just memorize the image in your mind so that you can use it to find me again," he explained. "Take my phone with you and keep checking for a signal. Call Chase as soon as you're able." The Snake gave her a military salute. "You can do this," he said. "Oh, and Ms. Maratinzano?" He called after her. "Keep your gun handy. Just in case."

She pulled the gun from the back of her pants, thankful it had not fallen out during their parachuting escapade. Then again, it had been wedged between her and the Snake so tightly that there was no way it could have fallen. "Call me Angel," she told him for the umpteenth time.

"I'll call you Angel when you call me Sean. Deal?"

"I thought you wanted to be called the Snake?" Angel puzzled.

"Only in front of the other bogata boys. It's my public persona," he joked and Angel smiled. "But in private I'm just Sean."

She put the watch on her left wrist and held the gun in her right hand. "I'll be back soon," she told him.

"I'll be here," he said with a nod. "Oh, and Angel," he paused as if he were debating on whether to say what was on his mind. "The pilot could have been flying low over this area for a reason, maybe even to land somewhere around here. Just because it blew up doesn't mean the pilot knew it was going to blow. So be careful."

Angel nodded. She hated the idea of walking off into the night all by herself and leaving him behind. She grunted as she trudged off due east through the dried-up corn field, wishing now that she had never watched the movie, Children of the Corn.

CHAPTER 2

Upon receiving an emergency text from Chase, Andrew and Tony immediately headed for the Towers to join him in the meeting room, which was a private floor Giovanni had specifically designed for high-level meetings. It could only be accessed by punching a secret code into the elevator key pad. Prior to the Russian attack on the Towers, which was led by a traitor in Giovanni's organization named the Shark, Giovanni had been the only person to know the code. Now, the code had been changed and Angel, Chase and Andrew were entrusted with the information.

Aware that Angel was returning home in the evening, Tony and Andrew were both in close proximity to the Towers, so when they received Chase's text, it didn't take them long to arrive. In fact, they arrived at exactly the same time and shared the elevator up.

"You just happened to be in the area?" Tony sarcastically asked, aware that Andrew was as anxious for Angel to return as he was. Their feelings for Angel had become a source of competitive tension.

"Same as you," Andrew quipped, while punching the code into the elevator keypad.

"How do you know the code?" Tony's eyebrows raised and he could tell that Andrew secretly enjoyed the fact that he had something over him.

"Giovanni gave it to me before he left for New York." He smirked, glancing sideways at Tony. "He didn't give it you?"

The elevator door opened and Tony pushed passed Andrew and made a beeline for Chase, who was sitting at the end of a rectangular mahogany table with two laptops open in front of him. "What's going on, Ace?" Tony asked.

Chase spastically twirled a pencil between the fingers of his right hand and clicked away at the keyboard with his left. He bounced his knees up and down and shook his head. "It's bad man, it's real bad."

"What's real bad?" Andrew asked, as he joined Tony to peer over Chase's shoulder. "Did you find more Russians in our families?"

"Worse, man," Chase shook his head. "Way worse."

"Few things are worse than the Bratva," Tony said.

"I've been tracking Giovanni's jet and all of a sudden it disappeared."

"What do you mean it disappeared?" Andrew and Tony blurted almost in unison.

"It just vanished off my radar," Chase shook his head. "So I tried to lock onto Angel's phone, but it's gone too."

"There's obviously something wrong with your equipment," Andrew began but Chase cut him off.

"No way, man, I checked everything. I double checked everything." He wiggled anxiously in his seat. "The Capo di Tutti Capi is always tracked by FBI security for obvious reasons," Chase raised his eyebrows as he spoke, "so I contacted Sal to see if he could locate the plane." Sal was a long-time FBI contact Andrew frequently used with police business. He had become a trusted friend. "Sal sent me some footage that was picked up by a department of defense satellite." Chase pulled up the video footage on his screen. "Here it is." He pressed a button as they all huddled around the screen, watching as the G4 exploded into a million tiny pieces.

They stared, stunned into silence. "There's no proof that was Giovanni's jet," Tony blurted.

"I compared the explosion coordinates to the last radar coordinates before it disappeared and they're the same, man," Chase explained.

"Where was the explosion?" Andrew asked.

"Somewhere over Fayette, Iowa," Chase answered. "Out in the middle of nowhere."

"Where's Fayette, Iowa?" Tony asked.

"Northeastern part of the state," Chase answered.

"I'm not following," Tony uttered. "Why would Giovanni's jet be flying over northern Iowa?"

"That's way off course," Andrew added.

"I know it is, man, it's crazy-ass off course," Chase admitted. "But it was his plane." Chase dropped his head. "I'm still trying to isolate the video and enhance the picture of the jet just before the explosion to verify that Giovanni's insignia is on the outside." He clicked rapidly on the keyboard until an image of the jet displayed. "But when it's magnified it's too blurry to see anything."

"It's a coincidence," Andrew exhaled and shook his head.

"Maybe they already landed in Chicago and then took off again. Maybe Angel's already on her way here." Tony's voice was filled with worry.

Chase lowered his eyes and shook his head. "No, man, it never landed."

"Tell me she wasn't on that plane."
Andrew's face was red and his teeth clenched as he

searched Chase's eyes. He raised his voice. "Tell me she wasn't on that plane," he yelled.

Chase stared up at him and for a brief moment sat perfectly still. No wiggling. No bouncing. No twirling pencils or fingers darting wildly over a keypad. He just sat, staring at Andrew. "I can't tell you that, man."

Tony paced wildly across the room and slammed his fist down atop the mahogany bar, spewing obscenities. "What do you mean you can't tell us that?" He hollered, his hands beginning to shake. "What does that mean? Was she on the plane or wasn't she?"

Chase dropped his head. "She was on the plane." His voice was almost inaudible, as if verbalizing it made it real and final.

"Are you positive?" Andrew asked. "Maybe Giovanni needed the plane for something else and she's still in New York. We need to call Giovanni and double-check that..." his voice tapered off.

"I already called, man," Chase cut Andrew off mid-sentence. "She and the Snake boarded the plane in New York."

Andrew sank slowly into a chair next to Chase and for several minutes no one spoke. The room was filled with silent agony.

"I need to know what happened," Andrew said quietly. "I need to know if it was an attack or a malfunction."

"I'm on it," Chase whispered, and then sitting up straighter, began clicking at his keyboard.

CHAPTER 3

Somehow it had been leaked to the press that Giovanni's private jet, with his granddaughter aboard, had been blown out of the sky, and now everyone wanted to catch a glimpse of the Capo di Tutti Capi in his hour of despair. Giovanni's house was buzzing with people. The long driveway leading to his two story, red brick with black trim, Victorian home was lined with cars as all his men responded to the news of Angel's death. The black gates that sequestered his estate were heavily guarded and the media were kept outside, chomping at the bit.

Giovanni's Compare, Carl Cusanelli, had promised to release a statement by morning and the paparazzi waited with baited breath.

Men lined the sidewalk and steps leading to the front door, poured into the foyer and lined the long hallway which emptied into the den where Giovanni sat in his deep brown leather studded arm chair. One by one the men entered the den through the glass French doors, kissed the top of his hand and offered their condolences. Giovanni sat rigidly somber, never uttering a word, but giving each man a mournful nod as a mere acknowledgment of the respect they had shown. Carl stayed until everyone, except Giovanni's select bodyguards, left; then he made his way to the den to join his life-long friend in his hour of need.

Closing the French doors behind him, he walked passed Giovanni's chair and straight to the built in bar that sat in the far left corner of the room, next to the red brick fireplace. He poured two Scotches, both neat, handed one to Giovanni and then sat on the brown leather couch across from him.

"This is a fine mess," he uttered as he exhaled and loosened the black tie from around his neck.

Giovanni gave a nod and sipped his Scotch.

"We've got the best men we have on the investigation. If there was foul play we'll find out who did this and they'll pay."

Giovanni's face tensed and then released in an exasperated sigh of sorrow. "Nothing I do will bring her back to me."

Carl leaned forward with his elbows on his knees and nodded his head in agreement. "No, we can't bring her back." His slicked back wavy gray hair curled up at the base of his neck and bounced slightly as he nodded his head. "What do you want me to tell the press?"

Giovanni gritted his teeth and tensed his jaw. "They take pleasure in my pain."

Carl replied, "We don't have to tell them anything. We can simply say that you are not ready to make a statement."

"Bah," Giovanni scoffed and raised his hand in the air. "Tell them to go to hell."

Carl rose from the couch and carried both of their empty glasses to the bar and set them inside the small sink. "I will stay the night and deal with the press in the morning."

"Si," Giovanni agreed. "Those vultures will be circling my gates all night."

Sophia lay in the guest room bed upstairs, sobbing into Olga's lap. With tears streaming down her cheeks, Olga stroked Sophia's dark brown hair and prayed in Italian.

"I just got her back," Sophia wailed, "only to have her taken from me. I should have been on that plane with her."

Sophia cried herself to sleep in Olga's arms, and as soon as Olga knew she could sneak away without waking her, she made her way downstairs to the kitchen to do what she did best. Cook. It didn't matter that it was midnight. She needed to cook.

Olga poked her head into the den and saw Giovanni sitting statue like in his chair.

"I'm making some ravioli and fresh cannoli," she said, waddling in and sitting on the couch beside his chair.

"I will not be eating at this hour," Giovanni mumbled in a low, soft tone.

"But you haven't eaten anything all evening. Starving ourselves won't change what's happened," she began but he cut her off.

"I said I will not be eating, Lucia!" His eyes flashed with a volatile mixture of anger and grief and Olga leapt to her feet, catching her breath.

"Merciful Heavens! You're not the only one mourning, you old coot." She shook her fist at him. "I've been with her longer than anyone. She was my Angel. MY Angel!" Olga broke into sobs and waddled quickly back to the kitchen. She plunked her rounded hips into one of the walnut chairs, buried her face in her palms and wept. When the ravioli and cannoli were finished, she put them in the refrigerator and went upstairs to bed. The weight of her grief left no room for hunger and she crawled into bed, empty.

CHAPTER 4

Angel's legs ached from traipsing through the corn fields. It was pitch black and the rough stalks stabbed at her ankles and scraped her shins. She had repeatedly checked the Snake's phone for a signal, but there was nothing. It was as if they had landed in a technological black hole. She used the light from the phone as a flashlight and now the battery was running low. Clouds hung overhead, blocking any hope of using the moonlight to guide her. She didn't want to admit it, even to herself, but she was scared. The country was foreign to a city girl like her and though she could handle the occasional rat, the thought of stumbling upon a snake or a coyote was enough to unravel her nerves. She reminded herself that she had gone to college in the small town of Columbia, Missouri, where she attended bon fire parties and hay rides that were out in the middle of the country; but she hadn't been alone then and being alone in the dark, in the middle of nowhere was the scariest part. *How can a woman who has faced a grenade launcher and been hurled out of an airplane be afraid of running into a snake?* She asked herself, but the answer didn't really matter. The truth was she was scared and nothing was going to change that.

The compass proved that she hadn't been walking in circles despite the fact that the scenery around her hadn't changed. Everything looked exactly the same. It was cornfield after cornfield after cornfield. The air was getting cooler and

Angel's mind began to wonder what would happen if she couldn't find a shelter and couldn't find her way back to the Snake. Her hands grew clammy and she gripped the phone tighter.

She was growing tired and walking slower, when she finally saw a dim light off in the distance and felt a surge of hope at the thought of finding help. She started to move faster toward the light, when a sudden crunching sound stopped her dead in her tracks. The crunching footsteps continued even after she had stopped and Angel instinctively ducked down among the stalks of corn. The footsteps were growing closer and with a lump forming in her throat, she slid the cell phone into her pocket and pulled the 9mm from the back of her waistband. Sliding the safety off, she held the gun steady while her mind raced with the unimaginable.

A sense of relief rushed over her when she heard a man's voice. At least she knew she wasn't being tracked by a wild animal. Still, she had to be cautious. The Snake's warning about the pilot flying low over this area for a reason was fresh in her mind.

"Who's there? I know you're out here. Show yourself," he called into the darkness.

Angel hesitated to move.

"You're trespassing on private property," he yelled. "I'll shoot if I have to."

Now that she knew he was armed, she felt less relaxed about the idea of standing up and showing herself; but what were the options? The Snake needed medical attention and she wasn't going to be able to help him alone. Should she trust a stranger who's out in a corn field in the dark with a gun?

Angel swallowed hard, trying not to let paranoia take hold as thoughts bounced around in her mind. *He's probably just some farmer who noticed someone trespassing on his land and came to check it out,* she told herself. *Then again, it's pitch black out so how in the world would he have noticed me?* She questioned. *Of course, I had the cell phone light on, so it's possible he saw a light from far away.* That seemed like a stretch. Staying crouched down she called out, "I'll come out, just please put your gun down."

"You're a woman?" He blurted. "What are you doing out here at night?"

"If you put down your gun I'll come out and tell you," Angel answered and heard him shuffle his feet.

"Okay, my gun is down, now come out."

Angel rose slowly and took two steps toward the shadowy figure of a man. "I'm right here," she said and he turned to face her. "You're not the only one with a gun so I suggest you don't make any sudden movements in my direction."

He had been holding it down, but now lowered his shotgun all the way to the ground and raised both hands into the air. "Listen lady, I don't know who you are, but I don't want no trouble with you. I came out here because I thought maybe some kids were out here messing around in the field."

Angel crept closer and used the cell phone light to get a good look at him. He stood about six foot four inches tall, had a body builder stature and light brown hair. She couldn't discern the color of his eyes, but his skin was sun-kissed brown and leathery, and he looked like he worked outside in the sun every day of his life. He had on blue jeans, a green and black flannel shirt which hung open over a tan tee and brown work boots, laced up into double knots. Judging from the contour of his face, she guessed him to be somewhere in his early thirties. "Do you live close?"

"Across the field," he said, pointing in a northeast direction.

"Do you live alone?"

"Nah, I live with the Nelson's. Well, I live on their land and I run their farm." He shuffled his feet. "Are you in some kind of trouble, ma'am?"

"What state is this?" Angel blurted.

"Fayette, Iowa," he answered slowly and Angel could tell by his inflection that her question surprised him.

Iowa, she repeated it in her mind, *why did it have to be Iowa?* Iowa reminded her of only one thing, Denny and his encampment, his link to the Russians and the fact that she still didn't know how deep their infiltration ran. She gripped her gun tighter. "I'm not alone. I have a partner who's been injured. He's straight west of here by a clump of trees. Can you take me to pick him up and then get us to a hospital?"

"The closest medical clinic is the Gundersen Clinic in downtown Fayette, but they ain't open after eight."

Angel was exasperated. How could a medical center close at eight o'clock? She lowered her gun. "Will you pick up my friend? We can figure out what to do from there."

He lifted his shot gun and carried it in his right hand with the barrel pointing to the ground. "My name's Michael, but my friends call me Big Mike," he said and extended his left hand toward Angel.

"Angel," she said, shaking his hand.

"That's a pretty name."

They walked in silence for a few seconds and then Angel asked. "Do you have a phone that works?"

29

"There's no cell phone coverage out here. This whole area's a dead zone. I don't have a phone at my place, but there's a land line in the Nelson's home. I'm sure they won't mind if you use it."

How can someone live without a phone? Angel wondered.

Big Mike opened the front door to a one-room, wooden cabin like something seen in an episode of Little House on the Prairie. There was a fire burning in the stone fireplace and one overhead light with antlers protruding from it that barely illumed the room. To the right of the door was a kitchenette area, with an oven and a stove top, a refrigerator, and a sink with two small cabinets above it. A small bar jetted out, dividing the kitchen from the rest of the room and two stools were tucked neatly beneath. There was a black leather couch in front of the fireplace with a colorful quilt thrown over the back and a wooden coffee table. A large plush rug in subtle earth tones covered the wooden floor and Angel noticed right away that there was a Moose theme. There were Moose on the rug, on the curtains and on the spread that covered the double bed in the far corner to the left.

"You like Moose?" Angel asked.

Big Mike chuckled aloud. "It sure looks that way don't it? Mrs. Nelson decorated the place."

There was a narrow door to the immediate left which led to a bathroom, where Moose hand towels and a Moose shower curtain hung. Angel couldn't help noticing how tidy the place was, especially since a single man lived here. There were no dirty dishes in the sink or even clean ones stacked on the counter to be put away. There was no toothpaste splattered on the mirror and even the bed was made complete with throw pillows set in a picturesque manner. "Were you expecting someone?" Angel asked, considering the possibility that he had cleaned because a visitor was arriving.

"Nah," Big Mike shook his head. "Why?"

"Where I come from single men living alone aren't usually so tidy."

"Mrs. Nelson cleans the place every morning when I leave for work. When I come home it's clean as a whistle."

"Wow, where I can get me a Mrs. Nelson?" Angel joked. *I have an Aunt Olga,* she thought to herself, *but cleaning's not high on her priority list.*

The Nelson's weren't home and Big Mike explained that he and Angel would have to wait until they came back to use their phone. "House rules," he said. "I'm not allowed inside when they're gone."

They climbed into Big Mike's black Ford pick-up and headed due west on a dirt road that ran alongside the corn field. Angel looked at herself in the side mirror and grimaced. From skydiving her hair looked like she had touched one of those static balls at the children's museum. It was sticking up all over. She also noticed her right silver hoop earring was missing. *Serves me right for jumping out of a plane with my good hoops on,* she sighed to herself. She casually tried to flatten her hair but it was no use. The tangles were so deeply knotted that it was going to take a wire brush to get through it.

Big Mike grinned at her and for the first time Angel saw the color of his eyes and the sincerity of his face. His eyes were green and they lit up when he smiled. "I was gonna say something about your hair but I figured, since we just met, it would be impolite."

31

Angel laughed. "That was considerate of you."

"So why is your hair like that?"

Angel inhaled and let out a loud sigh. "I jumped from a plane earlier today. Actually, I didn't really jump; I was strapped to someone who jumped."

Mike glanced over with sudden alarm on his face. "Your friend, the one we're going to pick up, jumped with you?" Angel nodded. "Are his legs broken? Is that why you left him where you landed?"

Angel described the jump and the landing. "I'm guessing it's broken because he couldn't even stand up."

Big Mike shook his head and pushed down on the accelerator. "Why did you jump?"

"It's a long story," Angel said, reaching up and grabbing the handle above her window as he sped up.

She couldn't ignore the fact that there was an intensity on Big Mike's face that hadn't been there before and that he was suddenly driving faster. "We don't have a skydiving center in Fayette. I heard they got one near Sumner, but I never saw anybody jumping around these parts."

"We weren't really planning on jumping. It was sort of an emergency evacuation."

He brought the truck to a stop, killed the lights and turned to face her. "Look, there are no skydiving places anywhere around these parts. I don't know what kind of trouble you're in, but if you want my help, you better come clean with me right here and right now."

His jawline tensed and Angel could feel prickly tentacles of fear working their way up her spine. "The jet was going to explode, so my friend and I jumped," she summed up, leaving out the relevant details.

"The plane DID explode," Big Mike said. "How did you know ahead of time that it was going to? Did you plant a bomb on it?"

"No, but the pilot had been compromised."

She could tell Big Mike wasn't buying her story. He leaned over, opened the glove compartment and pulled out a police radio. "It's a hobby," he said and turned on the radio. "I like to listen to what's going on. Do you want to know what's going on?"

Angel licked her lips. "I guess so," she answered slowly, trying to get a read on Big Mike.

He abruptly turned off the radio. "I'll just tell you. There's a warrant out for your arrest, at least I think it's you. You and a man. They said the two of you might have jumped from a plane and then blew it up. They also said that you are armed and dangerous."

Angel dropped her head and stared at the floorboard. *Why would the police think that we were armed and dangerous?* It didn't make sense. "Someone must have seen us parachute out," she mumbled more to herself than to him. "And if that's the case, then they'll be looking for us." She glanced over at Big Mike. Even though her gut told her that she could trust him, fear reminded her to trust no one, and pulling the 9mm from her jeans, she aimed it at him.

Big Mike's eyes widened. "What are you doing?"

She hated the fact that she had to resort to violence, but there was no other option. "Put both hands on the steering wheel and leave them there," she ordered and he followed her instructions. "My name is Michelangela Maratinzano and I am head of the Maratinzano Crime Family in Chicago.

Someone tried to blow me up today in my grandfather's jet. I don't know who and I don't know why. If the police are looking for me, that tells me that they are being paid off by whoever wants me dead. Right now I need to find my friend. Are you going to help me or am I pulling this trigger?"

CHAPTER 5

The ringing of Giovanni's doorbell jolted Olga awake. She threw on her yellow robe and slippers and waddled quickly down the hall to where Sophia slept. Sophia was already out of bed and heading for the staircase. They stopped at the top of the stairs and listened as Giovanni's bodyguards instructed two men to wait in the foyer.

"What's going on?" Sophia hollered down to the men.

"We've been instructed to talk directly to Giovanni," one of them answered.

"Only to Giovanni," the other one added.

Olga and Sophia crept down the steps toward the den, where Giovanni was just taking a seat in his armed chair and Carl was tying the belt on his black satin robe. "What's this all about?" Olga asked him.

"I do not know yet," Giovanni replied, adjusting himself in his chair. "You two cannot be present for this meeting. Go back to your rooms and if it is anything relevant to what has occurred, I will inform you immediately." His authoritative tone indicated that arguing or trying to persuade him otherwise was out of the question. So they left, but instead of returning to their rooms, like spying little school girls, they sneaked into the kitchen to eavesdrop.

Giovanni's bodyguards escorted the two men into the den. "Gentlemen," Carl greeted them and motioned with his hand that they should be seated on the couch. He then positioned himself behind Giovanni's chair. "It is late so I presume this information is of such importance that it could not have waited until a decent hour," Carl spoke with a hint of annoyance in his voice.

"It could have waited, sir, but we didn't think you'd want us to wait," the short, stocky man stammered, while running his fingers over his black goatee.

"Yeah, we thought you'd want to know right away," the leaner, younger man added.

Giovanni watched them with a scrutinizing eye. "What bogata are you from?"

"Cullato," the younger man said. "But we ain't Made yet."

Giovanni raised an eyebrow and motioned for Carl to bend down so he could whisper something in his ear. When he did Giovanni whispered, "Bring any information we have on these men." Carl excused himself and returned within a few moments with a manila file folder. He handed it to Giovanni.

Clearing his throat, Giovanni opened the folder and read from the file. "You," he pointed to the younger, leaner man. "You are John Paul Selento, twenty-six years old, born and raised in Brooklyn, arrested for small crimes, worked for the Cullatos for the past two years. Am I missing anything?"

John Paul's eyes widened. "No, sir, that's me."

Giovanni gave a nod and then turned the page and read from the file again, this time addressing the shorter, stockier man with the coal black goatee. "You're name is Michael Serci, son of Joseph and Maria Serci, born in Brooklyn, raised primarily by your Aunt and Uncle in the Bronx. Arrested for small crimes and you've worked the

36

past several years for the Cullatos and the Galantes. Am I missing anything?"

Michael looked up with disgust in his eyes. "Nope."

"Are you sure there isn't anything else you'd like the Capo di Tutti Capi to know?" Carl asked him.

Michael leapt to his feet. "My past don't matter. I got information for you now, so do you want it or not?"

Giovanni studied him and then pointed to John Paul. "Does he have the information too?"

The "yeah" just barely slid from Michael's lips when Carl pulled his .45 and shot him through the forehead.

John Paul dove to the side of the couch, cowering and wailing. "What was that for? Don't kill me. Please don't kill me."

"I didn't like his attitude," Carl said and slid the gun back under his robe.

The sound of the shot brought Giovanni's bodyguards into the room with their guns drawn. "Put your weapons away," Giovanni said as he rose from his chair, "and clean up this mess. We'll continue our conversation in my office."

Two of the bodyguards escorted John Paul out of the den and toward the office, while the other two began cleaning up Michael's body.

"My apologies about the couch," Carl said to Giovanni.

"Bah," he grunted. "Leather cleans up nicely."

Sophia and Olga sat motionless at the kitchen table, having overheard everything that transpired in the den. As soon as the men left the den, Olga grabbed Sophia's arm. "C'mon," she said, pulling Sophia toward the hall.

"Where are we going?"

"Merciful Heavens, don't you want to find out what John Paul has to say?"

Sophia shrugged. "Not really. He's probably going to end up dead too."

Olga convinced Sophia to sneak down the hallway and listen outside the office door. "We can sit in the living room and probably hear them through the wall," she said excitedly. They quietly made their way to the living room, which looked like it was rarely used. The furniture was old style Victorian, hard-backed chairs and a divan that sat against the far wall. Olga and Sophia sat facing each other on a loveseat and pressed their ears against the wall that stood between them and Giovanni's office. Olga had been right. They could hear every word, clear as a bell.

CHAPTER 6

Chase sat for hours clicking at the keyboard and re-playing the satellite feed of the G4 explosion. Over and over he watched it, hoping to find a clue as to what might have gone wrong. He enhanced the video until it looked like nothing but a big blur across the screen. Andrew told him to quit, but he couldn't. Something in his gut wouldn't let him accept the fact that Angel was gone. Not after everything they'd been through. Not this way. If there was even the slightest possibility she was alive, he was going to find her.

"Why don't you call it a night," Andrew said upon returning to the meeting room.

Chase rubbed his eyes. "No can do, not 'til I know what the hell happened up there." Andrew took a seat in the chair next to him. "Did you talk to Giovanni?"

Andrew nodded slowly and bit the side of his lip. "Yeah," he exhaled. "He's not good."

"What about Olga and Sophia? I bet they aren't so good either."

"None of us are." Andrew's eyes watered, as the words caught in his throat. "I'm going to go check on Tony. Let me know if you find anything." He rose from the chair, rubbed the corner of his eyes with his index finger and headed for the elevator.

"Where is Tony?" Chase asked.

"He went upstairs to the Penthouse. I told Giovanni, with his permission, we'd probably all stay here tonight."

"Right on," Chase agreed and turned back to his computer.

Tony stood on the roof top balcony, gazing up at the night sky. He leaned his elbows on the concrete surrounding wall and let tears of mourning roll down his cheeks. He couldn't believe she was gone. When he heard Andrew enter the Penthouse, he wiped his face with his t-shirt and stood up a little straighter.

"Tony?" Andrew called.

"I'm out here," he answered.

Andrew stood next to Tony and stared out at the city lights. "I told Giovanni we'd all stay here tonight just in case."

"Just in case what?" Anger seeped into Tony's tone. "She's not coming back."

"We don't know that yet," Andrew's jaw tensed.

Tony shook his head and bit his lip. "Yeah we do."

"Well, I'm not giving up hope yet," Andrew said softly.

"What do you think, Ace? You think she survived the explosion? You think she magically got off the plane before it blew up?" The veins were protruding from Tony's neck, as he screamed in Andrew's face.

"Back down," Andrew said, raising his hands in the air, gesturing for Tony to calm down. "All I'm saying is until we know what happened I'm choosing to believe she's alive."

"You're a fool, man," Tony said as he shoved Andrew's hands away and shook his head in disgust. Andrew grabbed Tony by his shirt and slammed him backwards against the wall. "You want to go, let's go!" Tony hollered, pushing Andrew away and taking a swing at his head.

Andrew retaliated with a swift fist to Tony's left jaw. He flew backwards, slamming into the wrought iron table and chairs. Tony growled and dove into Andrew, wrapping his arms around his waist and hurling them both to the ground.

Obscenities and name-calling filled the night air, as they pounded out their anger and grief in fists of rage.

The sound of Chase's voice brought their battle to an abrupt halt, and they stood bloody and bruised. "Are you freaking-ass crazy?" Chase yelled. "Are you trying to kill each other?"

"Good idea, Ace," Tony grunted and in one fluid motion, he grabbed the .45 from his waistband and pointed it at Andrew's head.

"Whoa, man," Chase blurted. "Take it easy, man."

Andrew slowly rose to his feet, panting from the fight. "Really?" He narrowed his brows and licked blood from his split lower lip. "Are you really going to shoot me? You think that's going to bring her back and make everything better?"

Tony lowered his piece and tucked it back into his jeans. "No, I just wanted you to know I could if I wanted to." Tony stormed passed Chase and into the family room. He needed to calm down and get his emotions under control, but he didn't know how. He sat down on the couch and buried his face in his hands.

Chase stared wide-eyed at Andrew. "That was some crazy-ass shit right there," he said, nodding his spikey head up and down.

"Yeah," Andrew said and ran his fingertips over his bottom lip. "Tony may be one helluva shooter, but he sucks as a fighter."

"I wouldn't say that to his face, man," Chase warned. "He's got a crazy-ass look in his eyes."

Andrew straightened his black shirt and adjusted his holster strap. "Did you come up here for a reason?" He asked, and Chase immediately jumped in the air and smacked his hands together.

"Yeah!" He said, "You guys got me all distracted. You've got to see this!" He dashed inside to the dining room table where he had set down his laptop. "I found something."

Chase started tapping at the keyboard and Andrew leaned in over his shoulder to watch the screen. "What are we looking at here?" Andrew asked.

"I pulled a picture from the satellite feed and increased it by 200%, which is why it's so crazy-ass blurry."

"Okay," Andrew said slowly, in a tone that made it obvious he wasn't following the relevance of Chase's actions.

"I started thinking, what if we're looking in the wrong place?" Chase's fingers flew wildly over the keys. "I've been looking for something ON the actual jet, but what if the key to what happened is something around the jet?"

"It doesn't matter," Tony exhaled and lifted himself from the couch.

"It does matter," Chase blurted. "Don't you want to know if the plane blew up because of a malfunction or if someone shot her out the sky?"

"Either way, it won't bring Angel back." Tony stared at the floor, his jaw tightening and his hands clenching into fists.

"What did you find?" Andrew asked, giving Chase a look that said to ignore Tony.

"I was magnifying the picture so it was crazy-ass close, right? But then it was too blurry to make out anything, so I started decreasing the image zoom little by little, and look." He pointed to the screen and at the very edge of the frame was a tiny dark dot.

Andrew leaned in closer and squinted. "What is it?"

Chase bounced his knee spastically up and down. "Dunno man, but it's something."

"What does that mean?" Andrew threw his hands in the air. "What does 'it's something' mean?"

Tony rose from the couch and joined them at the computer, taking a sudden interest and staring at the screen. "Can you make it bigger?"

"I just explained that when I zoom in closer, I lose clarity," Chase answered, twirling an ink pen between his fingers.

"No," Tony said, "can you isolate the dark dot and zoom in on it?"

"What good will that do?" Andrew said. "It's probably just smoke."

"Probably," Tony agreed. "But I was just thinking that she was on the plane with the Snake and he used to be Air force right?"

Before Tony could explain more of his theory, Chase blurted, "Right on." He stopped twirling the pen, stuck it horizontally between his lips and, using both hands, began rapidly punching keys. "That's a solid-ass idea, man" he said. "I don't know why I didn't think of it."

A few moments later, the dark dot was enlarged and full center on the screen. They all leaned in for a closer look. It was too blurry to tell what it was, but clear enough to see that it wasn't just smoke. "Hot damn," Chase exclaimed. "Either something or someone came out of that plane before it exploded."

"Would it even be possible to jump from a jet?" Andrew asked.

"You'd have to jump from the rear and it'd be one wild-ass ride, that's for sure," Chase said, "but not impossible." He clicked wildly on the keyboard, pulling up the last information he had before the jet disappeared from his radar. "Right before it blew up the plane was at 18,000 feet and had reduced dramatically in speed. If I didn't know better, I'd say it was getting ready to land."

Andrew squeezed Chase's shoulder. "Do whatever you have to do to get a clearer picture of whatever that is. Then I want to know the exact coordinates of where the jet blew up and projected coordinates of where whatever or whoever came out might have landed."

"Right on," Chase said.

"I want to know the location of the nearest landing strip to the jet's last known coordinates," Andrew barked and then turned to Tony. "We're going to need manpower, enough men to search a large area."

"I'm on it, Ace," Tony nodded and pulled out his phone.

Andrew grabbed his cell from his pocket and stepped out onto the balcony. "I need to speak to Giovanni," he said into the phone. "Tell him it's Andrew Venturini and it's urgent."

CHAPTER 7

Olga pressed her ear against the wall so that she could hear every word of the conversation between John Paul, Giovanni and Carl Cusanelli. Sophia was reluctant because she felt sure John Paul was going to end up dead at any moment.

Giovanni sat with his elbows resting on the walnut desk, while Carl stood to his right. "What is the information you have for us," Giovanni asked.

Even through the wall, Olga could hear John Paul's voice trembling. "We got a tip 'bout a job going down at the hanger," he stuttered.

"My hanger?" Giovanni gritted.

"Yes, sir," John Paul said nervously. "By the time we got there, the jet was gone so we couldn't confirm.

Giovanni and Carl shot each other a glance. "What was the job?"

"Hit the pilot. That's all I know."

"Who ordered the hit?" Giovanni demanded.

"I dunno, but I know who was in charge of clean up." Clean up was a nice term for disposing of the body. "He ain't a member of the family, but the Cullatos contract him out for certain clean up jobs."

"Who?" Giovanni asked.

"He's known on the street as Mr. Clean, but I don't know his real name," John Paul explained.

Giovanni looked to Carl, who gave a nod. "I've heard of him. We don't use him because he's pricey and some of his methods are a little too creative for our tastes," he explained. "But he works with many of the families."

Giovanni laced his fingers together. "You don't know who issued the hit on my pilot?" He asked again.

Olga could hear John Paul's voice crack from fear. "No sir, I swear I don't know. Michael knew but he never told me and well, now we can't ask him, sir."

Giovanni instructed his body guards to escort John Paul through the gates. "Then bring me Mr. Clean," he ordered. "I want to know who hired Mr. Clean and who ordered the hit on my pilot," he pounded his fists atop his desk and Olga could hear the rage in his voice.

As soon as the men left, the phone rang and Carl answered. "Put him through right away," he said and handed the receiver to Giovanni. "It's Andrew Venturini."

Olga gasped and hit Sophia on the arm. "Andrew's on the phone," she said excitedly, causing Sophia to sit up straighter and press her ear to the wall.

Only hearing one side of the conversation made it almost impossible to understand what Andrew was telling Giovanni; but Olga and Sophia got the gist of it. There was a possibility that Angel and the Snake had parachuted out before the explosion and were still alive. Without any forethought of being discovered eavesdropping, Olga maneuvered off the loveseat and rushed into Giovanni's office. "Merciful Heavens!" She exclaimed, waddling toward Giovanni and throwing her arms around his neck. "Is our Angel alive? Could she be?"

Sophia stood in the doorway, awaiting confirmation that that was indeed why Andrew had phoned.

Giovanni pried Olga's arms from his neck and motioned Sophia into the office, and then Carl closed the door. Olga and Sophia sat on the couch beneath the window. "Chase has reason to think that Angel and the Snake may have parachuted out the rear of the plane seconds before it exploded," he explained. "It is a long shot. But if they did and if they survived, they may still be in grave danger." Giovanni ran his hand over his jowls and let out a tired sigh. "We must assume that whoever ordered the hit on my pilot, replaced him with another pilot who was given instructions to fly to a particular location."

"Or was supposed to blow the plane up," Sophia added.

"Si," Giovanni nodded. "It is possible we are dealing with a form of suicidal terrorist."

"Whoever he was, he wasn't acting alone," Carl interjected. "We'll know more when we find out who ordered the hit on our pilot."

Giovanni rose from his desk. "We will leave for Chicago first thing in the morning. Carl, you will stay in New York and head up the investigation. Ladies, you will stay here where you will be under constant protection."

"Oh no you don't, you bossy old coot," Olga leapt to her feet and shook her finger at him. "I'm going back to find my Angel and I'll be damned if you or any of your big ugly goons are gonna stop me."

Sophia stood up and looped her arm in Olga's. "We're both going back."

"Don't make me get my Taser out," Olga warned.

47

Giovanni rolled his eyes. "You two have become a sore spot in my underside," he sighed. "Very well, you will travel to Chicago with me first thing in the morning."

Olga and Sophia hurried out of the office and back upstairs. Carl smirked at Giovanni. "Women."

"Si," Giovanni shook his head. "You can't live with them and you can't kill them because they'd find a way to nag and guilt you from the grave. Especially those two."

"Ah, friend," Carl put his hand on Giovanni's shoulder. "There is nothing in life like a feisty female spirit."

Giovanni chuckled a gruffly. "Indeed."

CHAPTER 8

Big Mike agreed to help Angel locate the Snake and get them both to a secure location. She wanted to believe that he was helping her out of the kindness of his heart, but when you have to shove a gun in someone's face and make them an offer they can't refuse, it doesn't leave a lot of room for kindness.

They searched the corn field for thirty minutes, but there was no sign of the Snake.

"This is like trying to find a needle in a haystack," Big Mike complained. "Unless you have some idea where you landed, we're never going to find him out here in the dark." Big Mike carried a flashlight and held it low to the ground so they could see where they were stepping.

Angel feared he was right, but she couldn't give up. If the shoe were on the other foot the Snake wouldn't stop looking for her. Another thirty minutes passed and Angel was beginning to feel hopeless, when Big Mike called out. "What's that?"

"What? Do you see him?"

"Something glistened in the light," he said, hurrying passed her. She followed the beam of light straight to the ground and gasped when she saw what it was.

"My earring!" She exclaimed and bent down to retrieve it. "I bet it fell out when we landed and I jerked the harness off." She took the flashlight from Big Mike and ran it over the ground. "This was where we landed," she blurted.

49

"You can see the broken stalks where we came crashing in."

"I see it," Big Mike said. "But I don't see your friend."

"He has to be here," she argued. "His leg is broken. He can't even stand up."

Big Mike searched an area about twenty feet wide in every direction. "He ain't here and there's no chute, no harness, no nothing."

"He has to be here," she insisted.

They searched for another forty-five minutes before Big Mike convinced Angel to give up. "We've been out here for almost two hours. Your friend is gone."

Angel felt heavy hearted and confused as she climbed into Big Mike's pick-up. Where would the Snake have gone? Even if he could have dragged himself by the strength of his arms, he couldn't have gone so far that they wouldn't have found him. If he was there, he would have seen their flashlight and called out. It didn't make sense.

Angel turned to face Big Mike, aiming the 9mm at him.

Big Mike started the ignition and then turned the truck around, heading back toward the Nelson's home. "You can put the gun away," he said. "I think that I've proven I'm not going to run off. I could have left you in the middle of that dark field if I had wanted."

Angel believed him, but she wasn't taking any chances.

As they approached the Nelson's home, they saw two police cars parked in the driveway. Angel's pulse quickened. "Do the police always visit the Nelson's?" She asked.

"Nah, never," Big Mike said.

"They're looking for me," Angel stammered.

"If you ain't done nothing wrong, why are you afraid?"

"It's a long story," Angel mumbled. "Let's just say the police in Iowa have been paid off before. Just the thought of being in this state makes me uncomfortable."

Big Mike brought the truck to a slow, quiet stop and Angel could feel his scrutinizing eyes on her. "I'm going to take my hands off the wheel now. Is that okay?" He asked.

"Yes, but why did you stop?"

He turned slightly to face her. "I don't know, but obviously you've got some trust issues. I get it. I'll help you hide from the cops and find your friend, but you have to stop pointing your gun at me."

Angel studied his face. There was something genuine in his eyes, something that made her want to trust him. She pushed the safety on and lowered her gun. She could see Big Mike breathe a little easier.

"I'll get you settled in my house and then I'll go over to the Nelson's and find out what's going on," he explained.

"What if the cops want to search your house?" Angel asked, realizing she probably sounded like a paranoid freak to him.

He winked at her. "Not a problem."

When they got close to his house, Big Mike killed the engine and Angel slid into the driver's seat while he got out and pushed the truck quietly toward the back of the house. Angel remarked that it was a pretty clever trick and Big Mike chuckled. "You don't learn that in the big city, that's for sure." Once inside, Big Mike kept the lights off and led Angel straight to the bathroom, where he opened the door to the linen closet. He pulled a string that hung from a single bulb in the ceiling, moved a stack of towels, and lifted a square panel in the floor. "This leads to the cellar. You can hide down there until I come back and get you. That way if the police want to search the place, they won't find you."

"Do the Nelson's know about the cellar?" Angel asked.

"I don't think so. They weren't the original builders and they've never mentioned it."

"How did you find it?" Angel questioned.

"I crawled in the linen closet during a tornado, scrunched down and felt something stabbing me in the ass. It was the hinge that opens the panel," he explained. "Lucky I found it too, because the storm blew the roof clean off."

He handed her the flashlight and Angel lowered herself into the dark hole below the house. Frightened didn't begin to describe how she felt. She shined the light toward the dirt floor, and then raised it to see that the walls were covered in black vinyl. Off to the right was a wooden handrail that led down three small steps into a slightly larger area where Angel could stand up straight without hitting her head on support beams. She shone the light around the room and stopped on a stack of plastic bins and a folding chair. Curiosity got the best of her and she crept toward the bins and opened the top lid.

Inside were photographs of a man she didn't recognize, a woman with a small boy and numerous pictures of various places in Sicily and Italy. There were Cubs ticket stubs from long ago and two guns; an older model of a Colt .45 and a .38. The second bin contained several Armani suits, all folded neatly in plastic, several ties, and a pair of perfectly shined dress shoes. At the bottom of the bin was a set of cufflinks with the letter M on them and a man's ring with an insignia that

looked oddly familiar, though she couldn't place
where she had seen it. Angel replaced the lids on
the bins and sat quietly in the dark, curious
thoughts whirling in her mind. There was
obviously more to Big Mike than met the eye and
Angel began to wonder if she really could trust
him.

She sat down, leaned against the black
vinyl wall, and felt something hard stab into her
back. There was obviously more than just dirt
behind the vinyl lining. Angel squatted down and
faced the wall, then ran her fingers along the
bottom of the vinyl searching for a loose area so
she could raise it up and see what was behind it.
The lining was tacked down but she was able to
loosen it enough to shine the light underneath.
Her heart stopped when she caught a glimpse of
what was behind that vinyl lining. It was rows and
rows of hanging guns. There were more guns than
she had ever seen in one place and most of them
looked of military orientation. The majority were
rifles, a couple grenade launchers and several
handheld Uzis. Angel knew firsthand how
powerful those guns were, because she had used
an Uzi when she shot and killed the Galante Boss.
If only Chase could see this, Angel thought. Then
she remembered that she had the Snake's cell
phone. She pulled it from her pocket, loosened the
lining a little more and angled the camera so as to
get the most guns in the picture. She then
returned to the bins and took pictures of the ring,
cuff links and several of the photographs.

When Angel heard footsteps above, she
quickly returned everything to the bins, made her
way back up the steps to the area directly below
the linen closet panel. She pulled her 9mm from
her waistband and held it steadily in front of her.
Uneasiness gripped her, making her hands

clammy. Could she trust Big Mike even though he was obviously more than he let on to be? What happened to the Snake? Had Chase, Andrew and Tony figured out that she was alive and were they searching for her? Who blew up Giovanni's jet and why? Angel turned off the flashlight and squatted down in the dark, keeping her gun aimed at the panel above. If anyone other than Big Mike opened the panel, she would fire.

CHAPTER 9

With the projected evacuation coordinates in hand, Chase loaded the last of his computer equipment into the helicopter and then headed down to the front doors of the Towers to wait for the delivery of guns he had ordered from his dealer named Trig, on the south side. Trig was a well-built African American man, with dreadlocks that hung to his shoulders and tattoos that covered both arms. Chase and Trig went way back and shared a mutual love and respect for weapons. As usual, Trig showed up right on time and backed an unmarked delivery truck right up to the front doors.

"You going to war or something, man?" He asked Chase as they lifted a large crate off the truck and carried it through the front doors. "This is one major load of power. You gonna ice a whole city?"

"Nah, man, it's more like a crazy-ass rescue mission," Chase said.

Trig stopped abruptly. "You need some extra hands?" He asked. "'Cuz you know these hands can handle the challenge, bro," he held his palms up toward Chase and raised his eyebrows.

Chase nodded in acknowledgment. It was absolutely true. Trig knew his weapons and Chase had never seen a more accurate shot. "If it were up to me, man, I'd cut you in. You know that," Chase explained.

When they sent the last of the weapons up in the elevator to the penthouse, Chase walked Trig back to his truck. "Thanks, man," Chase said. "I can always count on you to come through."

Trig closed the back of the truck and secured it with the locking mechanism. Then he leaned against it and crossed his arms over his chest. "Look, man, I'm gonna shoot it to you straight. Word on the street is that the Capo's plane blew up and your boss lady was on it. Now, either you know who blew it up and you're goin' on a revenge mission or you think she's alive and that's who you're goin' to rescue. Either way, bro, I can be of service."

Chase wiggled his fingers and tried to determine the best course of action. Trig could fly a chopper which would free Chase up to handle the technological side of things, like trying to get a trace on the Snake's phone. The problem was he didn't know if Andrew and Tony would be keen on the idea of bringing in an outsider. "I don't know, man. I gotta check with some people first," Chase explained.

Trig shook his head. "We go way back, bro. Give me a chance to prove myself to your people."

Chase exhaled, "okay, pull your truck into the garage beneath the building and meet me on the Penthouse level." He walked inside wondering what he was going to tell Andrew and Tony.

CHAPTER 10

Big Mike opened the floor panel in the linen closet, but instead of helping Angel climb out, he climbed in. "Angel, turn on the flashlight so I can see you," he whispered.

Angel froze. Was this a trap? Was Big Mike somehow involved in her plane blowing up? Could she trust him? She sat quietly crouched in the dirt, careful not to brush against the vinyl lined walls and make noise. She was still calculating the odds of being able to lift herself up through the opening in the linen closet floor before he could grab her and pull her back into the hole. The odds weren't in her favor.

"I know you don't have reason to trust me, but you don't have any other choice," he explained. "I can help you."

Angel's hands trembled. He was right. What choice did she have? *I can always give him a chance and then shoot him if he tries anything,* she thought. *That is, if he doesn't jump me and get my gun first.* Her heart beat rapidly with fear. *I could just shoot him right now.* She held her gun steady. She knew what Giovanni would do. If he were here Big Mike would already be dead; but somehow that didn't make it feel right.

"Angel, we don't have a lot of time," he said and Angel could tell he was moving as he spoke, probably trying to find her. "I'll tell you what, turn on the flashlight but keep your gun aimed at me. If I do anything you don't like you can shoot me."

That seemed reasonable. Angel took a deep breath, flipped on the light and shined it in Big Mike's face. "I know you're not who you pretend to be," she blurted. "I've seen what's in the bins. If you take one step toward me, you're dead."

Big Mike held his hands up. "I'm not going to touch you, but I need you to follow me down the steps and into the other room. We're running out of time."

Angel shone the light on his feet. "Walk. I'll follow you."

CHAPTER 11

Andrew came barreling through the penthouse door, holding his .45 to the back of Trig's head. "Do you want to tell me what this piece of crap dealer was doing in our garage?' He yelled to Chase.

"Tell him I'm with you, bro. Tell him, man, I ain't doin' nothin' wrong," Trig hollered.

"Shut up," Andrew barked, pressing the gun firmly against Trig's temple.

Chase, who had been sitting at the dining room table working on his laptop, jumped to his feet. "Take it easy, man," he exclaimed. "You got that crazy-ass Tony look in your eye. Trig's with me."

Andrew didn't lower the gun. "Who gave you permission to bring this scum here?"

"Hey, bro, I told you, I don't deal drugs no more. I ain't scum no more," Trig argued.

"It's true, man, he deals in arms now, and only low key stuff," Chase added. "He brought me a shipment and offered to help."

Trig kept his hands in the air. "That's right, bro. I heard the Capo's plane blew up and your boss lady was on it. I wanted in on the rescue or revenge mission."

Andrew gritted his teeth. "He has a rap sheet a mile long, and most of it is for selling drugs to kids," he seethed at Chase and then directed his attention to Trig. "How many times have I arrested you?"

"I'm telling you it ain't like that no more," Trig uttered. "I don't do that no more."

Andrew shook his head. "You give me one good reason why I shouldn't drop him right here, right now."

"He can fly a chopper," Chase blurted. "We served together in the Army and he saved my crazy-ass more than once. I trust him."

Andrew exhaled and pushed away from Trig, lowering his gun. "One wrong move and you're dead. You got that?" He said and then slammed him face first into the wall that stood between the dining room and the kitchen. "Let me be real clear," he twisted Trig's arm up behind his back and spoke inches from his ear. "I'm not talking to you as a cop. I'm talking to you as a Venturini. You get the difference?"

Trig didn't move. "Yes, sir," he uttered. "I'm pickin' up what you're throwin' down. Loud and clear, bro."

Andrew released him and glared at Chase. "Next time you feel the need to bring someone in, you clear it with me first."

"Right on," Chase said.

Andrew stepped onto the balcony to cool off. He was usually the level-headed one, but not knowing if Angel was alive or dead was too much for him. His nerves were shot and the only emotion his defenses allowed to surface was anger.

Tony paraded in the front door, and upon seeing Trig, he drew his .45 in one fluid motion and took aim at Trig's head. "What's he doing here and you better talk fast," he yelled to Chase.

"Shit, bro," Trig wailed. "Not again."

CHAPTER 12

Giovanni's limousine pulled up to the hanger at precisely 6:00am. His body guards escorted Olga and Sophia to the jet and then came back for Giovanni, who sat talking with Carl.

"This is my personal flight crew," Carl explained. "They'll get you there safely."

"In the event that something goes wrong, you know what to do," Giovanni told him.

"Yes, we've covered everything, but nothing will go wrong, friend."

Giovanni let out a long sigh. "I hope you are right."

"I'm always right," Carl gave him a wink. "Isn't that why you've kept me around for forty years?"

"Si, that and you have good taste in scotch," Giovanni teased.

"Now go, I will keep you informed as to what we learn from Mr. Clean."

Giovanni was escorted from the limo to the jet and sat down in a tan leather arm chair across from Olga and Sophia.

"Merciful Heavens, what is taking so long? I thought these private little jets were supposed to be faster than commercial airlines," Olga blurted and wrung her hands together.

Sophia patted her knee. "It's only been about twenty minutes," she said. "I'm sure we'll take off soon."

"It is all your luggage that delays us," Giovanni smirked. "My men are still loading your fifteen suitcases."

"Hush up, you old coot," Olga shook her finger at him. "A lady never knows what she'll want to wear so she has to pack it all."

"I imagine a lady does," Giovanni grinned, "but what does that have to do with you?"

Sophia rolled her eyes and leaned back in her seat. There was no sense in trying to interject into their conversation. They were going to bicker like school children, just as they always did, and she would just have to tune them out. Thankfully, Giovanni's cell phone rang and brought an abrupt end to their arguing.

He answered the call and moved to the back of the jet. Carl Cusanelli's jet was considerably smaller than Giovanni's but equally as nice. It had been a gift from Giovanni, as a thank you for his loyalty and friendship through the years.

By the time Giovanni returned to his seat, Olga was dozing. "I thank the Lord for small favors like putting my sister to sleep," Giovanni said to Sophia and then chuckled.

Sophia grinned and shook her head.

"That was Andrew on the phone. He tells me they feel strongly that our Angel is alive and that they will find her." He took Sophia's hand in his and gave it a tender squeeze. "He also tells me that you placed a call to Joseph Venturini, asking him to send men to help in our search. Is this true?"

Sophia lowered her eyes and nodded. She knew she had overstepped her boundaries and that she should have sought Giovanni's approval before involving a Boss from another family. "I'm sorry," she began and then raised her eyes to meet his. "I could not sit by and do nothing. She is my daughter."

Giovanni nodded. "I must ask you something personal and I expect a direct answer." He cleared his throat and released her hand. "Do you have romantic feelings for Don Venturini?"

Sophia felt her face flush and a tiny grin form on her lips. She didn't expect the question and she suddenly felt embarrassed, like a nervous adolescent with a crush. "I believe he is a good man…"

Giovanni cut her off. "I did not ask your opinion of his ethics. I asked if you love him."

Sophia pursed her lips together. "What concern is this of yours?" She felt defiance rising within her, as if she were speaking to her own father.

"All things pertaining to the families are of my concern. But when a member of my own executes poor judgment, judgment that can cause potential risk to my own men, I must question the motive behind such an act. When I look at your motive, the only thing I can imagine that would cause you to blindly trust Joseph Venturini is the fact that you are in love with him."

"I don't blindly trust him," she defended. "I trust him because he has not given me a reason to not trust."

Giovanni took her hand again and held it tightly. "Sophia, like it or not you must accept who you are in this world and stop running. You are Sophia Buscetta, only child to Salvatore, head of the Cosa Nostra. You are also mother to my granddaughter, who became head of the Maratinzano family in Chicago and is predestined to one day be the head in New York as well. Salvatore will want you to return to Sicily and lead the family there. I would ask that you consider staying here, especially if, God forbid, we have lost our Angel."

Sophia wrenched her hand from his. "We haven't lost her. I can feel she is alive." She swallowed the lump in her throat.

Giovanni leaned back in his seat. "Joseph Venturini has called a private meeting with me. I presume it is to ask your hand in marriage. You understand if Angel is gone and you become a Venturini that would mean the end of the Maratinzano family? You understand I cannot allow that to transpire?"

Sophia clenched her teeth together. "With all due respect," she gritted, "you have no power over matters of my heart." Sophia got up and moved to the back of the plane.

Olga cracked one eye open. "What are you gonna do when Angel wants to marry Andrew or Tony?"

"You have been eavesdropping?" Giovanni narrowed his eyes at her.

"Oh, pish posh, you old coot. Answer the question."

"I will forbid it."

"Even though she loves them?"

"I have chosen a suitable husband for her. He is a good man and has association only with our family. He will make a fine husband."

"Merciful Heavens, you're living in the dark ages," Olga blurted. "She won't marry someone because you tell her to. That child would rather die an old maid."

"I will convince her it is the right thing for the family," Giovanni said.

"Good luck with that," Olga rolled her eyes and then shook her finger in his face. "Mark my words, one day you will push her away forever and then you'll never see her again. She's not like you, Giovanni, she has a heart."

"Bah," Giovanni waved his hand and angled his chair toward the window away from Olga.

CHAPTER 13

Angel cautiously followed Big Mike down the wooden steps into the larger room. She stopped at the bottom of the steps and kept the light on his feet, as he crossed the room, to the wall opposite where she had seen the guns and plastic containers.

"Can you shine the light a little higher so I can find the door?" He asked.

Door? She hadn't seen a door, but then again she had been immediately distracted by the plastic bins and hadn't investigated the other side of the room. She watched as he removed the black vinyl wall covering, revealing a small wooden door. Pulling a key from his pocket, he unlocked the deadbolt and pulled it open. Then he walked to the center of the room and pulled a string that lit a single light bulb. Angel followed him inside and turned off the flashlight.

As she glanced around the room, she couldn't believe her eyes. There were no windows, as they were completely underground. Black vinyl covered the walls and floor and wooden shelves lined all four walls. The shelves to her right were packed full of canned goods and military MRE's, which was short for Meals Ready-to-Eat. There were large jugs of water, toilet paper and what looked like basic camping supplies, including sleeping bags and weather resistant rain gear. The shelves to her left held weapons of all shapes and sizes. There were hand grenades, boxes of shells in every size, bullet proof vests, protective headgear and goggles, handcuffs, rope, duct tape, and several large hunting-type knifes. On the shelves along the back wall was an overwhelming display of technological equipment; computers, police radios, transponders, GPS tracking devices, a radar screen, and a screen that looked like it was hooked directly into a satellite view of the area. Big Mike closed the door and locked it from the inside with another deadbolt.

He turned to face Angel. "There's a chair over there," he said, pointing to a folding chair. "I'll answer your questions but first I need to tell you what's happening."

Angel kept her gun pointed at Big Mike as she walked to the chair in the back of the room and slowly sat down.

"My real name is Michael Maletta and I'm Italian, more specifically, Sicilian. I know your grandfather, Salvatore."

Angel's eyes widened with surprise.

"I know who tried to kill you in the plane and I know they have found your friend."

"How do you they have the Snake?" She blurted.

"The cops at the Nelson's house weren't really cops. They're members of a militia group called the Black Brigade, or Brigatte Nero in Italian," he explained. "They only asked if I had seen a woman meeting your description. That means they either already have your friend or they don't know he exists, or..."

Angel interrupted him. "How do you know they're with this group?"

"There is a marking on the inside left wrist of each member. It is a tiny BN and I have studied this group extensively," he said. All of sudden Angel noticed that he had lost his country boy persona and now spoke like one of the brotherhood.

"I've never even heard of this group, so what would they gain by killing me?"

"They weren't planning on killing you, at least I don't think so, not yet. They have a history of taking hostages and holding them for ransom. It's how they fund their organization."

Angel shook her head. "So, I was randomly chosen as a money-making scheme?"

Big Mike chuckled. "If only," he said. "I'm pretty sure you were targeted because you're Salvatore's granddaughter." He walked closer to Angel, pulled out another folding chair, placed it in front of her and sat down. "You can keep your gun, but could you not hold it right in my face while we talk?"

Angel lowered it slightly.

"I was born in Italy at a time when the Brigatte Nero were running rampant. They kidnapped my father, held him for ransom for thirty days and then executed him, releasing the picture of his execution to the public." Angel could see Big Mike's jaw tighten as he spoke about what had happened. "My father was an Italian politician named Aldo Maletta and he was also a personal friend of Salvatore."

"The ring and the suits and the cufflinks in those bins were your father's?" Angel asked.

"Yes. When they murdered my father, Salvatore sought revenge and killed many, many of the Brigatte Nero members. I have heard it said that Salvatore's men murdered well over one hundred BN members." Big Mike smiled. "Salvatore took me and my mother in, to protect us and honor his commitment to my father."

"What happened then? How did you end up here?" Angel asked.

Big Mike sighed and leaned back in his chair. "It became a big political mess. What was the KGB at the time backed the Brigatte Nero and there was much bloodshed between the Italians and the Russians. I think it was the only time in history that the Cosa Nostra teamed up with the Italian police."

"How did you end up here?" Angel asked again.

"The Brigatte Nero knew Aldo Maletta had a son and they knew Salvatore was protecting me. Their threats grew and grew until Salvatore feared he could no longer protect me and my mother, so he sent us to the States. At that time, we were unaware that the BN had spread to the western world." Angel saw his face soften as he recanted the journey to the States with his mother. "I was a small boy and my mother was instructed to find Salvatore's daughter, Sophia."

"My mother," Angel said more to herself than to him.

He nodded. "But when we arrived in Chicago, your father had just been murdered and Sophia had disappeared."

Angel was stunned by how their lives were so intricately connected.

"My mother couldn't contact Salvatore and she knew no one else in the States, and so we had to make it on our own." Big Mike's eyes softened. "My mother was a tough lady."

"How did she pass away?" Angel tentatively asked.

"I was fifteen and I came home from school and found her dead." His brows narrowed and Angel saw the anger in his eyes. "Somebody broke into our apartment and killed her."

"I'm so sorry," Angel said. "Did they ever find who did it?'

Big Mike pursed his lips together and nodded his head up and down. "They carved BN into the top of our kitchen table. The police never found them but I knew exactly who they were. They were the Brigatte Nero."

"So, you left the city and moved out here?" Angel asked.

He cleared the emotion from his throat. "I quit school and hooked up with a street gang called the Cobras. I told them my story and they took me in, even though I was the only white kid in the gang. They hid me for years, showed me the ropes, trained me on weapons and when I caught wind that the Brigatte Nero had a compound in Iowa, I reinvented myself here and started laying the groundwork for my revenge." Big Mike rolled up his sleeve and showed Angel the cobra tattoo on his right forearm.

"Where is the BN compound?" Angel asked. "Maybe that's where they've taken the Snake?"

Big Mike hung his head. "Listen, if they took him, he is as good as dead. But I think you need to look at the possibility that he didn't break his leg and maybe he's secretly one of them."

The thought had never entered Angel's mind and it formed a pit in her stomach. Was it possible? It couldn't be. Why would he have saved her life in a fight against the Russians if he was just going to set her up to be killed by the Brigatte Nero? Why would he have parachuted her out of the plane? She shook her head no. "That's not possible," she said.

"I'm not saying he is one of them, but I think you need to keep an open mind about it and not rule it out completely."

"He would have let me die in the plane..."

He cut her off. "No, the Brigatte Nero are kidnappers. They are famously known to take hostages and make public their demise. My father was only one of many, many hostages taken by the BN group. Some were set free but most were murdered. If your friend is one of them, then he would not have let you die in the explosion, but would have rescued you, faked an injury so that you would have to wander into the dark alone and set you up to be easily kidnapped."

It made Angel sick to think about. Five minutes ago she trusted the Snake implicitly, but now she was engulfed with doubt. "He's a good guy," she mumbled more to herself than to him.

"I hope you're right."

Big Mike got up and moved to the radar screen and began explaining how he tracked planes in and out of the area. "I've set up a transponder and multiple receivers so I can get high-resolution surveillance of the area," he explained but Angel had no idea what he was talking about. "What it means is that my data is pretty accurate and your plane was on course for the BN compound when it exploded." He tapped around on a keyboard. "What I don't understand is why it blew up and how your friend knew it was going to blow up?"

Angel suddenly remembered the picture of the knife the Snake had taken with his cell phone just minutes before they jumped form the plane. She pulled out the phone and scrolled through the pictures, stopping on that one. Handing the phone to Big Mike, she explained in detail what had happened on the plane, how the co-pilot was pushed into her and the knife was sticking out of his chest.

Big Mike studied the picture. "I'll be damned," he said and then motioned for her to move in closer to the phone. "See this marking?" She nodded. "That's their insignia. It's a tiny BB overlaid with an upside-down BN. Black Brigade and Brigatte Nero."

"The Snake recognized it because he told me we were dealing with terrorists and we had to get off the plane," Angel recalled. "See, so he's a good guy."

Big Mike had a faraway expression, like he was deep in thought. "Let's say he's a good guy for now," he said slowly, "but it still doesn't answer the question of who blew up the plane?"

"The pilot blew it up," Angel shrugged.

"Not if he was Brigatte Nero," Big Mike argued. "BN would gain nothing from blowing you out of the sky. They either want you alive so they can blackmail Salvatore or they want to publically kill you for revenge."

Angel swallowed hard. He made it sound so nonchalant. "So, what do we do now? With all this equipment is there a way for me to reach my people in Chicago or New York?"

"Not without risk," he said.

"But I need to let them know I'm okay and have them come get me."

Big Mike shook his head. "That's the last thing you want them to do. They'll track your men coming in and ambush them. It'll be like lambs to the slaughter. The best thing you can do for now is let them believe you died in that explosion."

That idea felt so harsh that it pierced her heart, yet the last thing she wanted to do was to put Chase, Andrew or Tony in harm's way. "How will we get to the Snake? How will I get back home?"

Big Mike stared at her with eyes that felt strangely piercing. "You don't, not until things quiet down. Right not the Brigatte Nero are going from farm to farm looking for you and since you and this Snake guy landed on the Nelson's land, they're going to be circling this particular area like vultures."

"I have to get home," Angel protested.

Big Mike shook his head. "If you show your face anywhere, you're as good as dead. I'll get you out of here in a few weeks after the Brigatte Nero decides to believe that you died in the explosion."

A few weeks! Angel didn't scream it aloud, but she was screaming in her mind. How could she stay here that long? How could she allow her family to believe that she was dead for that long? It felt cruel and suffocating. There had to be another way.

CHAPTER 14

At the request of Sophia, Joseph Venturini
sent four of his men to assist in the search for
Angel, and Tony brought two men from the
Andriachini family. Surprisingly, the Cullato Boss
agreed to loan them a helicopter for the mission
but would not supply any men for the search.
Andrew was certain Giovanni must have made
Carlos Cullato an offer he couldn't refuse, which
resulted in them being able to borrow his chopper.
The Galante family, still in ruins from the murder
of their Boss and Underboss, were not asked to aid
in the search. They all knew this was because
Giovanni was not convinced that the Galantes had
relinquished all ties to the Russian Bratva.

Trig flew the Cullato's chopper and Chase
flew the Russian one which they had confiscated
after killing Selovich, the Russian arms dealer who
had worked with Denny. Chase took Andrew, Tony
and the two Andriachini men, while Trig flew the
four Venturini men. Prior to leaving, Chase
printed out an aerial view of Fayette County
marking projected coordinates of where someone
parachuting from a plane might have landed. He
and Trig chose a target landing zone where they
would set the choppers down. The plan was that
Trig and his group would head straight to the
target landing zone and begin a search, while
Chase would head to where he projected the plane
was intending to land had it not blown up. It was
a longshot, but Chase had estimated, based on the
plane's elevation and direction that they were on a

purposeful descent for landing. He approximated landing coordinates and they all agreed to do a fly over to see if such a landing strip existed. If it did, they would set the chopper down and ascertain who directed Giovanni's plane to this location and why. If they couldn't find an air strip, they would fly back to help Trig and his group with the search for anyone or any debris from the jet.

As they approached Fayette County, Chase gave Trig the thumbs up sign and each chopper flew to their designated zones. Chase handed Andrew, who was in the co-pilot seat, the aerial view and pointed to the coordinates which were circled in red. Andrew nodded that he understood. As they neared the zone, Chase pointed to a small air strip seemingly in the middle of nowhere, surrounded by fields of corn on all sides.

Andrew hollered back to Tony and the two Andriachini men, "There's an air strip, so we're setting down."

Tony checked the clip in his handheld Uzi, instructed his men to ready their weapons, and then gave Andrew a thumb's up.

"It doesn't look like anyone is down there," Chase hollered to Andrew. "I'm gonna set her down." Chase lowered the chopper and swung around to circle the strip, when suddenly he saw them. There were six camouflaged roofs that led to underground bunkers, three on each side of the air strip. "Holy..." he didn't finish his sentence, but quickly pulled the chopper up and away.

Andrew gripped the side of the chopper. "What are you doing?" He yelled, but before Chase could respond, the answer became obvious. Bullets soared from the ground toward the chopper.

"We're taking ground fire!" Chase screamed and maneuvered evasively to avoid the shots.

Tony and his men fired back, taking down three of the men on the ground. "We need one of them alive," Andrew hollered.

"Then get me low enough to aim," Tony shouted back.

"No can do, man!" Chase yelled. "We're outnumbered. I'm pulling out."

Chase lifted the chopper higher and headed back. "Damnit!" Tony blurted.

"Sorry man, but staying would be a crazy-ass suicide ride," Chase said.

Tony pounded his fist against the top of the chopper. "Take it easy," Andrew said. "We know where they're at. We'll get more manpower and come back."

Tony frowned. "What if she's down there right now? What if they move her somewhere else before we get back?"

"We don't even know if she's alive," Chase reminded them. "This is a wild-ass longshot and chances are we're not going to find her."

They all went silent, as Chase's words brought them back to the reality they didn't want to face.

Tony gritted his teeth. "If those are the people responsible for her death, I won't stop until each of them suffers."

No one argued. They all felt the same.

They flew in silence to where they were supposed to rendezvous with Trig. "Keep your eyes peeled," Andrew instructed. "These people could have underground bunkers all over the place." Each man intently scanned the ground with his weapon ready.

When they arrived at the targeted zone, Chase spotted Cullato's chopper on the ground and lowered to set down next to it.

"We got trouble," one of the Andriachini men yelled.

"What do you mean trouble?" Tony blurted, and moved to the right side of the chopper to see whatever his man was seeing. On the ground, surrounding Cullato's chopper were all four Venturini men, shot to death. "Son of a...." Tony blurted but Chase cut him off.

"I'm pulling up to get an aerial view. Look for vehicle tracks, shooters or any sign of Trig," he yelled. "The shooters are probably in camouflage so look closely."

He flew low over the corn fields but they saw nothing. Chase then flew back to Cullato's chopper and set down.

"What are we doing Ace?" Tony asked.

"I want to look at the ammo, man," Chase said, grabbing a large hunting knife, and the Pistol Makarova, which had been given to him by the Shark. "Maybe the weapons they're using will tell us who we're dealing with."

"What's the knife for?" Andrew asked.

"In case I need to dig a bullet out," Chase explained and climbed out of the chopper. He turned and poked his head in the doorway. "Could you guys get your lazy asses out here and give me some protective cover?" He rolled his buggy eyes and shut the door.

Tony and his men took all the weapons from Cullato's chopper and from the Venturini men and loaded them into the other chopper, while Chase and Andrew checked the bodies.

"This was one wild-ass ambush," Chase said.

"They were on foot," Andrew said, "and there were at least two of them because there are two different sets of footprints, one on each side of the chopper."

"There's a set of prints over here too," Chase said, "but the tracks are different."

Andrew put his police investigative skills to work and analyzed each set of prints. Chase was right. The two coming from the rear of the chopper, flanking up each side were similar in shape and left similar groove marks in the ground, which Andrew believed were made by some form of military boot or work boot. It appeared that they had approached and exited from the same direction, as footprints led to and from the chopper. The other set of footprints looked like the bottom of tennis shoes and led away from the chopper. Andrew looked at Chase. "How well do you know Trig?"

"Why?" Chase asked defensively.

"Because I think these are Trig's prints and they lead away from the chopper, which tells me either he somehow magically escaped the killing-spree or he was in on it."

"Impossible, man, truly impossible," Chase shook his head emphatically. "Trig is a right on guy, totally straight up."

Tony narrowed his brows. "It's not looking straight up to me, Ace."

"I'm telling you man, he's clean, totally squeaky-ass..." Chase paused without finishing his sentence. He stared blankly at the body in front of him.

"What's the matter?" Andrew asked. "You look like you just saw a ghost."

Chase motioned for Andrew to come closer and then he explained what had stopped him dead in his tracks. The three bodies of the Venturini men in the back of the chopper were shot in the front, seemingly while they were trying to exit the chopper. Two were shot in the chest and one in the forehead. The fourth Venturini man, who had been riding in the co-pilot seat, was shot in the back of the head.

"Maybe he took a stray bullet from the shooter to the left rear of the chopper," Andrew suggested.

"Or maybe he turned his head to look toward Trig who was in the pilot seat and the shooter to the right rear of the chopper shot him in the back of the head," Tony added, but Chase and Andrew both shook their heads to indicate no.

"His body fell forward, out of the chopper. If it went down your way he would have fallen forward toward the pilot's seat and his body would still be inside the chopper," Andrew explained.

Tony grimaced. "Could you two CSI wannabes hurry this whole thing up? I don't want to end up like these guys."

Chase looked to Andrew. "There's more, man," he said and opened his hand to reveal shell casings. Four were identical but the fifth one was different.

"Let me guess," Andrew said, "the odd casing was located behind the co-pilot seat next to Trig, who just happened to be the only one who made it out alive." Chase nodded. "You still think Trig is a straight up guy?" Andrew sarcastically asked.

Chase shrugged. "I don't know what to think, man. I'm crazy-ass dumbfounded right now."

One of the Andriachini men whistled for Tony and the rest of them to follow him. "Look," he said, pointing forward, "there's a body over there."

Tony took the lead with his .45 held steady in front. Andrew joined him and then Chase. "You two wait at the chopper," Tony instructed his men.

The three of them stared down at the body. The man was dressed head to toe in camouflage with only his eyes showing. He wore black military boots and black gloves. Andrew determined he had been shot in the heart at close range. He re-enacted the shooting using Chase. "The shooter must have jumped out and surprised him, physically grabbed him, shot him through the heart and then lowered his body face down to the ground."

Chase winced. "Take it easy, man, you don't have to play rough."

"Tony," Andrew said, "have your men search the field on the other side of the chopper. I'm guessing we'll find another body there." Then he turned to Chase. "Find out if the gun used to kill this guy was the same one used to kill the guy in the co-pilot seat."

"I'm on it," Chase said and quickly bent down over the body to extract the bullet.

Andrew was right. They found another body, dressed in full camouflage, black boots and black gloves lying in the corn field on the other side of the chopper. This body was further away from the chopper and was also lying face down but had been shot in the back. As soon as Chase retrieved the bullet from the first body, he went to work on the second one. When he came back to the chopper his hands were completely covered in blood.

"That was a nasty-ass job, right there," he said, and then spit on his hands, trying to wipe them clean with corn leaves.

"Here you go, Ace," Tony hollered and tossed him a bottle of water that he found in the chopper.

"Well, was it the same gun?" Andrew asked.

Chase gawked at him. "You got one crazy-ass brain up inside that head, man," he grinned.

"'Cuz you were right on." He opened his hand and showed them the bullets. The two men in camouflage and the man in the co-pilot seat were all shot with the same gun.

"Nice to know all my years on the force are paying off," Andrew uttered.

"Yeah, yeah, we all know you're Chicago's finest," Tony mumbled with an eye roll. "Can we get the hell out of here now?"

As they climbed in the chopper Chase asked, "I don't suppose any of you knows how to fly a chopper?" No one answered. "I'm no mob-ass expert, but I'm pretty sure the Cullato Boss is gonna be wild-ass pissed when we return without his chopper."

Tony grinned ear to ear. "I can't wait to see that. Let me tell him."

Chase lifted her up and they headed back to Chicago.

CHAPTER 15

When Big Mike saw a helicopter
approaching on his radar, he jumped out of his
folding chair, grabbed two guns from the shelf and
rushed toward the door.

"Where are you going?" Angel asked.

"I've got to get to that chopper before they
do," he gritted.

"Why?" Angel blurted. "How do you know
the chopper isn't just more Brigatte Nero members
searching the area?'

"All the BN choppers are the same and this
one is different, smaller." He grabbed Angel by the
shoulders. "Listen, if it's your guys, I've got to get
to them before the Brigatte Nero do, otherwise
they're dead."

Angel studied his eyes, trying to assess
whether or not he was telling the truth. What
choice did she have but to believe him? After all,
he hadn't killed her and his story sounded
believable. "If it's my men, will you bring them
here?"

"Yes," he uttered quickly. "Now, deadbolt
this door behind me and don't open it unless you
hear the secret knock. Six quiet raps and a
seventh hard one."

Then he was gone and Angel sank into the
folding chair. She couldn't help but wonder if the
helicopter could be Chase, Andrew and Tony
coming to search for her. She felt hopeful, but
reality quickly chased the thought from her mind.

How could they know she had made it off the plane alive?

Sitting in the dark and waiting nearly drove her crazy. Questions whirled through her mind. Who blew up the plane? Where was the Snake? How long would she have to hide out before it would be safe to go home? Her heart ached at the mere thought of the agony her mother and Olga and even Giovanni must be going through. If only she could somehow reach them. If only there was a way to get a signal to Chase. If anyone could find her, he could. The scariest question of all was what if something happened to Big Mike and he never came back? How long should she stay hidden underground? Who else could she trust? The Nelson's maybe? She knew she needed to be patient but patience wasn't exactly a prevalent virtue in her DNA.

Angel's heart pounded when she heard the front door open, followed by footsteps above her. She could hear men talking but couldn't make out what they were saying because the room was virtually soundproof. She lifted her 9mm slowly, slid the safety off and waited. *If it's Big Mike, he will come down and get me right away,* she told herself. *Maybe he found the Snake or Andrew or Tony or Chase and that's who he's talking to upstairs,* she wondered, trying not to get her hopes up. After a few minutes she heard the door open and close and whoever had been there was gone.

Angel waited another thirty-five minutes before she heard the door open again and the sound of footsteps upstairs. This time they walked immediately to the left, into the bathroom and came down through the linen closet floor. Angel kept her 9mm handy, though she felt certain it was Big Mike returning. When she heard the six light raps followed by a seventh hard one, she unlocked the deadbolt and opened the door. Big Mike stepped inside and Angel immediately lifted her gun on Trig. "Who is he?" She blurted, taking aim at this chest, where even if he moved, her shot would still do considerable damage. Tony had tried to convince her to always aim for the head, but the head was so small a target that Angel felt better aiming at the chest.

Trig's face drained of color and he threw his palms in the air. Big Mike laughed. "I've never seen you turn white before."

"What's wrong with you people, man? Everybody's always shoving a gun in my face," Trig moaned.

"He's okay," Big Mike said to Angel. "He's an old friend."

She stepped back so Trig could enter the room. "Yo, bro, you got some nice artillery down here," Trig said as he walked closer to view the shelves.

Angel kept her gun aimed at Trig. "What were you doing in a helicopter in the middle of nowhere?"

Trig turned and grinned at her. "Looking for your pretty face."

"Who are you?" Angel blurted, un-amused by his flirty smile.

He reached out his right hand, "My names Trig..." he began but Angel cut him off.

"What's your real name? Your full name?"

He retracted his arm and the smile left his face. "Laveil Walter James III," he enunciated slowly. "My birthday is in June and I'm a Cancer. My momma died when I was five and I ain't seen my daddy since I was twelve. Anything else you want to know?"

"Why are you called Trig?" Angel met his tone will equal fervor and sarcasm.

"Because I pull the trigger faster than anyone. You want me to show you?"

Angel raised her gun. "How do you know Big Mike?"

"You wanta help me out here, man?" Trig said to Big Mike, who was tapping away at the equipment and trying to pull up images on the radar screen.

"Nah, I think you're doing fine on your own," Big Mike said.

"We go way back, man," Trig answered.

"How far back?" Angel demanded.

Trig pulled up his sleeve and Angel saw the Cobra tattoo on his forearm. It was the same tattoo Big Mike had on his arm. "Who are you working for?"

His smile came back and Trig raised his palms upward and out. "You, Boss lady."

The way he called her Boss lady made a wave of emotion sweep over her, as it reminded her of Chase and everyone back home. "Who sent you here?" She asked, but before he could answer Big Mike was on his feet and heading for the door.

"We got another chopper. It's already on the ground and I don't know how long it's been there," he explained.

"It's gotta be Chase," Trig said.

"Chase!" Angel blurted. "I'm coming with you."

"It's too dangerous," Big Mike said and Angel whirled around and pointed her gun mere inches from his face.

"I'm coming with you."

Big Mike rolled his eyes and Trig burst out laughing. "She's a real ball buster," he said and slapped Big Mike on the back.

CHAPTER 16

Carl sat in the back of his black town car behind tinted windows and waited patiently for Giovanni's men to arrive at the hangar with Mr. Clean. He had promised Giovanni answers and was determined to do the interrogating himself.

When two men entered carrying a large black body bag and dropped it onto the ground, Carl's driver leapt from the car and quickly opened the back door. Carl stepped out and stared down at the body bag. "What is this?" He demanded.

"We found the body that Mr. Clean dumped," one of Giovanni's men said.

"And you brought it to me, why?" It was obvious by Carl's tone that he was not pleased by their actions. "I asked you to bring me Mr. Clean."

"We did, sir," the other man's voice shook. "Our guys are bringing him in, but we thought you might want to take a look at this first."

He bent down, unzipped the body bag and pulled open the deceased's shirt. A Brigatte Nero emblem was burned into his flesh. Carl's face turned bright red and he seethed, "Brigatte Nero!"

"We thought this information would help you question Mr. Clean," Giovanni's man explained and Carl nodded.

"Si, you have done well. Photograph the emblem so I may show Giovanni and then get rid of this mess, Capisce?"

"Si," they answered in unison.

"And bring me Mr. Clean!"

Loosening his gray tie and straightening the sleeves of his black suit jacket, Carl didn't like to be kept waiting. He motioned for his driver to open the car door and then he climbed back into his town car. Pulling the cell phone from his inside jacket pocket, he dialed Giovanni and left a voicemail. "Brigatte Nero," he seethed into the phone. "I will have more information for you later, my friend." He disconnected the call.

When Giovanni's men dragged Mr. Clean into the hangar, his hands were taped behind his back and a pillow case was draped over his head. They slammed him down into a folding chair and taped his ankles to the chair. Carl stepped slowly from his car.

"Scorpra la sua testa," Carl ordered and one of the men immediately pulled the pillow case from Mr. Clean's head. His hair was dark brown, almost black and cut military short. His eyebrows were dark and bushy over narrowed brown eyes.

Mr. Clean squinted as the daylight hit his face. Then he slowly leaned forward and spit on Carl's black, shiny shoes. Giovanni's men and Carl's driver immediately drew their guns, taking aim at Mr. Clean; but Carl held up his hands and motioned for them to lower their weapons.

"I would expect nothing less from someone who works for the Brigatte Nero," Carl remarked.

Mr. Clean smirked. "I work only for myself."

"Bugiardo!" Carl blurted. "You branded the Brigatte Nero emblem into the flesh of Giovanni's pilot."

"I don't know what you're talking about," Mr. Clean answered. "I didn't kill him."

"Bugiardo," Carl seethed.

"I'm not a liar," Mr. Clean rebutted in English. "I work for a lot of bogatas and I have a reputation for getting a job done right, but I don't make 'em.   The hits are done before I show up."

"Then who killed Giovanni's pilot?"   Carl demanded.

Mr. Clean shrugged his shoulders. "Dunno. My job was to come get the body, brand it and dump it. That's all I did."

"Who contracted your business for this particular job?" Carl asked, holding his hands behind his back and pacing back and forth between his town car and Mr. Clean.

"I can't tell you that," he answered flatly.

"Look at this guy," Giovanni's man to the left of Mr. Clean uttered with a chuckle. "He thinks he's some kind of attorney or something."

Giovanni's other man piped in. "Yeah, like he's got some kind of attorney client privilege thing going on."

"I have a reputation," Mr. Clean answered calmly. "If I told people who hired me then no one would ever hire me."

"And if you don't tell me, you won't live long enough for anyone else to hire you." With that remark still hanging in the air, Carl quickly pulled his gun from inside his jacket and took aim at Mr. Clean's head.

Mr. Clean's eyes widened.

"I wonder who will clean him up?" Giovanni's man joked and the other one laughed out loud.

"Is there a Mr. Clean junior we could call," Giovanni's man chided.

Mr. Clean kept his brown eyes locked on Carl's gun. "Yes, there is a Mr. Clean junior. His name is Benjamin. He's eight years old and he's my whole world." He cleared his throat as if he were fighting to hold back emotion. "I don't do hits, I don't make threats and I don't ask questions. I'm a simple businessman. When someone has a mess they need cleaned up, I show up and clean it up."

Carl moved closer and pressed the barrel of the gun against Mr. Clean's forehead. "Bugiardo!" He yelled.

"I'm not lying," Mr. Clean screamed and his voice broke into sobs. "I never meet the people who hire me. I only talk to them on the phone and then they wire my fee to an offshore account. I've never heard of this Brigatte Nero other than the emblem I was supposed to put on the body. Please. You've got to believe me. I didn't kill anyone. All I was paid to do was brand and get rid of the body."

"You did a crappy job at that because it was easy to find," Giovanni's man to the left snorted.

"Yeah," Giovanni's man to the right added, "ain't you the guy with the reputation for hiding bodies so good, ain't nobody gonna find them?"

"You really screwed up this job," the man to the left said and they both chuckled again.

"Silenzio!" Carl hollered and Giovanni's men instantly shut up. "You were supposed to leave the body where we would find it, weren't you?"

Mr. Clean nodded. "Most of the time my job is to make sure bodies never surface, ever. But this time my instructions were to ensure that this one would be found."

"By whom?" Carl asked. "Found by whom?"

"I don't know. They didn't say. They just said it needed to be easily found."

Car lowered his gun and stepped back from Mr. Clean. "I have one last question for you. Who hired you?"

Mr. Clean dropped his head. "I don't know names. I only know numbers. If you reach in my pocket I'll show you the phone number of the guy who called me. That's all I know. I swear."

Carl's cell phone rang and when he saw that it was Giovanni, he stepped away from Mr. Clean and took the call. "My friend, I was just about to get rid of Mr. Clean," he answered and then explained all he had learned. "Our Mr. Clean is not what I expected."

"How do you mean?" Giovanni asked.

"I can't determine exactly what it is, but he is weaker than I expected," Carl struggled to explain.

"Do not kill him yet," Giovanni uttered. "He may come in handy later. I want you to join me in Chicago. Have my men detain Mr. Clean until you return."

"Friend, have you found Michelangela?"

"No, and it is time you and I start considering a new Boss for the family. I would like you here by tomorrow so we can start looking at recommendations," Giovanni explained and sighed heavily. "There has been enough chaos."

"I will be there first thing tomorrow," Carl said.

"Grazie, il mio amico," Giovanni said and disconnected the call.

Carl turned to face Mr. Clean. "It appears you have been given an extension on life. Giovanni wants you detained for further questioning."

"Giovanni? As in the Capo di Tutti Capi?" Mr. Clean uttered nervously.

"Si."

"Where will I be detained? For how long? Can I arrange for someone to look after my son?" Mr. Clean asked.

Giovanni's man kicked Mr. Clean's chair with his foot. "You ain't exactly in a position to be asking no favors."

90

"Where is your son's mother?" Carl asked and studied Mr. Clean's face.

"She left us, right after Ben was born."

Carl stared at him and then directed his attention to Giovanni's men. "Allow him one phone call to arrange care for his son, but monitor the call and the location, and then bring me his cell phone." Carl lowered his eyes to Mr.Clean's in a piercing stare. "If you do not cooperate, your son will die." He climbed into his town car and closed the door.

CHAPTER 17

Big Mike was the first one out of the front door, followed by Trig and then Angel. No sooner had Angel pulled the door closed behind her than Big Mike grabbed her by waistband and pulled her back flat against the side of the cabin. "We got company," he said and pointed toward the Nelson's house. Angel peaked around the corner of the cabin and saw two men dressed in camouflage standing outside the Nelson's front door. They both had military crew cuts, wore black boots, black gloves and carried machine guns.

"Looks like tweedle dee and tweedle dumb are standing guard, keeping somebody out or keeping somebody in," Trig observed.

"That's not good," Big Mike sighed and Angel could hear the concern in his voice. She guessed he was worried about the Nelsons and by the looks of these men, his concern was valid.

"What do you want to do?" Angel whispered.

"Yeah, man, there's three of us and only two of them. You wanta take 'em out?" Trig asked.

Big Mike peered around the corner. "No, they're probably looking for Angel and questioning the Nelsons to determine if they've seen anything."

"Or they know about their men getting whacked in the field," Trig added.

"You killed their men in the field?" Angel gasped.

"I had to," Big Mike exhaled. "They took three of your guys out and the other guy was about to take Trig out."

Angel's heart skipped a beat and she felt her throat go instantly dry. Three of her men were dead, but which three? Was it Andrew? Tony? Chase? Without any forethought, Angel reacted, pushing her 9mm into Trig's temple.

"What the hell, man?" Trig wailed. "Have you lost your frickin' mind?"

Angel narrowed her eyes and glared at him. She knew Big Mike and Trig probably thought she was crazy but she didn't care. She needed to know who was on that helicopter and who had died trying to find her. "I want to know who was with you," she demanded, pressing the gun harder against his skull. "I want names."

Trig shot a glance to Big Mike. "Do something, man!"

Big Mike was still staring at the Nelson's house. "Keep it down."

"That's all you've got to say, 'keep it down' when some white chick is going all crazy up in my face?"

"I've already saved your ass once today," Big Mike shrugged. "You'll have to talk your way out of this one."

Trig raised his hands in the air and stared at Angel. "Look, I don't know nobody's names. They were all Venturini's. That's all I know."

Angel suddenly felt like she was going to vomit. Her head pounded and she couldn't catch her breath. All she could think of was Andrew. *Andrew. Sweet Andrew.* Her fingers trembled as she lowered her gun and slid down the house into a squatting position. "Andrew," she mumbled quietly.

"Andrew?" Trig blurted. "Oh, no, he wouldn't fly with me and that was a good thing too because he was all crazy up in my face before we left."

Angel sprung to her feet. "Andrew wasn't with you?" She exclaimed. "But you said Venturini's, and that's Andrew's family..."

Trig cut her off. "Yeah, he sent his four guys with me. Andrew and Tony and his couple of dudes flew with Chase."

Angel was overcome with relief. She couldn't have forced the smile from her face if she wanted to. Big Mike raised his hand and again motioned for them to be quiet.

"I'm gonna go talk to them," Big Mike said.

"That don't seem too smart, bro," Trig responded and Angel shook her head in agreement.

"They've already been here once, posing as policeman. They know I live in the cabin and they'll probably come search here next."

Suddenly Angel remembered that she had heard footsteps and voices earlier and had forgotten to tell Big Mike because when he showed up with Trig, she had been distracted. Big Mike was visibly annoyed when she told him about the intruders.

"That settles that," he said and handed Trig his gun. "I've got to go talk to them now, otherwise they'll be back for sure."

"We'll wait for you here," Angel said, but Big Mike shook his head.

"No, you need to take advantage of my distracting them and get to that chopper," Big Mike explained.

"We can't just leave you," Angel argued. "What if they know you killed their men?"

94

Big Mike ignored her question and looked at Trig. "Get her to the chopper and if you can, get the hell out of here."

Trig shook his head, "I can't leave if you need back up, man, you know that." He said, covering the Cobra tattoo on his arm, as if honoring some covenant vow.

Big Mike grinned, and nodded his head, as if the mere gesture took him back to a different time and place. "I appreciate it, but you're standing next to the granddaughter of the man who saved my mother's life and mine. I need you to get her to safety while I distract the bad guys. You can come back for me later."

Angel started to object, but Big Mike held her face between his palms and planted a kiss on each of her cheeks. "Vada con il Dio," he said softly. "Fino a che non ci incontriamo ancora."

Angel didn't understand the second part of what he said, but she knew the first part well. She grew up hearing Aunt Olga say it over and over, every time she left the apartment. No matter where she was headed, to school, on a date or to work, Olga would holler, "Vada con il Dio," which meant "Go with God."

Touching Big Mike's hand, Angel whispered, "Grazie per tutto." She felt a strange connection to him and now knew it stemmed from the fact that her grandfather, Salvatore, had taken him in; yet the connection went even deeper. He had lost his mother, she had lost her father, and they were both trapped in circumstances of their birthright. Now, looking into his eyes she saw an understanding heart that she'd never known before. It felt as if they were already family.

Angel watched as Big Mike approached the Nelson's house, was patted down by the two men guarding the door and then ushered inside.

"Do you think he'll be okay?" She said to Trig. "Maybe we should stay and wait for him to come out."

Trig took Angel by the arm and pulled her toward the corn fields. "Nah, we better get to that chopper if you wanta catch Chase."

"We don't even know for sure that it is Chase, right?" Angel pulled her arm away. "What if it's more Brigatte Nero? What do we do then?"

"What if it IS our boy, you wanta take a chance at missing him?" Trig grimaced and she conceded to go, though she felt conflicted. There were too many unknowns to feel comfortable and her mind whirled with possible outcomes, as she quietly ducked into the corn field behind Trig.

By the time they arrived to where Trig had landed Cullato's chopper, there was no sign of Chase and no sign of another helicopter. Any hope Angel had of getting home quickly faded. She and Trig stayed low in the field and surveyed the area, looking for any sign of movement.

"They'll all be wearing camo," Trig whispered. "And they'll just appear out of nowhere, like bam, in your face."

They quietly circled the chopper, careful to stay hidden. When they felt certain that no one was there, Trig stepped toward the chopper and Angel followed. "These are the Venturini men?" She asked, seeing the four bodies.

"Yeah, but their guns are gone and their bodies have been moved," Trig answered. "Chase must have been here or someone else."

"Trig," Angel stopped moving and stared at him. "Can you fly us out of here?"

"Girl, I flew this baby in here," he mumbled under his breath.

"No, I mean is there any damage to the chopper or can we fly out right now?"

Trig's face lit up and Angel could see the wheels spinning in his mind. He immediately walked around the outside of the chopper, peering underneath and giving it a once over. Then he peeked inside at the console. "We got to move that body out of the back, but then I think we'd be good to go."

Trig climbed in the chopper and lifted the body up and out while Angel grabbed the legs and pulled. There was a time when this would have sent her running into the weeds to puke, but those days were gone. She had become desensitized to gunshots, gunshot wounds and even dead bodies. As long as she didn't know the person, she could face it without vomiting; though that didn't seem like something one should brag about.

The body dropped with a thud to the ground, Angel stepped over it and climbed into the front of the chopper. There was blood splattered all around, but she tried to ignore it and focus on the fact that Trig was going to get her home.

"Buckle up," Trig said. "The minute I get her going we're gonna take off like a bat on crack."

"Got it," Angel said, though she wasn't familiar with the bat on crack analogy, she assumed he meant they would be flying very fast.

Trig looked over at her. "There's a chance the minute I take her up they're gonna shoot us out of the sky."

Angel felt her adrenaline surge as fear once again gripped her. She returned Trig's stare and tried to mask her fear. Reaching over, she placed her hand on top of his. "I've already been shot out of the sky once and I'm still here. We can do this."

"Rock on Boss lady," Trig gave Angel a half-smile and started the chopper, immediately lifting her from the ground and flying low and fast over the field, then lifting her high into the sky. Angel watched as the ground grew further and further away. Her heart beat faster. Had they made it? Was she on her way home? Her stomach was in knots as she held her 9mm with a white knuckled grip and scanned the ground for any sign of danger.

A few minutes later, Trig glanced over and smiled. "I think we're clear, man."

Angel wanted to shriek with joy but couldn't help tempering her excitement. She had seen too much to ever completely let her guard down, and she knew this was far from over. The Brigatte Nero were still out there. The Snake was still missing. They'd have to come back and make sure Big Mike was okay. Angel took a deep breath and exhaled, feeling her muscles relax just a little for the first time since the Snake had hurled her out of Giovanni's jet. "Can you contact Chase and let him know where we are?"

Trig handed her his cell phone. "As soon as you see a signal, call."

CHAPTER 18

The Snake awoke to find himself lying on a wooden bench in an underground barracks. The room was small with benches lining three of the four dirt walls. The barracks looked more like an underground bomb shelter than a military bunker. An opening to his left led to wooden steps ascending to the surface and he could only assume that the opening to the right led to more rooms. He couldn't remember being transported from where he and Angel had crash landed. He was able to sit up without pain which probably meant that he had been injected with some type of drug, which he assumed was also responsible for his memory loss. Without his watch or his phone, he had no idea what time it was or how long he had been there. He scooted himself backwards across the bench so he could lean against the dirt wall and keep his right leg elevated atop the bench.

"Sean Shepherd," a voice came from the doorway and the Snake turned to see who was speaking. "Or should I call you the Snake?"

The Snake didn't answer but instead did a quick up and down analysis of the man now standing in front of him. He was Caucasian, dressed in camouflage, black military boots and a black belt that held two guns. The gun on his right hip was a PM, or Pistol Makarova, which the Snake remembered was a Russian made weapon that was no longer manufactured. PM's were the guns used in the massacre at Tetterbaum's Pub several weeks earlier and the same gun the Shark had given to Chase before they realized the Shark was a traitor. The gun on his left hip was an Italian made Beretta 92 edition, semi-automatic pistol fitted with an 18-capacity clip that protruded three quarters of an inch below the frame of the gun. The Snake knew this gun well, as he had been issued a Beretta 92S-1 in the Air Force.

The man stood five feet, eleven inches, his blonde hair was a tight crew cut and his green eyes looked like mere slits in his face. Tattooed on the top of his right hand was a BB overlaid with a BN.

"Black Brigade," the Snake uttered.

"Yes, Mr. Shepherd, we are Black Brigade," the man smirked. "But you already knew this."

"What business do you want with me?" The Snake asked.

"What makes you think we want anything to do with you?" The man seethed.

"If you didn't want something, you would have killed me already."

"We still may," the man chuckled. "But first, let me introduce myself. I am Johan Bernardelli, first officer in charge of this operation."

"And what exactly is THIS operation?" The Snake folded his arms over his chest and glared at Johan.

"We will get to that in due time, Mr. Shepherd, but first..."

The Snake cut Johan off mid-sentence, a purposeful tactic to show that he did not respect his authority. "Call me Snake."

"Very well, Mr. Snake," Johan narrowed his eyes and pursed his thin lips together. "I know you are quick on your feet," he paused as a sardonic grin crossed his face, "that is, when your leg isn't broken." He walked closer to the Snake. "You were the easiest captive we've ever taken. We don't need to tie you up or cage you in. The doorway to freedom is right there and yet you can't get to it," he taunted. "It must be terribly frustrating."

The Snake felt his temper rising but he forced himself to control it. He knew from his years of military training and missions in the Air Force that the most powerful stance was one of controlling one's emotions and maintaining a perspective of logic. Still, Johan was beginning to piss him off. "What do you want?" The Snake gritted.

"Oh, Mr. Snake, I think you know exactly what I want," he said, pacing slowly in front of the Snake with his hands held tightly behind his back. "You took away what I wanted and forced me to institute plan B."

"What was plan A?"

"Plan A was simple," his voice raised. "My pilot was to land the plane; we would take Ms. Maratinzano off, kill you, kill the pilot and then destroy the plane."

"Then what? Demand ransom from Giovanni and murder his granddaughter publically? That's what the Black Brigade is known best for, right?" The Snake glared at him.

Johan chuckled aloud. "Perhaps I have given you more credit than you deserve. We don't demand ransom anymore. Those days are long gone."

"Then what DO you want?" The Snake blurted.

"What everyone wants. Revenge. Power. Money," Johan grinned. "Enough talking now. Our medic will set your leg and give you medication. We will keep you alive as long as you are useful and then you will die."

"How do you think I will be useful? If you think for one moment I will betray Giovanni you are fooling yourself. You might as well kill me now, because I will never help you." Anger was beginning to show in the Snake's voice and he fought to control it.

Johan stared at him, his eyes oozing evil. "We have our ways. I am certain, Mr. Snake, we will be able to help you make the right decision to help us. If there is one thing we know for certain it is that Ms. Maratinzano has a soft-streak and when she sees you in need, she will come."

"I wouldn't underestimate her, if I were you," the Snake warned. "She's not as soft as you think."

Johan laughed aloud. "And you are not as smart as you think."

CHAPTER 19

By the time Chase, Andrew, Tony and the Andriachini men arrived back at the Towers, Giovanni, Sophia and Olga were already there. As soon as the chopper landed on the rooftop patio, Sophia and Olga rushed out, hoping to see Angel's face, but all they saw was the sadness and anger in Andrew and Tony's eyes.

Andrew stepped out of the chopper and Olga grabbed his arms. "Tell me good news," she begged. Andrew lowered his eyes and shook his head, then slid from her grip and walked inside to find Giovanni.

Sophia searched Tony's face as he climbed from the chopper. "Tony?" She cried out.

Tony shook his head. "Non c'è speranza," he mumbled and walked passed her.

Sophia burst into sobs and Olga held her tightly. "Merciful Heavens! Don't listen to him," Olga exclaimed. "There is still hope. There is always hope."

Giovanni ordered them all into the family room for a meeting. He sat in his armed chair, Sophia and Olga took the couch, Tony and the two Andriachini men stood behind the couch in front of the windows, Chase sat at the dining room table, booting up his laptop and Andrew leaned against the wall between Giovanni's chair and the fireplace. Sadness and anger hung so heavily in the room that it felt palatable.

Giovanni cleared his throat. "Upon the conclusion of this meeting we will go to the meeting

103

room where I will be briefed on the details of your trip. At that time we will discuss a strategy for taking revenge on the Brigatte Nero."

Chase jumped from his chair. "That's it!" He yelped, "That was the tattooed mark on the right hands of both the men we found dead in the corn field. It was driving me wild-ass crazy!"

"You found Brigatte Nero men in a corn field?" Giovanni asked. "I was speaking of the Brigatte Nero who killed my pilot and branded their emblem into his flesh."

Andrew chewed on his bottom lip. "You mean the Black Brigade? The faction from Italy who were supported...."

Tony cut him off. "By the Russians." Tony grabbed a pillow from the couch and hurled it against the wall. "Bratva!" He yelled, his face turning dark red and the veins protruding from his neck.

Giovanni raised his hand in a gesture to quiet everyone. "We cannot undo what they have done to us, but I promise you we will avenge Michelangela's death, and we will ensure that no Bratva member or Brigatte Nero member ever breathes air again!" Giovanni's voice grew louder and gruffer as he spoke.

Chase clicked away at his keyboard.

"Chase, are we keeping you from something?" Giovanni sarcastically remarked.

Chase whirled around in his seat. "No sir, I mean no disrespect sir, it's just that I'm trying to pull up the footage from the cameras on the chopper so I can get a better look at the bunkers around the air strip." Giovanni's face remained stern and Chase finally stopped talking, took his hands off the keyboard and turned to face Giovanni. "It can wait."

Giovanni continued. "My compare, Carl Cusanelli, will be arriving tomorrow morning and we will begin talks for a new Boss to the Maratinzano family."

"Isn't this premature?" Sophia said. "Shouldn't we wait and see if..." her voice cracked with emotion. "We don't even know if Angel is..."

"Merciful Heavens! Think with your heart for once in your life, you old coot!" Olga shook her fist at Giovanni. "If I had my Taser I'd zap you right now just for being insensitive."

"Tony," Giovanni said, "please escort the ladies to their bedrooms."

Tony gave a nod and took Sophia and Olga each by the arm. Sophia pulled her arm away. "I can walk by myself," she tearfully spat.

Olga yelled over her shoulder, "Then I'd zap you again for being stupid." Tony tugged at her but she kept yelling. "Then I'd zap you again just for fun!" Tony tugged at her. "Maybe I'll zap you while we're eating again so your head will go THWOP right into your pasta. Ha! That was the greatest moment of my life!"

"Lucia!" Giovanni growled and Tony forcefully pushed her down the hall and into her bedroom.

When Tony returned to the family room, Giovanni continued. "If you have any men you would like to recommend, please let me know. We have some internal candidates in mind but they are all from the New York bogatas and I would like to examine some from the Chicago bogatas as well." The men all nodded signaling that they understood. "We will adjourn now to the meeting room." Giovanni rose from his chair. "Tony, release your men to go home."

While Giovanni, Chase and Andrew took the elevator to the secret meeting room, Tony escorted his men to the ground level and out of the building. Placing a hand on each man's shoulder, he thanked them for their help. "Listen," he said, drawing his face close to theirs. "I want you to scour this city and anyone, and I mean anyone, with the tiniest tie to the Bratva or the Brigatte Nero, I want dead. Capisce?"

"Capisce," they answered in unison.

"How you want it done?" One of the men asked.

"I don't care, Ace, I just want them dead," Tony shrugged.

"I was thinking," the man explained, "they branded one of Giovanni's, what do you say we brand theirs?"

"Yeah," the other man agreed. "It's disrespectful to brand one of the Capo di Tutti Capi's men. God rest his soul."

Tony nodded. "Fine. Brand them. Do whatever you want to them. Just make them dead."

CHAPTER 20

With all of the men downstairs in the meeting room, Olga ventured out of her bedroom and began to futz around in the kitchen. She grumbled under her breath as she slammed dishes down on the counter top and pulled out her recipe book intending to whip up some homemade cannoli.

Sophia crept into the kitchen, her eyes still puffy from crying. "What are you making?" She asked.

"My Angel's favorite," Olga said with her bottom lip quivering. "Cannoli."

Sophia embraced Olga and they wept together for several minutes.

"It isn't right what Giovanni said to you on the plane," Olga drew back from their hug and patted Sophia on the cheek. "Don't let that old buzzard tell you who you can and cannot marry."

Sophia gawked at her. "Were you pretending to be asleep on the plane and eavesdropping on our conversation?"

"Merciful Heavens, child, I'm always eavesdropping. It's what I do best."

Sophia tied an apron around her waist and began to help with the Cannoli. "He's right," she sighed. "I couldn't marry a Venturini. It would just further complicate our families."

"Why? You're not a Maratinzano," Olga blurted and stuck her hands on her rounded hips. "Are you forgetting that small fact, my dear?"

Sophia smiled. "No, I guess I'm not."

"Merciful Heavens, child, not marrying you was the greatest gift Joseph ever gave you." She reached over and took Sophia's hands in hers. "He loved you so much that he gave you freedom from this, from all of this."

Olga spoke the truth. Joseph Maratinzano had never officially married her. He loved her and she him and they had Angel together, but despite her wanting him to, he would not marry her. It was once the cause of much heartache, but as she aged, she understood that it was the only way he could protect her. She now knew that feeling all too well. When Angel was eighteen Sophia had to leave her in Olga's care to ultimately protect her. Sometimes the only way to love someone is to let them go. Sophia took a deep breath. "Joseph Venturini hasn't asked for my hand in marriage," she said.

"But Giovanni seems to think he is going to," Olga interjected.

"Si," Sophia sighed.

Olga squeezed her fingertips. "If he does, you follow your heart, you hear? I'll take care of Giovanni." Olga gave her a wink. "I'll zap the old coot as many times as it takes to zap some sense into him."

"Aren't you the slightest bit afraid of him? He IS the Capo di Tutti Capi," Sophia said.

"He's nothing more than a pain in the ass with a title, that's all he is," Olga spat. "Besides, he won't hurt me; I'm the only sibling he has left."

"I hope you're right," Sophia said.

After several minutes Sophia wiped her hands on her apron. "If you were in my position, what would you do?" Sophia leaned against the counter and wrung her hands together. "I mean, if Angel is..." she stopped and fought back tears. "If

Angel isn't coming back, and you were me, would you marry Joseph Venturini?"

"If I were you and my only tie to this lifestyle was gone, I would get out and start my life over."

"What if you loved him?" Sophia blurted out.

"I wouldn't," Olga said and then winced at the direct harshness of her answer. "Unless I really loved him," Olga paused and looked at Sophia. "Do you really love him?"

Sophia shook her head. "Loving him would be foolish."

"Love is always foolish," Olga smiled. "That's what makes it so much fun." Olga turned her attention back to her recipe but continued to talk. "The question is, do you want love or do you want freedom? At my age I would choose freedom, but that's only because I don't have some rich Italian Boss who's not half bad looking wanting my affection. If that were the case, I'd choose his hunk-a-hunk-a-burning love stick."

"Olga!" Sophia gasped, her face blushing.

"What? Just because I'm old doesn't mean the furnace isn't kicking on."

Sophia laughed and made the sign of the cross over her body.

"If somebody were fanning these flames, I'd be known as one hot Italian mama." Olga danced around in a circle, gyrating her hips and Sophia hit her lightly with a dish towel.

"You're already one crazy Italian mama, I'll give you that," Sophia laughed.

Tony poked his head into the kitchen and startled both women. "I don't mean to intrude on your hot Italian mama conversation, but..."

"You were eavesdropping on us? Shame on you," Olga scolded.

"Like you're one to talk," Sophia scolded Olga.

"I'm old. Old people are allowed to eavesdrop," Olga said matter-of-factly and raised her chin in the air.

"Why is that?" Sophia asked.

"Because we have wisdom to impart and we can't impart it unless we know what's going on," Olga said, then turning back to her Cannoli, she mumbled under her breath something about how she shouldn't bother eavesdropping because nobody listened to the wisdom she imparted anyway.

Sophia shot Tony a glance and an eye roll that made him smile and then Olga whirled around with a wooden spoon in her hand and shook it at Tony. "Shouldn't you be at the meeting? What are you doing up here?" Olga blurted.

Tony held his hands up. "Whoa, I came to apologize to Sophia," he said and Olga lowered the spoon.

"Merciful Heavens, get on with it then," she barked.

"Sono spiacente," Tony said to Sophia, clearing his throat as his voice cracked.

"What are you sorry for?" Sophia questioned.

Tony shuffled his feet in an uncomfortable manner. "When I got off the helicopter I told you there was no hope and I'm sorry for that. I'm never giving up hope and you shouldn't either."

Sophia placed her hands on the outside of his shoulders and looked deeply into his eyes. "La amavate molto…"

Olga interrupted, "well, of course he loved her very much. We all loved her."

Tony fought back tears. "Era la mia vita," he uttered almost inaudibly and Sophia embraced him.

"Era la mia vita anche," Olga wailed and burst into tears, waddling over and joining their embrace.

"She was my life too," Sophia cried.

In the midst of the emotion, it took a few moments for the whirring sound of a helicopter to register in their minds. Finally, Olga pulled back, wiped her face on her apron and asked, "Merciful Heavens, where is Chase flying off to now?"

"Giovanni probably sent him on another mission," Sophia said, squeezing Tony's fingers and returning to the Cannoli.

"Not without me," Tony said, "and I didn't hear anyone walk through, did you?"

Sophia and Olga both shook their heads to indicate they hadn't.

Tony pulled his .45 from the back of his jeans and instructed the women to remain quiet and stay put. "I'll go get my Taser," Olga shrieked, "just in case they get passed you."

Ignoring Tony's advice to remain in the kitchen, Olga waddled quickly down the hall toward her bedroom. "Keep an eye on her," Tony ordered Sophia and then he crept slowly toward the patio door.

Tony peered outside and saw the helicopter parked in its usual spot. It wasn't running and no one was in it, though he could still hear the whirring of chopper blades. He slid outside, staying close to the wall and beneath the narrow overhang of the roof so as not to be seen by whoever was in the chopper hovering above. Tony watched as the helicopter dropped lower and lower. He squinted to see who was in it but the glare from the sun obliterated all visibility. Whoever it was,

was hovering way too long for Tony's comfort. He moved quickly around the wall to see if he could get a better view of the chopper from a different angle. When he looked up and realized Trig was the pilot, Tony walked forward with his gun in front and ready. They had never ascertained whether Trig was good or bad and Tony wasn't taking any chances.

He took aim at Trig's head, with his finger on the trigger and then stopped as the chopper turned sideways and the co-pilot door opened. Angel waved her arms and Tony dropped his gun as he crumbled to his knees.

Since there wasn't enough room on the rooftop for Trig to land the chopper, at least not without taking out tables, chairs and possibly the blade of the other chopper, he lowered the helicopter as far as he could and then Angel jumped, landing on her feet and dropping to her knees next to Tony.

His hands shook uncontrollably as he grabbed her and pulled her to him. She curled up against his chest and they rocked back and forth, Tony stroking Angel's hair and repeatedly kissing her forehead, her cheeks and her neck. There was so much to explain but it could wait. There were no words to express what she was feeling at this very moment. Relief. Joy. Comfort. Love.

"Il mio amore, il mio amore," Tony whispered over and over again with tears streaming down his face. Angel clung to him, not wanting to let go; never wanting to let go. "I will not let you go," he said, as if he had read her mind. He took her face in his hands. "I will never let you go."

Tears ran down Angel's face as his lips closed on hers in a kiss of passion and warmth, love and life. It was different than any other kiss they had shared and Angel didn't want to pull her lips away. She was home in his arms.

"Ti amo. I love you," he uttered in between kisses.

"I love you too," she whispered. "Always."

"Sempre," he said. "Always."

He drew her into a deep kiss that was abruptly interrupted by Olga's scream from the patio door. Olga threw her Taser to the ground, grabbed her chest and waddled toward Angel with such speed that Angel was certain she was going to topple right over, but instead she dropped to her knees right beside her. Olga made the sign of the cross over her body, touching each shoulder, her head and her heart and then kissed her fingertips and threw the kiss toward the sky. "È un miracolo!" She exclaimed. "È un miracolo!" She grabbed Angel's face and kissed both cheeks. "Il mio Angel è vivo, elogio è al nostro signore santo, il mio Angel è vivo," Olga uttered, gripping her chest and smiling through giant tears. Before Angel could say anything, Olga pushed herself to her feet and waddled quickly into the house yelling, "Sophia, Angel è vivo! Angel è vivo!"

Angel looked at Tony and grinned, "Everyone looks like they've seen a ghost."

"Or an Angel," Tony winked.

"What was she saying in Italian?" She asked him.

"She said you need to learn the language, Babe," he smiled, ran his hand up around her neck and pulled her lips into his. Their kiss only lasted a few seconds before Sophia came out screaming and crying and pulling Angel from Tony's arms; but it was a good few seconds.

Olga waddled out to Giovanni's men standing guard outside the penthouse door and ordered them to go and get everyone from the meeting room, while Sophia and Tony escorted Angel inside. Angel glanced around the penthouse, feeling her muscles finally start to relax. She was home and it felt good to be there. Sophia stroked her matted hair and Tony interlaced his fingers with hers, obviously, neither one of them wanting to let her go for even a moment. She knew what it felt like to think someone you loved was gone, and she knew these past two days had been harder on them than on her.

Olga waddled back to where they stood and looked at Angel. "Merciful Heavens, child, you look like you've been thrown out of a plane," she said and gave a wink. "How about a hot shower and some freshly baked Cannoli?"

Angel's mouth watered. She couldn't remember the last time she had eaten or drank anything, much less used a bathroom. The hours since the explosion all seemed to run together. "That sounds wonderful," she said. "I want to clean up before everyone else attacks me like you three did." She gave Tony's fingers a squeeze and kissed her mother on the cheek. "I'm just going to the bathroom, you guys can let go of me now." Sophia patted her arm and headed to the kitchen to help Olga.

"I don't think so, Babe," Tony teased. "You probably shouldn't shower alone. I better go in with you just to be safe."

Olga poked her head out of the kitchen. "Merciful Heavens, they'll be time for shenanigans later," she spat.

"Stop eavesdropping," Angel scolded.

"I can't help it, it's a God-given talent and it's blasphemous to waste a God-given gift." Olga put her hands on her hips and looked at Tony. "Now, let the poor child clean up," she snorted. "Her hair looks like rats have been nesting in it."

Tony grinned. "Now that you mention it, you do have a rat-infested look about you."

"I was hurled out of a plane at eighteen thousand feet," Angel objected.

"Well, in that case you don't look half bad," Olga smirked and then clapped her hands together as an idea popped into her head. "Merciful Heavens, why didn't I think of it before? I'll take you down to Elsa at my hair salon. She'll get you all fixed up."

"No thanks," Angel grimaced. "I've seen Elsa's handy work, remember? She had me so teased I looked like Elvira."

Olga snorted out a laugh. "Oh, that's right, you had Ho hair." She chuckled out loud. "I forgot all about that." Olga went back into the kitchen and began telling Sophia about Angel's Ho hair episode while Tony gave her a light kiss on the lips and headed downstairs to make sure everyone knew Angel was back.

She walked into her bedroom to see her two cats, Midnight and Mo, laying on top the bed. "Hello boys," she said and scooped them up, one in each arm. "Did you miss me?" They purred like little motorboats and Angel kissed each one on the nose. "I missed you." She put them down, walked into her bathroom and almost shrieked aloud when she caught her reflection in the mirror. Olga was right; her hair was a rat's nest. She wondered if conditioner would even begin to work through the matted knots.

The warm shower massaged her back and began to melt away the tension. She was safe now and her family was no longer tormented by thinking that she was dead. A sense of normalcy, even in the tiniest form, had been restored and she would finally be able to sleep. She had only managed to doze off and on while underground in

Mike's cabin and the exhaustion was now catching up with her. Angel wrapped a towel around her torso and opened the shower door to step out but stopped abruptly when she saw him leaning against the bathroom wall with his hands folded over his chest.

Their eyes met and she could see the emotion, although he was obviously trying to conceal it. "I'm beginning to think you have nine lives just like those mangy felines of yours," he said.

Angel smiled. "Me too."

When he took several steps toward her, Angel felt like she couldn't catch her breath. She couldn't even move. Just seeing him sent a rush of familiar emotion through her.

"We're even," he said, taking her hand and pulling her out of the shower.

"Even?"

"You thought I was dead and now I thought you were dead. We're even," he explained, closing the gap between them.

Angel's heart was pounding wildly. "How did you get in here? I locked the door."

"Locks mean nothing. I'm batman, remember?"

"Where is everyone?"

Andrew placed his hands on her waist and pulled her against him, his lips less than an inch from hers. "Giovanni's in his chair." His lips inched closer. "Sophia and Olga are in the kitchen." His lips were almost touching hers and she was suspended in breathless anticipation. "And Tony and Chase went to meet Trig."

Angel closed her eyes as his lips closed over hers with a passion that told her everything she needed to know. She was wanted and needed and deeply loved. As Angel wrapped her arms around his neck, her towel slipped to the floor. His hands moved gently down her back, wrapped around her hips, and pulled her forcefully against him. Their kiss deepened and Angel was on the verge of complete surrender, when Andrew pulled back and took her face in his palms. "Not this way," he spoke softly. Her eyes searched his for understanding. "I want to make-love to you when we can take our time and I can savor every inch of you."

She hated when Andrew was right. She hated when his logic messed up the magic of the moment. He was right; this wasn't the time or the place, but so what? *Sometimes you just have to go for it,"* she thought. When Andrew left her to get dressed, she couldn't help but compare him to Tony. If she had been naked in the bathroom with Tony, he would have ravished her. He would have pushed her against the wall and made-love to her right then and there. If Tony knew anything, it was how to seize the moment. That was one of the things she loved about him. Logic didn't control Tony's passion the way it did Andrew's, and there were moments like these when she wished for a little more action and a lot less thinking.

CHAPTER 21

Johan Bernardelli was summoned away from the Snake by an urgent phone call.

"She got away!" His voice raged on the other end of the line.

"That isn't possible," Johan answered, "we're still looking, but I'm sure she couldn't have gotten far."

"Then explain to me why she just landed on the roof of the Towers in Chicago!" He screamed into the phone.

All the color drained from Johan's face and he stuttered for words. "That can't be."

"Have you forgotten how long it has taken to lay the groundwork for this operation?" He yelled into the phone. "How long have we waited for the perfect opportunity? Do you know how much money I have invested in this?"

"Yes. I mean, of course I know," Johan sputtered.

"Ready your men for transport to Chicago. Get them set up immediately and inform them that I am coming to lead this mission personally."

"But, don't you want us to find out how she escaped?" Johan asked. "Someone local must have helped her."

"I don't care how she escaped, I need her dead!" He hollered. "I need Giovanni scrambling for a replacement as head of the family. Do you understand?"

"Yes," Johan stammered, but the call had already disconnected. His face was flushed with anger as he briskly strode down the dirt hallway and into the main area of the bunker, spewing out obscenities. There were computer screens, radar and surveillance monitors lining the walls and men working at every station. He pulled a whistle from his front pocket and blew it loudly until every man was on his feet at attention. "Angel Maratinzano has escaped and returned to her home in Chicago. I want to know how this happened. I want to know who helped her and I want them dead!" He seethed. "Prepare to move the operation to Chicago. We leave after dusk. You have until then to find out who helped her." He stormed out of the room in a huff.

The Snake overhead the whole thing and smiled to himself. "That'a girl, Angel. That'a girl."

CHAPTER 22

After the hugging and the crying had subsided, and Olga had fed everyone to overflowing, Angel and the men returned to the secret meeting room to discuss what had transpired and develop a plan of action. They gathered around the long mahogany table with Giovanni at the head, Angel to his left, followed by Chase, and then Trig. Andrew and Tony sat on the other side. Two of Giovanni's men stood guard at the elevator.

Since Trig was responsible for returning Angel alive, Giovanni blessed him with pseudo-acceptance into their group, but Angel knew his scrutinizing eye would be watching Trig closely; as were Tony and Andrew.

Angel informed them of what had happened on the plane, how the Snake saved her life and how she left him injured in the field to go for help. She slid the Snake's cell phone to Chase. "There's a picture of the knife on it."

Chase retrieved it like an excited child. "Yep, that's the Brigatte Nero emblem, right there." It confirmed what they already knew. "Why would the crazy-ass Brigatte Nero want to kill Angel?"

"We will return to that issue later," Giovanni uttered and something in his expression let Angel know there was more to the story.

Angel told them about meeting Big Mike, and then she and Trig pieced together the rest of the story.

Tony glared across the table at Trig. "So let me get this straight, Ace. You show up out of nowhere and just happen to be an ex-gang member with this Big Mike guy who lives in the middle of Podunk-ville Iowa; who just happened to rescue Angel?" He narrowed his eyes. "Somethin' smells fishy."

Andrew crossed his arms over his chest and leaned back in his chair. "Agreed. It's all a little too coincidental for my taste."

"Look, man, I told you already. Me and Chase, we go way back and when I heard that the Capo's plane blew up, and then he called me looking for ammo and guns, I thought this was my chance to be Made," Trig explained with his usual, flare.

No one spoke. They all just stared at him. Angel felt a twinge of guilt for not speaking up; then again she was beginning to feel like she'd been burned too many times to give anyone the benefit of the doubt. She never wanted to become as cold and jaded as Giovanni or Salvatore, but as time passed, she was beginning to understand how easily it could happen.

"Besides, man, if I was the bad guy why would I have brought her back here?" Trig asked. "That don't make no sense."

Chase fidgeted in his seat, bouncing his knee up and down. "I told you he was squeaky-ass clean."

Angel exhaled, rested her elbows on the table and rubbed her temples. She was tired. "We need to focus on the Snake," she said. No sooner had the words escaped her lips than Tony, Andrew, Chase and Giovanni all grumbled under their breath. "What?" Angel asked. "We can't just leave him there."

"I'm no mob-ass expert, but the Brigatte Nero, man, they've got a mean-ass reputation. If they took him, he's already dead," Chase said while twirling a pen between his fingers and shaking his spikey-haired head back and forth.

"We don't know that," Angel rebutted. "He was alive when I left him so we have to assume he's still alive."

Everyone grumbled again. "Brigatte Nero will have no use for him. I guarantee you he is dead," Giovanni said. "It is not worth our time to consider him otherwise."

Angel gawked at each of them. "I'm glad you didn't take that same attitude when I was missing."

"That's different," Andrew said.

"Apples and oranges, Babe," Tony added.

Angel stood up and slammed her palms on top the table. "I wouldn't be standing here if it weren't for the Snake. We're going back to look for him." Her jaw tensed and no one in the room dared to speak. They all glanced from Angel to Giovanni and back to Angel.

Giovanni cleared his throat. "Very well, Michelangela, you may send some men tomorrow morning to look for the Snake, but you are not to go with them." He pointed his finger at her. "You will remain here," he said, his tone emphasizing the fact that this was not negotiable. Angel opened her mouth to object but Giovanni cut her off. "You will meet with myself and Carl Cusanelli tomorrow morning."

"Carl Cusanelli?" Angel scrunched up her nose. "Your Compare is coming here?"

"Si," Giovanni answered.

"Why?" Angel asked, lowering herself back into the chair.

"Originally it was to discuss candidates for a new Boss, now it will be of a more personal nature."

"A new Boss? I wasn't even dead for thirty-six hours," she rolled her eyes. "Good to know you'd all take some time to mourn my loss."

"Everyone mourns differently," Giovanni mumbled, "but the experience was a reminder that certain positions need to be filled. We cannot endure more chaos. We are weak and vulnerable in this city and it must end. When people in our world smell weakness, they pounce on it and that is what has been transpiring in this city." Giovanni's face flushed with anger and he pounded his fist atop the table. "I will not tolerate it any longer!"

By the time everyone left, Angel was exhausted and longed to fall into her comfortable bed and pretend the rest of the world didn't exist. She snuggled in next to Midnight and Mo and lay on her back, starring at the ceiling. If only she could turn off her mind, but her thoughts bounced rampantly from concern for the Snake, to questions about Big Mike, to worrying about the Brigatte Nero and the Bratva, to the never-ending saga of her mixed-emotions for Tony and Andrew. She closed her eyes and prayed, *"God, thank you for bringing me home safely and help me know the right thing to do."* She sighed and added, *"Please help me with everything."* Then she drifted off to sleep.

CHAPTER 23

Angel awoke with a jolt and glanced at the clock. It was 5:03 am and there was as much commotion going on outside her bedroom as there was in her head. She threw on her cream colored, satin robe and cracked open the door, listening for voices. She could hear Giovanni's voice and several others, so she closed her door, brushed her teeth and her hair, threw on slippers and some lip gloss, just in case Tony and Andrew were there, and headed toward the family room.

"Michelangela," Giovanni called out upon seeing her, "we have awakened you. "Sono spiacente."

"I don't know what that means," Angel said with a yawn.

Giovanni moaned and rubbed his hand over his jowls. "We must have you learn Italian."

"Yeah, I'll get around to that in my spare time," Angel sarcastically uttered and sat down on the couch next to Giovanni's arm chair. "What's all the noise about and why so early?"

"Your new friend Trig showed up at the Towers causing quite a commotion this morning," Giovanni explained.

"At five o'clock in the morning?"

"Si," Giovanni exhaled a long, deep breath. "He demanded to be seen." Giovanni rolled his tired eyes. "This had better be important."

Angel got up to get coffee from the kitchen. As she walked by his chair, Giovanni reached out, grabbing her hand and stopping her. "We have big decisions to make today," he uttered. "They will not be easy."

Angel nodded, but she had no idea what he was talking about. When she returned from the kitchen with two cups of coffee, Giovanni was staring off toward the windows, as if he were lost in thought. "Grandfather, are you okay?" Angel asked.

Giovanni leaned forward, taking his coffee from her. "Michelangela, today everything will be different." Angel studied his face but she couldn't get a read on what emotion he was projecting. Was it sadness? Subdued anger? She didn't know, but there was something strange in his tone. Before she could question him, Giovanni's men entered with Trig in tow.

"I told you, a million times," Trig blurted, "I'm friends with the Boss Lady."

"Shut up!" One of Giovanni's men barked and Trig crossed his arms and bulged his eyes.

"Tell them," Trig said to Giovanni and Angel.

"I said shut up!" Giovanni's man gritted and twisted Trig's arm behind his back, making him holler with pain.

Angel leapt to her feet. "Let him go," she ordered. "He's with me."

Giovanni motioned with his hand for his men to bring Trig over to him. "Selo sieda là," he said and pointed to the dining room chairs. His men immediately dragged a chair from where it had been neatly tucked beneath the dining room table and placed it in the middle of the family room, facing Giovanni; then they pushed Trig into the chair. "Leghilo con un nastro," Giovanni uttered and his men immediately began taping Trig to the chair.

"What are you doing?" Angel asked.

"What must be done," Giovanni responded without taking his eyes from Trig.

"You DO realize that he saved my life. He brought me back home. If it weren't for him, I would be in a corn field in the middle of nowhere and you'd still think that I was dead." Her voice grew louder as she spoke and the uneasiness in her stomach intensified.

"We tolerate no traitors," Giovanni uttered flatly. "Not even when they do one good deed."

Trig started to argue but his mouth was quickly slapped shut with duct tape.

"What did he do? Why do you think he's a traitor?" Angel demanded.

"He is a Cobra!" Giovanni seethed and Angel threw her hands in the air.

"So? We don't have anything to do with the Cobras or any other street gang," Angel argued.

"We do now," he huffed.

Angel plunked back down on the couch and grunted aloud. "What the hell is going on?"

"We received word late last night that two of the local street gangs have been commissioned with a hit," Giovanni explained and Trig started shaking his head violently back and forth and squirming in the chair.

"Who's the mark?" Angel asked.

"You are," Giovanni uttered, taking a sip of his coffee and then leaning forward, returning the cup to the coffee table.

"What?" Angel was on her feet again. "Why?"

"It would seem that there is a substantial bounty on your head," Giovanni sighed.

Trig squirmed harder and squealed beneath the tape, until Angel walked over and ripped the tape from his mouth. He yelped and sucked in air.

"What is wrong with you people?" He gasped. "Don't you know this brother can't breathe out of his nose! You all got issues, man, fat funky issues is what y'all got goin' on up in here," he ranted.

"Shut him up," Giovanni ordered his men, who quickly drew their guns, but Angel moved in front of Trig.

"You're not murdering someone in my family room!" She yelled.

"That's the part that bothers you?" Trig blurted. "Damn, girl!"

"Shut up!" She yelled at Trig, as his words sank in and she found herself in a state of disbelief over the fact that she was more appalled by the possibility of a killing occurring in her family room, than the fact that someone was about to die. *Something in my psyche has gone terribly wrong,* she thought, but there was no time to ponder the subject. "I refuse to let you kill him until we hear his side of the story," Angel said, and then turned her attention to Trig. "You better start talking and you better have the right answers," she said, trying to warn him of Giovanni's rage more than actually threatening him herself.

"Look man, I came here to warn you," Trig said. "When I heard we was given a hunting order and it was for you, I hustled over." Angel studied his face. "Why else would I come here at five frickin' o'clock in the morning?"

"What's a hunting order, exactly?" She asked.

"Your head stuffed on a wall," he blurted, "and one mil in the hands of the hunter."

"One million dollars?" Angel exclaimed.

Trig nodded his head up and down. "Yeah, man, one mil and the order went out to the Cobras AND the Knights which don't make no sense."

"Why not?" Angel asked.

"Because the Cobras, we hate the Knights and the Knights hate us. Everybody knows that, so why give the same order to both of us unless it's an order you want done really fast."

Angel turned and looked at Giovanni, who had that far away expression again.
"Grandfather?" Angel said and drew his attention back to the conversation.

He narrowed his eyes at Trig. "Who sent you this hunting order?"

"I dunno, man, I heard it through Chito."

Giovanni folded his hands in front of him. "And who is this Chito?"

"He's like our mini-boss, like the head dude, only we don't have official rankings like you guys do," Trig quipped. "It's just sort of understood that Chito runs the show."

Giovanni looked to his men. "Bring me Chito," he said and they moved quickly toward the door.

"Wait!" Angel yelled and turned to Giovanni. "What if we send Trig back to gain information? If we bring Chito in, we run the risk of him lying to us, but if we send Trig back, we could use him to get accurate information."

"Wait a second," Trig blurted. "I don't wanta be no freaky spy. Do you have any idea what they'll do to me if they find out I'm spyin' on 'em?"

Giovanni motioned his men back over. "Do you understand what we will do to you if you do not cooperate?"

Trig shook his head. "I see, man, this is one of them offers I can't refuse."

"It's an offer you shouldn't refuse," Angel clarified.

Trig ran his tongue across his lips. "What do I get? I mean, a brother's gotta get something in return right?"

Giovanni glared at him. "You get to live."

Trig's eyes widened. "That sounds fair."

Giovanni's men left to retrieve Chase, who was several floors down in a one-bedroom apartment. Chase had no family to take care of him after he had been shot in the leg by the Shark, so Giovanni allowed him to stay in one of the apartments, where there would be people close by to help him. When Giovanni's men returned to the penthouse with a groggy Chase, Angel met him at the door and laughed out loud.

"Nice jammies," she teased.

He was wearing a white t-shirt and navy-blue flannel pants that were covered in pictures of little cell phones, lap tops and wire connectors. "Vogue says your clothing should fit your interests," he quipped, sarcastically.

"Even your pajamas?" Angel grinned.

"I'm not a freaky-ass clothing designer. I just liked 'em," he shrugged and then stopped abruptly when he saw Trig taped to the chair. "What kind of dumb-ass thing did you do to get yourself taped to a chair?" He blurted and moved toward Trig.

"Nothin' man, I swear. I came here to warn the Boss Lady and this is the funky thanks I get. They taped my black ass to a chair and almost suffocated me."

Chase looked at Angel for an explanation. "They taped his mouth and he couldn't breathe through his nose," she said, throwing her hands in the air.

Angel filled Chase in on the details about the hunting order being given to the Cobras and the Knights. "So you want me to hook Trig up with a bug," Chase said. "No problem."

"I can't wear no wire," Trig mumbled. "They see a wire on me and its lights out for Trig; you know what I'm saying, man?"

"It won't be a wire and it won't be detectable," Chase assured him.

Giovanni's men removed the tape from his ankles and wrists. "How is it not gonna be detectable?" Trig asked. "Everything on the outside is detectable." His eyes widened and he gawked at Chase. "Oh, no, you ain't gonna stick nothin' inside this brother."

Chase grimaced. "You got that right."

Giovanni's men escorted Trig and Chase downstairs to Chase's apartment so Trig could be adequately wired, and Angel couldn't help but wonder where Chase was going to hide the bug. She turned to Giovanni, "where do you think he's going to put it?"

Giovanni shook his head wearily and sighed. "There are some questions to which I prefer not to know the answers. This is one of those."

Angel laughed. "I'm just curious."

"And I am not," Giovanni grinned.

CHAPTER 24

Big Mike was still in bed when he heard vehicles approaching. He jumped up, raced to the window and realized immediately that the Brigatte Nero were back and they weren't coming peacefully this time. He couldn't imagine why they had returned, as he and the Nelson's had already answered all of their questions. He threw on a pair of blue jeans, stepped into his brown work boots, and pulled on a white t-shirt that clung to his muscular biceps. He grabbed a .45 from his night stand drawer and stuck it in the back of his jeans, then grabbed a .38 with a silencer from beneath his mattress and set it on the bed. He slid into a black leather jacket, picked up the .38 and rushed toward the front door. Peering through the peep hole he watched as two Brigatte Nero men approached his door. He moved behind the door and slowly, quietly unlocked it; then he readied the .38 and waited.

The Brigatte Nero knocked several times before trying the knob and pushing the door open. Big Mike knew he needed to move swiftly and kill both men before either one got a shot off. The challenge was that he needed to make sure he killed them inside the house, so he would have to delay the first kill until the second man was all the way inside. It was risky and had to be perfectly executed. Big Mike stood statue like behind the door, trying to control his breathing.

The first man entered and called out, "Hello? Is anyone home?"

The second man entered. "Check the bathroom," he ordered, causing the first man to turn to the left and meet eyes with Big Mike. He raised his gun, but before he could fire, Big Mike shot him through the head, leapt over his body in one fluid motion and planted three bullets into the second man's chest, sending him backwards onto the couch. He unscrewed the silencer from his .38 and slid the gun into his right jacket pocket and the silencer into his left pocket. Each Brigatte Nero carried a handheld Uzi, which Big Mike now slung over his shoulder. He then slipped outside, shut the front door and locked it. Peering around the side of the cabin, he checked to make sure he could make it to the Nelson's house without being seen by anyone. When he saw the coast was clear, he made a mad dash toward the front door, flanked his back against the wall next to the door and peered sideways into the front window. There were two Brigatte Nero inside, but no sign of the Nelsons. Big Mike took a deep breath, slid one of the Uzi's down from his shoulder into his grip and slowly pushed open the front door. He listened for any sign of sniveling or crying; any indication that the Nelson's were still alive. He heard nothing except the voices of the two Brigatte Nero men.

"We don't know if they helped her," one man said.

"It doesn't matter," the second one barked. "We tell Johan they confessed to helping her, then he will be pleased and we can get to Chicago, kill Michelangela and be done with this."

Their voices grew louder as they approached the door and Big Mike tightened his grip on the Uzi. He spun around the corner surprising them and taking out the first man at the knees. He fell forward, screaming and writhing. Big Mike stepped in the center of his back and held the other man, who was fumbling in shock to grab his weapon, at gunpoint. "Get your hands up now or die," Big Mike ordered.

The man was visibly shaken. His hands trembled and Big Mike could tell that he was trying to decide if he could get a shot off before Big Mike did.

"Even if you get a shot off," Big Mike warned, "you're a dead man."

The man raised trembling hands and locked his fingers behind his head. "Please," he said, "I have a family."

"The Nelson's were my family," Big Mike clenched and he could tell by the fear on the man's face that the Brigatte Nero had killed them. "Where are they?"

The man motioned with his head toward the kitchen. Big Mike kept his gun aimed on the man, but walked toward the kitchen and peered in. Mr. and Mrs. Nelson had obviously been sitting at the kitchen table when the Brigatte Nero entered. Their coffee cups and breakfast plates were still in place, but their bodies lay in a heap of blood on the floor. Big Mike screamed at the top of his lungs, strode aggressively into the front room, aimed the Uzi at the man on the floor and fired several rounds into him. The other man burst into sobs. "Omigod!" He wailed. "Please don't kill me. Please!"

Big Mike could feel the adrenaline and the anger violently surging through his veins as he whirled around and aimed the Uzi at him. Grabbing the .45 from the back of his jeans, he shot the man just above his right knee. He fell over, gripping his leg and begging for life.

After taking the man's gun, Big Mike taped his wrists behind him, taped his mouth and threw him in the back of his pick-up, strapping him down and snapping the pick-up bed cover in place. He loaded two canisters of gasoline and the Uzi's into the cab of his truck and then headed down the dirt road away from the Nelson's farm. It would be a five hour drive to Chicago.

CHAPTER 25

The barracks were alive with action as men loaded trucks and supplies into a cargo carrier. Johan barked out orders and the Snake could tell by the intensity in his tone that things were not going as he had planned. Not only had Angel somehow escaped, but several men hadn't returned from their search and weren't responding via radio.

Johan spewed obscenities. "We cannot wait for them!" He yelled. "Board the plane. Our focus now is to kill Michelangela." Johan stopped at the bench where the Snake was seated and yelled down the hallway, "Someone carry this trash to the plane." He looked at the Snake and an evil grinned formed on his lips. "You're going to become bait."

"It won't work," the Snake said. "If she's in Chicago, she's so heavily guarded you won't get near her."

"I won't," he smirked, "but you will."

CHAPTER 26

Giovanni's men escorted Carl, his son Miguel Cusanelli, and his grandson, Salvo Cusanelli from the private jet to the black limousine. Giovanni was notified that they were on their way and sent word for Angel to meet him in the secret meeting room.

Sophia and Olga had already warned Angel about the brashness of Carl Cusanelli, and Angel was certain that their descriptions added to her uneasiness.

"He's a tough son of a you know what," Olga had said.

"Just don't cross him," Sophia had warned.

"You want to take my Taser with you?" Olga had asked and Angel shook her head no.

"I'll be fine," she had assured them. "It's just a meeting." Now, looking in the mirror, she tried to reassure herself. She had chosen a black business suit, with a white blouse and black pumps. She put on silver hoops and her father's silver and diamond cufflinks. They were her good luck charm. Angel wasn't sure why she felt so tense about meeting Giovanni's Compare, but she did. Maybe it was because Giovanni had been acting strangely. Maybe it was because of all Sophia and Olga had told her about him. Maybe it was because Giovanni had said tough decisions were going to be made and everything would change, and she didn't really know what that meant. Whatever the cause, she had butterflies in her stomach, as she left her bedroom and headed toward the door.

Freddie opened the penthouse door and escorted her to the elevator. He was one of Giovanni's men from New York and had been with him for a long time. Freddie stood well over six feet tall, had shoulder length dark, brown hair that he kept tied back in a low pony tail, a neatly trimmed dark goatee and round brown eyes that reminded her of a hound dog.

"Ms. Maratinzano," he said, giving his head a slight nod as he held the door open.

"Thank you, Freddie," she responded.

"May I say you look lovely this morning ma'am," he smiled at her and it was the first time she'd ever seen him smile. Usually he stood staunch and expressionless at the door. His compliment stopped her and she turned to face him.

"Thank you," she uttered awkwardly.

"Are you ready to meet with your grandfather?" He motioned her toward the elevator.

"Yes, but first I'd like to ask you a question. What do you know about Carl Cusanelli?"

She couldn't help but notice the change in his demeanor. His shoulders straightened, his jaw tightened and the casual smile that had filled his face quickly disappeared. "He's Giovanni's Compare," he answered flatly.

"I know that, but what else do you know about him?" Angel studied Freddie's face.

"Nothing. Nobody knows anything about him," he said.

Angel could tell she wasn't going to get any more information out of Freddie, even though she sensed there was something he wasn't telling her. The elevator opened and she and Freddie stepped inside. He entered the secret code and they began to descend. When the elevator stopped, just before the doors opened, Freddie turned to her with a voice of warning. "Don't cross him," he uttered.

"Who?" Angel asked as the doors opened.

"Cusanelli," Freddie whispered. "Don't cross him."

Giovanni was already in the meeting room, seated at the head of the mahogany, rectangular table, which sat in the middle of the room in front of the windows. "Michelangela," he said, rising from his seat and gesturing for her to come closer. "Come sit." One of Giovanni's men escorted her over and pulled out her chair.

"What's all this about?" Angel asked. "Why do I have the feeling I'm about to be blindsided?"

Giovanni folded his hands on the table and smiled at her. "You have your father's smarts," he said with a sense of pride, "and his heart." Giovanni drew in a deep breath and gazed at her. "It is time we solidify our family here. Build it stronger. Unify it with the bonds of matrimony."

"Matrimony?" Angel gasped, feeling her throat go instantly dry.

"I have tolerated your playful banter with Tony and with Andrew, but it must end now. You cannot build a family with an Andriachini or a Venturini. You must be with someone from the Maratinzano family."

Angel's mouth fell open. "You're arranging a marriage for me? Are you insane?"

"No, Michelangela, the choice for a husband will be yours, but I will supply the candidates," Giovanni explained.

Angel couldn't believe what she was hearing. It was as if her grandfather were setting himself up to be her own personal dating service.

She pushed her chair back and stood up. "With all due respect I can find my own candidates."

"Sit down," Giovanni ordered and Angel sank into her chair in a huff.

"You need an Under Boss and a Compare and a husband. The meeting this morning will be to outline what is needed and review appropriate candidates for each."

"I'm fine with the whole Under Boss and Compare thing, but no one reviews husband candidates for me," Angel argued. "Besides, I don't even know if I want a husband."

Giovanni appeared shocked by this statement. "Why would you not wish to marry and start a family?"

That was a hard question. Actually, it was an easy question but a difficult answer. The truth was, she did want children and a husband, at least she did when she thought she was just Angel Martin, a regular woman from Chicago whose most adventurous thing in life was owning Tetterbaum's Pub. Ever since she found out she was Michelangela Maratinzano, head of the Maratinzano mafia family, that desire had changed. It wasn't so much that the desire was gone, but that it was now buried beneath a suffocating fear that something would happen to the people she loved. She couldn't tell him, but there was still a part of her that wanted to run away from this life. A big part of her heart wanted to be normal again. She now understood why her mother had run and why Olga had run. The mafia world isn't all glamour and power, the way it is portrayed in the movies. It is filled with heartache and fear. How could she bring a baby into such a world? Angel dropped her chin and drew along the edge of the table with her finger.

"It's too risky right now," she said. "I have too much to learn and I'm not ready to teach anyone else."

"Michelangela, I don't want you to ever be alone in this life. I am aging and the time I have left is short. Your aunt is aging and her time is hopefully shorter than mine." He looked at Angel and gave her a wink and a cunning grin.

Angel rolled her eyes. "That's not funny."

"Alas, we cannot control the aging process and you are surrounded by an older generation. We must build for you a family of support that will last your lifetime." Giovanni reached out and took her hand in his. "What we do here today, the decisions that we make, we make for your lifelong benefit and protection."

Angel gave him a nod. She didn't like it but somehow it made sense.

Moments later, Carl, Miguel Cusanelli and Salvo Cusanelli were ushered inside. Carl approached Angel with a smile illuminating his face and his arms out-stretched.
"Michelangela," he spoke breathlessly, "it is as if I have awaited my whole life to see you. The last time my eyes beheld you, you were a baby." He kissed each of her cheeks and then turned to Giovanni. "She is even more beautiful than you described," he said.

Giovanni beamed with grandfatherly pride and all the attention made Angel blush.

"May I introduce you to my son, Miguel Cusanelli," he said to Angel. "Miguel knew your father."

Miguel stretched out his hand and shook Angel's. His grip was firm and she could see the family resemblance between him and Carl. Their six foot, upright stature was identical, as was their semi-crooked smile and brown eyes. "This is my grandson, Salvo Cusanelli," Carl said, and Salvo stepped forward to shake Angel's hand. Salvo looked to be about her age, maybe a couple years older, but he didn't look anything like his father or grandfather. He was a little taller with darker, shorter hair that didn't have the same natural waviness as theirs. His eyes were blue green and his smile covered his entire face. Angel had to admit, he was oddly handsome.

As they each took a seat around the table, Freddie arrived to serve coffee and Olga's homemade Cannoli. Angel locked eyes with Freddie a couple of times and sensed that he was trying to send her some sort of message. She wished she could pull him aside and have a conversation.

"Shall we get down to brass tacks," Carl asked and Giovanni nodded.

Carl stood and passed out a spreadsheet with four columns. The columns headings read: Under Boss, Compare, Husband, Members. Beneath each heading was a list of names. Angel scanned the list and noticed right away that Salvo Cusanelli's name was listed in each column and Miguel Cusanelli's name was listed in the Compare column. *That explains why they're here,* she thought, and gave herself a mental head slap. *I should have seen this coming.* Glancing up, she met eyes with Salvo from across the table, and then quickly dropped her gaze back to the spreadsheet. Awkward didn't begin to describe how Angel felt. She continued scanning the list. "I'd like to add some names to this," Angel said.

Giovanni looked surprised. "Who?"

"Chase, for one. He needs to be in the member column."

Giovanni looked as if he were in deep thought and then nodded. "Agreed," he said and Carl jotted down Chase's name.

"Sean Sheperd, or the Snake," Angel clarified. "He should be on the list."

"He is dead," Giovanni said.

"We don't know that and until we do I'd like him added."

"To which column?" Carl asked.

"All of them," Angel said and she could feel Giovanni's eyes on her. She knew what he was thinking. He was wondering if she would seriously consider the Snake for a husband and she guessed by his raised eyebrows and surprised grin that he would approve of such a selection. After all, he was a Made member of the Maratinzano's out of New York so he already met that criteria. Angel playfully raised her eyebrows back at him and then continued scanning the spreadsheet. She didn't recognize any of the other names listed and she noticed right off the bat that neither Tony nor Andrew were in any of the columns. Two of her dearest, most trusted men couldn't make the cut in any category. *That's because they're not MY men,* she reminded herself. They belong to other bogatas. Still, it didn't seem right. There had to be a way to change the rules. She cleared her throat. "My Compare can be anyone I want, right? I mean, he doesn't have to be part of our family."

"He should NOT be part of your family," Carl interjected. "The Compare is a trusted friend from outside the family, which allows his views to remain uncompromised."

"Can he or she be from another family?" Angel asked.

"No," Giovanni and Carl blurted in unison.

"Why not?" She rebutted.

"It just isn't done. It has never been done," Giovanni exhaled.

"That doesn't mean it can't be done," Angel argued.

"I think what your grandfather is saying is that it shouldn't be done," Carl explained. "If loyalty is divided it can become a conceivable detriment down the road."

Angel bit her lip and held her tongue, though every part of her wanted to rant about how ridiculous this whole thing was. Surely, she was capable of selecting her own Compare, Under Boss and members. She was certainly capable of choosing her own husband. Anger and indignation rose within and Angel sighed loudly. "So, what now? Do you introduce me to every man on this list and I decide who I want or is this meeting just a formality and you've already made the decision?"

"I like you," Miguel said. "You cut right to the chase."

Flattery will get you nowhere, she thought but kept it to herself and forced an outward grin. *He's just trying to butter me up because he wants to be my Compare.* Angel felt suddenly repulsed.

"Yes, we will introduce you to everyone on the list and you will offer input as to which column you feel they best fit," Carl explained.

Angel nodded her head. "I see. So, this is like a Mafia dating service. I mean, all of these men already made the cut, right? We're just determining which one I'm going to sleep with."

"Michelangela!" Giovanni reprimanded.

"What?" Angel threw her arms in the air. "Let's just call it what it is. You're basically arranging a marriage for me." She pushed her chair back and stood up, her blood beginning to boil. "I'm very impressed with your spreadsheet Carl, but there's one column missing. There needs to be a Lover column because if Giovanni makes me marry someone I don't love, I can promise you I'm going to have at least one or two men on the side. In fact," she ranted, "why don't you just fill in their names right now." She paced across the room. "I'll be sleeping with Andrew Venturini for sure because he's the slow, sensual Italian lover and I'll be bedding down with Tony Andriachini too because he's the passionate, forceful lover. Oh, and be sure to leave a few extra lines because I'm sure I'll want to add more to the list." She wadded up the spreadsheet and stuffed it into her suit pocket. All four men stared wide-eyed at her with their mouths agape. It looked as if her words had stunned them into silence. "Excuse me gentleman, but I'm going to take a little break." Angel stormed across the room and out the door.

Carl leaned back in his chair and looked at Giovanni, who lifted his arms in the air and rolled his eyes. "È ardente," Carl exhaled.

"You have no idea, friend," Giovanni sighed.

"She's more than fiery," Salvo added with a grin and a raised eyebrow. "She's hot."

Miguel buried his face in his hands. "Il dio li aiuta," he mumbled.

"May God help us indeed," Giovanni repeated in English and Carl chuckled out loud.

"She is exactly like you," Carl said to Giovanni. "Exactly like you."

"Il dio li aiuta," Giovanni mumbled. "May God help us."

CHAPTER 27

Big Mike pulled off to the side of the road and poured one of the canisters of gasoline into his tank. He then uncovered the Brigatte Nero man and poured a gulp of water into his mouth. "Please," the man begged. "I'm going to bleed to death."

Big Mike took a bungee cord and wrapped it tightly around his thigh, just above the gunshot wound. "There," he said, "you'll live for a while."

"Where are you taking me?" He asked, his face pale with fear and pain.

"To the Capo di Tutti Capi," Big Mike answered and, ignoring his pleas to kill him, he refastened the cover and climbed into his truck.

They were now only two hours from the Chicago city limits and Big Mike pulled back onto the road and dialed Chito.

"My caller ID says this is my main man, Big Mike calling, but that can't be right 'cuz I ain't heard from Big 'ol Mikey in years," was how Chito answered.

"It's me, bro," Mike said.

"For reals, man?" Chito sounded genuinely surprised.

"Yeah, man, for reals," Big Mike said. "I need help."

"Listen, man, once a brother, always a brother. What do you need?"

"A place to stay for a couple days," Mike said.

"Mi casa es su casa, bro, you know it," Chito said. "Just like old times."

"Yeah," Mike sighed. "Old times."

"What brings you back?" Chito asked.

"I'm tracking the Brigatte Nero."

"You still on that quest? I thought you followed those jackasses to Iowa?"

"I did, and they're headed to Chicago now and I know exactly where to find them. I'm gonna finish this."

"Alright, man, alright. You know you got back up here. We got your ass covered, anything you need. I'll rally the brothers and we'll see you tonight, man." Chito disconnected, and Big Mike was flooded with a rush of memories. It had been a long time since he left the city and it felt strange to be heading back. He also felt as if retaliation for his mom's death was just around the corner. He would finally be free to start living his life.

CHAPTER 28

Angel stormed passed Freddie, who was standing guard by the penthouse door.

"Everything okay Ms. Maratinzano?" He asked as he reached to open the door for her.

"No," she blurted and kept walking.

Once inside, Angel kicked off her black pumps and grunted loudly.

"Merciful heavens," Olga exclaimed, "what has gotten into you?"

"Giovanni," Angel moaned.

"What did that jackass do now?" Olga waddled to her side and wrapped her arm around Angel's waist, leading her toward the dining room table where Sophia, Olga and Chase were having breakfast.

"He wants to pick a husband for me and he has a list of men." Angel plunked down into one of the dining room chairs and reached for a Cannoli. "The problem is none of the men I would want to marry are even on the list." She shoved a bite of Cannoli in her mouth and resumed her rant. "I don't even know the people on the list except for Carl's grandson, Salvo, and I mean, he's cute but I don't want to marry him."

"Merciful heavens, child, no one's going to marry you if you keep talking with your mouth full," Olga scolded and handed Angel a napkin.

"I don't even know if I want to get married," Angel said with Cannoli squishing from in her mouth.

"You keep chewing like that and you won't have to worry about it," Olga snorted.

"That's it," Angel exclaimed. "Maybe I should go back down to the meeting and act really disgusting? Then Salvo won't want to marry me."

Chase shook his head side to side. "That won't work," he said. "You could pick your nose, eat your boogers and go all crazy-ass gross at the table and he'll still want to marry you."

"Why?" Angel grimaced at the visual Chase painted.

"Power," Sophia chimed in. "Giovanni will position it so that your husband, whoever he may be, will also fill the Under Boss role and take over the family in the event of your demise."

Angel scrunched up her eyebrows. "So that's why I can't marry someone from another family."

"Merciful heavens, no," Olga threw her hands in the air. "Your grandfather will never allow it."

"I'm no mob-ass expert, but I have to agree with Olga on this one. He's not gonna hand his only granddaughter over to another family," Chase remarked as he fidgeted in his chair like a shaky Chihuahua.

"Then I'm never getting married." Angel threw her hands in the air. "I'm just going to have unsolicited sex whenever I want and with whomever I want and see how he likes that."

Chase's mouth dropped open. "Damn, Boss Lady, you are one rule-breaking bad-ass."

"Damn straight," Angel retorted and wished she felt as confident on the inside as she acted on the outside. The truth was that deep down she really did want to marry and have children, but the white, picket fence dream didn't fit into the dark violent mafia world she now knew, and her heart was utterly torn between two men, both of whom she would not be allowed to wed. Leaning her head back against the chair, Angel sighed.

Freddie poked his head in the door. "Ms. Maratinzano?" He called out.

148

"In the dining room," Angel answered.

Freddie stepped into the foyer and walked to where he could be seen from the dining room table. "Giovanni asked that I remind you and Chase of the meeting, which is scheduled to begin in thirty minutes. He asked that I tell Chase to remind Tony and Andrew that they will also be expected at the meeting." Before she could respond, Freddie turned and left.

"He's one I'd like to have unsolicited sex with," Olga blurted, staring after Freddie.

"Lucia!" Sophia exclaimed and Angel laughed out loud, partly at Sophia's reaction and partly at the fact that Chase was so surprised by what Olga had said that his mouth fell open and a piece of Cannoli dropped out.

Olga nudged Angel with her elbow. "Uh-oh, I'm in trouble now. It's always bad when your mother calls me by my real name."

Sophia got up and carried dishes to the kitchen. "You're not setting a very good example," she said to Olga.

"Merciful heavens, the girls had more lovers than you and I put together," Olga blurted and Angel felt blood rush to her face.

"Damn!" Chase blurted.

"I have not," Angel defended.

Olga stood up and waddled toward the kitchen. "She's had Grayson Galante and there was that hot fireman, but that was short-lived, and then there was Tony and of course Andrew..." Her voice faded as she disappeared into the kitchen.

Angel glanced over at Chase, who was staring at her, wide-eyed and with a big grin. Angel pointed at him. "Don't say a word," she ordered. "Not one word."

Chase pursed his lips together but couldn't hide his smile. When Angel stormed off to her bedroom, Chase burst out laughing. "These are some wild-ass women," he said to himself and then stuffed in another bite of Cannoli.

CHAPTER 29

Giovanni sat at the head of the mahogany table with Angel to his left, followed by Chase. Andrew sat to Giovanni's right, and then Tony.

"Where is Carl?" Angel asked.

"He will be joining us shortly," Giovanni replied.

"And Miguel and Salvo?" Angel asked.

"They will not be a part of our meetings here," Giovanni stated.

"Ever?" Angel asked, with a hint of sarcasm in her tone.

"Today," Giovanni answered flatly and then turned his attention to Chase. "What have you found concerning Mr. Clean's phone?"

Chase clicked away at his keyboard. I did a trace on all the numbers to and from his cell over the past several weeks." He pressed a button and his data appeared on the larger screen across the room so they all could see the numbers. "The most frequent incoming and outgoing number is his home number. There are other numbers though, that could be relevant in our search for who hired him."

"Explain," Giovanni said.

"Mr. Clean claims that he never meets the people who hire him, that they call, give him instructions and then wire money to an offshore account. Once the money is received, he waits for confirmation as to where to find the body and clean it up," Chase explained. "He said they sometimes make specific requests, as in the case of your pilot."

"Refresh my memory. What was the request for my pilot?" Giovanni asked.

"They wanted his body to be easily found and to have the Brigatte Nero emblem burned into his chest." Angel grimaced and Chase continued. "Yeah, I know, it's a real whacko-ass request, but that's what Mr. Clean says they wanted and that's what he says he did."

"I know some families hire Cleaners, but that's usually done for more gruesome jobs," Tony noted.

"I'd say branding someone's chest is pretty gruesome," Angel added.

"Nah," Chase fidgeted in his seat, "that ain't nothing. You should see some of the crazy-ass stuff that's out there."

"No thank you," Angel exhaled.

"Most of the families use their own people for the hit and the clean up," Andrew explained, "but there have been situations where their own members don't have the stomach for the job."

"Like what?" Angel asked.

"An ice and dice," Tony and Andrew said in unison.

Angel shuddered. Just the sound of it gave her the willies. "A lot of guys have no problem icing someone, but if they got to dice up the body afterwards, they can't do it," Tony explained.

"So, Mr. Clean never kills anyone, he just cleans up the mess and gets rid of the body in whatever manner the client requests?" Angel clarified.

"Yep, that's the weird-ass truth of it," Chase quipped, clicking rapidly on his keyboard. "And he makes a crap load of cash doing it."

"Let us remain on task with the telephone numbers," Giovanni said.

"Right on," Chase responded. "All the numbers have a 212 area code, which is New York City. There's nothing weird there, but one of the numbers is from Chicago, with a 312 area code and another one is 515, which is in Iowa."

"Did you trace the numbers?" Andrew asked.

"They're all cell numbers, so the area code doesn't necessarily indicate to whom or from where the call originated," Chase said, "but from this point forward we can track the phones via satellite.

"Make it so," said Giovanni.

"I had a crazy-ass notion you were gonna say that, so I already did. I'm pulling up the live data we have for each number," Chase said with his fingers dancing rapidly across the keypad. "Here it is." He pointed toward the big screen and they all turned their heads to watch.

"It looks like our Iowa number is actually in the Chicago area," Andrew pointed out.

"So are a bunch of the New York numbers," Tony added.

"Weird," Chase sighed. "They were all in separate spots earlier today."

"Do you have ID's for the numbers?" Andrew asked.

"Not yet, I'm still running them through various data bases. I know that one of the New York phones is a cell throw away and has no name associated with it."

"Is it still in use?" Andrew asked.

"I haven't been able to track any data from it since the last call made to our Mr. Clean, but I'm still working on getting all the traces to go live," Chase explained.

"Why not bring Sal in on this?" Andrew directed his question more to Giovanni than to Chase. "Sal could run the numbers through the FBI security database and pull up satellite links to any of the numbers that are still active."

"I can do all that," Chase blurted, bouncing his leg up and down and rapidly drumming a pen against it.

Andrew held his hands up in the air as if to motion for Chase to calm down. "I was just suggesting that Sal take over this part to free you up."

"Free me up for what? This is what I do," Chase defended.

"Work in conjunction with Sal," Giovanni instructed. "We want to locate whoever is behind this operation as quickly as possible."

The conversation came to a screeching halt when Freddie entered the room at a brisk pace, leaned down and spoke directly into Giovanni's right ear. "Bring them immediately to me," Giovanni uttered with his lip tightened. "Then ask Carl to join us.

Freddie left as quickly as he had entered and Giovanni rose from his chair. "A man has shown up at the front doors with an injured Brigatte Nero member. He claims he knows you, Michelangela."

"Who is he?" Angel asked.

"He calls himself Big Mike."

Instinctively Angel's hand covered her mouth as she gasped. What was he doing here? Had he driven all the way from Fayette County? Surely, with all his technology he could have found a way to call her and give her whatever information he had. Moments later Big Mike was standing in the secret meeting room and the Brigatte Nero member was being taped to a chair in the corner.

Angel ran to Big Mike and gave him a hug. "How did you know where to find me? How did you know we made it out alive?"

"The chopper was gone so I figured Trig made good on his word and flew you back here."

Everyone's eyes were glued on them as Angel and Big Mike stood by the doors talking. "Michelangela, would you like to introduce us to your friend?" Giovanni said.

Taking Big Mike by the arm, she led him over to the table and introduced him. He dropped his head in a gesture of respect toward Giovanni and slid into a chair near the end of the table. Angel sat down next to him, as she shared the history of his involvement with the Brigatte Nero, telling how they had killed his father and later murdered his mother. He filled in the gaps of information, including how the Brigatte Nero had murdered the Nelsons.

"You have brought us a very important piece of the puzzle," Giovanni said, gesturing toward the Brigatte Nero man, who sat in the corner, taped to a chair.

Big Mike nodded. "He can answer your questions, but you need to know the Brigatte Nero are here now."

"How many are there?" Tony asked.

"Dunno, but I've taken out five of them since yesterday," Big Mike said.

"You were the dude who picked them off in the field by the chopper," Chase snapped his fingers in an a-ha fashion.

"Yes, sir," Big Mike answered.

"You shot them with a Glock G22 didn't you?" Chase excitedly asked.

"Yes," Big Mike said.

"Whoo hoo, I knew it!" Chase blurted.

Big Mike lowered his brows and shot Angel a glance that asked, "Is this guy for real?"

"He likes guns," Angel shrugged. "He would love your hideout."

Angel could tell Andrew was studying Big Mike with his logical detective eye. After Chase's excitement died down Andrew said, "Chase, didn't you say one of the Venturini men was killed by the same gun as the two Brigatte Nero members in the field?"

"Yeah, I did. I mean, yeah, he was," Chase rambled.

Tony folded his arms over his chest and grinned. "Lucy, you got some splaining to do," he mumbled teasingly.

Andrew turned his glare to Big Mike. "You want to tell me why you killed one of my men?"

Big Mike returned Andrew's stare with equal fervor. "Your guy turned his weapon on Trig, one of my brothers and I did what I had to do."

"Are you sure about that?" Andrew asked. "Maybe in all the confusion, isn't it possible that he drew his weapon to defend himself, unsure whether Trig was good or bad?"

Big Mike shook his head. "No."

Tony leaned forward. "How can you be so sure, Ace?"

"First of all, the Brigatte Nero took out the other three and purposely didn't take him out. Secondly, I watched him turn intentionally toward Trig, who was unarmed and running away from the chopper, and take aim." Big Mike raised his eyebrows. "I had a millisecond to determine motive and make a decision and I did what I needed to do to protect Trig."

"If what you are saying is correct, that means we had a traitor within the Venturini family," Giovanni pointed out. "Chase, I want to know everything about that man."

"I'm on it," Chase answered and began clicking away on his keyboard.

Carl entered the room with Freddie and two of Giovanni's men, who stood by the door, while Carl and Giovanni consorted quietly in Italian. This made Angel angry. She hated when Giovanni, or anyone for that matter, conversed in another language in front of her, as if they were taunting her because she didn't know the language. After several seconds Angel cleared her throat obnoxiously loud, drawing all eyes to her. "I'm sorry," she quipped sarcastically, "did I interrupt your private conversation?"

Giovanni gave her an I-know-what-you're-up-to look and turned to his men. "Prepare an apartment for Big Mike and place the Brigatte Nero in the holding room."

"With all due respect, sir," Big Mike said. "I'd like to return to the Cobra's tonight. I have plans for the Brigatte Nero and my brothers are going to help me."

"And it would seem your brothers have plans of their own," Giovanni retorted.

"One of which includes a million-dollar bounty on Angel's head," Andrew chimed in, keeping an analyzing eye on Big Mike.

"A hunting order given to the Cobras and the Knights," Chase chimed in and it was obvious by the expression on Big Mike's face that he considered this to be dangerous news.

"Who gave the order?" Big Mike asked.

"We can only assume it came from the Brigatte Nero," Giovanni answered.

"How did you find out about the order?" Big Mike glanced around the room, as if he were searching all of their faces for answers. "And how do you know it went to the Cobras and the Knights?"

"Trig told us," Angel said. "He came here this morning. He said he heard about it from someone named Chito."

Big Mike's brows narrowed and he shook his head side to side.

"We also received a call last night, warning us that Angel was the target," Giovanni added.

This was news to Andrew and Angel could see the peaked interest on his face. "Who called last night?" He asked.

"The caller remained anonymous," Giovanni said, "but the information he gave was confirmed when Trig showed up."

Andrew directed his attention to Chase. "Did we trace that call?"

"Nah, man, this is the first I've heard of it."

"Well, trace it, Ace," Tony blurted.

"I'm not a crazy-ass mind reader. If I'm not told about a wild-ass phone call, I can't just wake up and know I'm supposed to trace it," Chase mumbled to himself. "Geeze."

"What time did the call come through and to what number?" Andrew asked.

Freddie piped in. "It came through on the main Towers land line and it was a little before 1:00am."

"How many people have access to that number?" Tony asked.

Andrew's lips curled into a grin at the corners. "It's the main land line so pretty much everyone, Sherlock."

Angel could see by the clenching of his teeth and the redness in his face that Tony didn't appreciate Andrew's sarcasm. "You got somethin' you want to say to me?"

"Yeah, why don't you leave the detective work to the professionals," Andrew quipped.

"Near as I can tell the so-called professional in this room is the only person whose family has a traitor involved. Nice work catching that one, Ace," Tony rebutted with equal sarcasm.

"Enough!" Giovanni hollered.

Big Mike moved closer to Giovanni with a stern stare. "Sir, the Cobras are my brothers. If you let me go and meet with Chito, I can explain to them what's going on and call the order off."

"How do we know you won't help them?" Carl asked. "One million dollars to a street gang of low life thugs is a lot of money."

Angel saw Big Mike's jaw tighten and in one fluid motion he grabbed Carl by his collar and lifted him slightly from the ground. "The only low life thug I see here is you," he seethed and Giovanni's men drew their weapons.

Angel threw her arms in the air, motioning for her grandfather's men to stand down. "Big Mike, put him down. You're free to go meet with Chito." Giovanni turned his angry stare to Angel, but before he could question her decision she explained. "He brought us a Brigatte Nero member who will give us more information than he can. If he can't stop the hunting order we are no worse off than we are right now; but if he can bring the Cobras to our side then we will have more power against the Brigatte Nero."

All eyes in the room bounced between Giovanni and Angel as he considered what she had said. "Or, we get rid of the riff raff now and wipe out any Cobra and Knight that makes an attempt on her life," Carl spewed.

Angel held her hand up in a gesture to silence Carl. "We don't do things that way," she blurted, locking eyes with him, "not anymore."

159

She took a few steps closer to Giovanni. "Grandfather, do I have your blessing to proceed?" She didn't want to walk on his authority and she didn't want to battle against him, so she approached him with respect.

"Si," Giovanni nodded. "But one wrong move and we take out Chito and the rest of the Cobras. Capisce?"

"Agreed," Angel said and then she took Big Mike by the arm and walked with him to the door. "Chase, see to it that he has a way to reach us and us him," she instructed.

"I'm on it," Chase answered.

"Freddie, once Chase has him squared away, escort Big Mike from the Towers," Angel ordered.

"Yes, ma'am," Freddie answered.

Angel turned and faced Big Mike. "Thank you," he said.

"You helped me and now I'm helping you back. Please understand, though, if the Cobras come after us we will have no choice but to retaliate."

He bit his lip. "I know."

She took his hand and squeezed it gently. "I don't want that to happen."

"If I can find out who gave the hunting order, I'll contact you," Big Mike promised.

"Good," Angel smiled. "If you can find that out for us, then I promise we'll help you shut down the Brigatte Nero and avenge the deaths of your family

Chase joined them near the door and handed Big Mike a cell phone. "State of the art, bro," he said. "I'll be able to track you anywhere and if you push this button it'll work like a wiretap, feeding the sound back to me. I'll hear you but you won't be able to hear me."

Big Mike nodded and slipped the phone into his pocket. He turned back to Angel and gave her a goodbye hug. "I'm glad you made it home safely," he said.

"You come back safely too, okay?"

"I'll do my best," he said with a wink and then climbed into the elevator with Freddie.

Angel took a deep breath before heading back to the meeting room. She was worried for Big Mike.

CHAPTER 30

Johan and his men unloaded the cargo
carrier and set up their equipment in the hangar of
an old air strip just south of downtown Chicago.
The Snake knew this location well. It was the
same place where he had flown a chopper over the
Russian Bratva during a bloody battle that ended
with the death of the Galante Boss. It was the
same place where Angel had almost sacrificed
herself trying to save Scotrovi, the Russian
operative who went undercover in the Vamloskaya
gang and never came out.

Two Brigatte Nero men carried the Snake
off the plane and into the hanger, placing him in a
folding chair in the corner next to the hangar door.
The frustration of not being able to move was
almost more than he could bear. It taunted him to
be so close to the doorway to freedom and be
unable to get up and walk. He watched carefully
and listened intently to everything, hoping to get a
handle on their plans.

When a black van with dark tinted windows
approached the hanger, Johan rushed out to meet
whoever was on board. The van door slid open and
Johan stepped inside. The Snake strained to see,
but it was impossible to make out who was in the
van. A few minutes later Johan stepped from the
van and began walking toward the hangar. Three
shots rang out and Johan went down. He took two
hits to the back of the head and one to the lower
spine, falling forward onto the pavement in a heap
of blood. The van door closed again and the van

sat motionless. The Snake expected it to immediately speed off and when it didn't, he realized that whoever was inside was so powerful that he feared no repercussions from Johan's men. Whoever was in that van was behind the whole operation and if he could only catch a glimpse, his questions would be answered. If he could only roll himself out of the chair and drag himself across the ground without being seen; but that was impossible.

Before he could devise a better plan, two men made a beeline for Johan's body, gripping it beneath the armpits and at the ankles and carrying it passed him into the hangar.

"Who killed him?" The Snake blurted. "Who's in the van?" But they didn't answer.

A moment later another Brigatte Nero man approached the van and climbed inside. The Snake guessed that he was going to be appointed as Johan's replacement, and he was right. Within minutes the man climbed out of the van, slid the door closed and the van drove away from the air strip.

With an air of confidence, the man strode into the hangar and passed The Snake. "Congratulations on your promotion," the Snake blurted, causing the man to turn, sneer at him and continue on. "If he killed Johan what makes you think he won't kill you too?" The Snake yelled after him.

This time the man stopped, whirled around on his heels and took several steps toward the Snake. "Because I will succeed where Johan has failed," he said with a heavy Russian accent. "I will kill this Angel and the man will be pleased with me."

"You'll never get close enough to kill her," the Snake remarked. "And then you'll be lying face down with your brains splattered everywhere." The man turned in a huff to walk away. "Unless you have someone helping you from the inside," the Snake added. "Someone who knows the layout of the Towers, knows the people and can get you closer than you'll be able to get on your own."

The man grinned with a mouth full of crooked, yellowing teeth. "And you think I am stupid enough to trust you to help us?"

"No," the Snake uttered, "I think you're smart enough to do something Johan wouldn't do. Let me prove myself useful to you."

"How will you prove yourself?" He asked and the Snake could tell that his interest had been peaked.

"Give me a phone and I will set a time and place for you to drop me and for her men to pick me up. When they do, you ambush them and then we return to the Towers in their vehicle. I can tell you where Giovanni stations his men and I can tell you how to get to Angel."

The Snake could see this new leader was studying his face intently. "I will consider your proposal," he said and walked briskly away.

The Snake took a deep breath, leaned his head back and exhaled long and low. If he could get them to allow him to make the call, he could somehow warn Chase that it was a trap ahead of time and reverse the plan. The problem was he wouldn't know for sure whether Chase decoded the message until everything actually went down. It was risky, but he couldn't think of any other way.

Less than an hour later, two men moved the Snake to the back of the hangar, next to the surveillance monitors. The leader met him there and explained the Snake's plan. "Wire him so we can monitor what transpires," he ordered his men. "Also, wire him with a c4 vest."

The Snake looked up. "That wasn't part of the plan," he said.

"That is my part of the plan. I will hold the detonator. If anything goes wrong, you will explode," he said with a sardonic grin spreading across his face.

"How do I know you won't detonate it even if everything goes according to the plan?" The Snake argued.

"You don't," he sneered.

"Fine," the Snake said, "but I want to at least know the name of the man I'm working for now."

"My name is Vladmir Gro..." he began but the Snake cut him off.

"I want the name of the man in the van," the Snake seethed.

This made the yellow-teethed Brigatte Nero leader laugh out loud. "You have no leverage here and no room to make demands." He looked to his men. "Wire him and bring me the detonator."

CHAPTER 31

Angel paced across the family room, chewing on her index fingernail. Carl and several of Giovanni's men were interrogating the Brigatte Nero member. Her head reeled with questions. Was the Snake really dead, as everyone seemed to think? How did the Brigatte Nero know that she had returned to Chicago? Could Big Mike and Trig be trusted? All of that, plus the fact that Giovanni wanted her to marry someone, find a Compare and build a family in Chicago; not to mention that the Galantes were still without a Boss and she had yet to confirm that all the traitors within the five families had been vetted. She exhaled aloud.

"Merciful Heavens, child, you're going to wear a hole in the carpet," Olga said, waddling in from the kitchen and plunking her round hips onto the couch. "Come," she patted the couch, "sit next to your old aunt."

"I can't sit," Angel sighed. "I'm too anxious."

"That's why you sit. To calm yourself down. That's why God gave us bottoms."

Angel knew that arguing with Olga over whether she should sit or not was futile, as Olga would eventually win; so she conceded, sat down and leaned her head against the back of the couch.

"I want to talk to you about something," Olga said and then reached inside her apron and pulled out the spreadsheet Carl had made, noting the candidates for Compare, husband and Made members.

"Where did you get that?" Angel asked, surprised that Giovanni would have given her a copy.

"I took it from your room," Olga winked.

"You snooped in my room?"

"Oh, don't get your panties in a wad; I thought we covered this already. I snoop. I eavesdrop. It's what Italian women do. We're gifted in it," Olga explained. "Besides, your mother refused so she forced my hand. I had to do it."

Angel rolled her eyes. "Whatever makes you feel better."

"I feel wonderful," Olga smiled, "but the point is we need to make you feel better."

Angel narrowed her brow and looked at Olga, as if to say, *I don't know what you're talking about.*

"You certainly can't marry anyone on this list," Olga spouted matter-of-factly. "They're not your type."

"My type?" Angel questioned, honestly unaware that she even had a type. How could she have a type when the two men she loved were so different? Tony was handsome in a rugged way, hot-headed and passionate. Andrew was GQ kind of handsome, logical and romantic.

"Everyone has a type. Take me for instance, I like my men young, hard and hot." Angel laughed out loud. It was true. Olga's taste in men hadn't aged with the rest of her. "Of course, there is something to be said about power. I wouldn't mind having me a piece of that Salvatore pie."

"Olga!" Angel gasped.

"I can't help myself. There's something about that man that makes me want to bake for him and gets me all willy-nilly inside." Olga made the sign of the cross over her body. "He looks like a wrinkled-up toad, but merciful heavens, there's something about that man."

Angel couldn't help but chuckle as she watched Olga describe her feelings for Salvatore. Her round little cheeks were a flushed shade of pink and her eyes sparkled. "You really have the hots for him, don't you?"

Olga's expression grew stern and she shook her finger at Angel. "You repeat any of this, Missy, and I'll take my Taser to you."

Angel held up her hands in surrender. "I don't know what you're talking about," she smiled.

"Good, because I think that Grayson Galante Tasered you enough for a whole lifetime," Olga teased. "Elsa, down at the hair salon, says these Tasers cause brain damage; but I don't know if I believe that. I think I should zap Giovanni a few hundred times and test the theory." Olga made herself chuckle aloud and rubbed her hands ghoulishly together. "The thought alone excites me."

"You're bad," Angel scolded.

"We all have our special God- given gifts," Olga patted her knee with a smile.

"I thought yours was snooping and eavesdropping."

Olga shook her finger at Angel in a teasingly scolding manner. "Don't sass your old aunt." She directed her attention back to the spreadsheet. "The point is you can't let that old coot tell you who to marry. You won't be happy and if you don't have happiness, child, you don't have anything." Olga patted the side of Angel's cheek with her palm. "Choosing a husband is your choice and no one else's."

A long beeping from the kitchen sent Olga jolting off the couch and waddling away, mumbling something about her homemade manicotti. Angel sat quiet, reflecting on their conversation and wondering if she would ever marry and if the choice would really be hers, or would she be confined to the traditional rules of Italian Mafia families.

Freddie entered the front door, disrupting her thoughts and announcing that Giovanni was requesting her presence in the meeting room right away. She followed him out of the penthouse and into the elevator, and as he reached to enter the secret code into the keypad, Angel noticed a tattoo on the inside of his left wrist.

"You were Air Force?" She asked and could see he was startled by the question.

"Yes, ma'am," he said and continued entering the code. Stepping out, Freddie escorted her inside and immediately left the room.

"Michelangela is here, we may begin the meeting now," Giovanni stated and Carl, Tony, Andrew and Chase sat around the table. Giovanni gave a nod to Carl. "Begin," he said.

"We interrogated the Brigatte Nero member. He didn't know the name of the man calling all the shots, but he gave us the name of one of the contacts. Vincent Carlachi."

"Stefano's uncle?" Angel blurted.

"I thought he was in police custody?" Tony directed the question to Andrew.

"We had no grounds to hold him," Andrew explained. "He was released the day Angel left for Italy."

"Nice going, Ace," Tony quipped and Andrew shot him a warning scowl.

"I should have killed him when he was here," Giovanni shook his head. "I let compassion cloud my judgment again." He grit his teeth and slammed his fist onto the table, causing Chase to jump and fling his pen across the room.

"We think Carlachi is a liaison between the Brigatte Nero and whoever is calling the shots," Carl explained. "Probably getting paid a lump sum to coordinate hits and meetings but not directly involved with motive, is my guess," he said.

Chase immediately jumped on his laptop and started clicking rapidly at the keyboard. "Gotcha!" Chase blurted aloud, drawing everyone's attention.

"Explain," Giovanni ordered.

"Remember how I said that there was an Iowa phone number listed on Mr. Clean's phone?" Chase blurted, bouncing excitedly in his seat. "Well, it's registered to a John Doe, which clearly tells us that someone has no imagination for making up fake ID's."

"And?" Tony asked.

"And, when I lock the number into the police database here and in Iowa and then cross-reference it with Sal's FBI mob files, it lists potential candidates based on their last known location, aliases, etc. It's this wild-ass new technology that tries to assign ID's based on whatever data you enter," Chase explained in his usual spastic manner.

"Who are the candidates?" Andrew asked.

"One is Carlachi." Chase grinned and raised his eyebrows into his forehead.

"Who are the other candidates?" Angel asked.

"Stefano is the only other one listed," Chase said. "But we know that ain't right."

"Even if we know that Carlachi contacted Mr. Clean, we do not know what was said," Carl pointed out.

"No, but we can find out," Chase interjected, his fingers dancing across the keyboard.

"Whalah! I love crazy-ass technology!" He blurted, clicking some keys and making a giant satellite picture appear on the screen across the room. They all turned to look and Chase narrowed the view until it showed an airstrip just south of the city, a guard station and a hangar. Angel gasped when she saw the image.

"I've seen this place," Tony said, "and I didn't like it."

"Nobody liked it," Andrew added.

Angel lowered her eyes and swallowed hard. Seeing the hangar and the air strip brought back a flood of memories that she didn't want to remember: Stefano being in the car with her, Scotrovi exploding in the plane, Boglevich blowing his cover to save her, the helicopter whirring around overhead, the gun fire erupting on every side and Kristen shooting her three times in the chest. Thank God she had been wearing a vest.

Giovanni looked to Chase. "Explain the relevance."

"Carlachi is here, or at least his cell phone is," Chase said. "He's in that hangar right now."

Angel could feel the anger rising in her throat, as she clenched her teeth together, pushed back her chair and rose. "Bring Carlachi to me, now."

CHAPTER 32

Big Mike remembered the Cobra hang out well. It was located on the south side of town, just past what was now a vacant hotel, under the viaduct and down the sewer opening. After descending the ladder into the sewer, there was a large open room immediately to the right. Big Mike looked at the graffiti painted on the walls and it brought back a flood of memories. He remembered the first time he met the Cobras. It was right after his mom had been killed and he was running for his life, afraid the Brigatte Nero were going to come after him too. He had stopped beneath the viaduct to rest and that was when Chito found him, listened to his story and took him in. Big Mike ran his fingers over the painting of his name on the damp wall and felt a certain excitement to be back again.

He exchanged the customary handshake with Chito and his other Cobra brothers and was impressed with himself for remembering it.

"Damn, Bro, I think you're even bigger than I remember," Chito remarked, stepping back and gawking up at him.

"And you're still skinny and wiry as ever," he said. Chito launched into a crouched position and moved quickly back and forth.

"Like a cheetah," he said. That's how his nickname came to be. Over time Cheetah was shortened to Chito.

Chito and Big Mike walked into the main sewer area, where they wouldn't be overheard and Chito filled Big Mike in on the phone call he had received from the mysterious man, who gave them the hunting order on Angel. Big Mike then filled Chito in on the Brigatte Nero and seeing Trig in Iowa.

Big Mike slid his hand inside his jacket pocket and pushed the button on the phone that would transmit their conversation to Chase.

"So, you don't know who gave the hunting order but they promised you one mil?" Big mike shuffled his feet. "Tell me about the money," he said. "If you make the hit, how is the money transferred? Where's your drop point?"

"Small airstrip south of town. We make the hit and bring the body there," Chito explained. "But from what I hear, getting close enough to the Capo's granddaughter to take her out ain't gonna be easy." Chito picked up a small rock and threw it down the corridor and it echoed as it hit against the sewer wall and rolled across the concrete floor. "One mil, bro. One mil. That's a lot of dough."

Big Mike studied his face. "If you take out the Capo's granddaughter you won't live long enough to see the dough."

"Probably not," Chito mumbled and shook his head. "Unless we can figure out a way to get the money and disappear real quick like."

"There's no guarantee whoever gave you the order will even pay up," Big Mike argued. "Do you even know if the caller is trustworthy? What if you show up with the body and they kill you anyway."

"We won't show 'em that we got the body until we have the money, bro," Chito rebutted.

Big Mike put his hand on Chito's shoulder. "It doesn't work that way. Listen to me, these guys are the real deal, they're not like us. I've looked in their eyes and they're cold. They'll get what they want and then kill you."

"Well, one thing ain't gonna happen, bro. We ain't gonna let the Knights walk away with one mil, you can bet your white ass on that," Chito said.

Big Mike exhaled. He knew the mindset of a Cobra and the fierce hatred and competition between the Cobras and the Knights. Whoever had given the order to both gangs knew exactly what they were doing. Big Mike shuffled his feet and tried to think of a plan. "I got an idea," he finally uttered after several seconds of silence. "I'll help you get to Angel but first, you have to help me find out who's calling the shots; because I'm not sticking my neck out when we don't even know who we're dealing with and there's no guarantee we'll get the money."

"How the hell am I supposed to find that out?" Chito snorted. "What you think, I'm some FBI, pc hacking sucker?"

Big Mike shook his head. "No, but I think you must have a phone number or some way to reach whoever called you."

"Nah, man, I told you, we was instructed to bring the body to the old air strip."

Big Mike's patience was wearing thin. "Can I see your cell phone?"

Chito gave him a strange look and then dug in his front jean pocket and pulled out a phone. "What you need that for, bro? Don't you got your own phone?"

"Yeah, I do, but a mystery caller didn't call me on my phone and offer me one mil for a hunting order, he called on yours," his voice escalated, as he was clearly becoming frustrated by the conversation.

"Chill out bro, here." Chito slapped the phone into Big Mike's palm. "Knock yourself out."

Big Mike scrolled through the list of incoming calls. There was a blocked number that came through at 1:15am. "Was this the call?" He asked.

"Yep," Chito took the phone back.

"And it doesn't bother you that the number is blocked?" Big Mike asked.

"Nope, everybody blocks their numbers; it's a matter of personal privacy." Chito slid the phone back into his jean pocket. "So, you gonna help us get the money?"

Big Mike leaned against the sewer wall and let out a sigh. "Let me see what I can find out, you know, about where she'll be, how many guards will be with her, that kind of stuff; and I'll let you know. But make me a deal, you don't mobilize your guys and send them out until you've got the go ahead from me. Deal?"

Chito grinned, "Deal, man. We'll wait for you to lay out the plan but make it quick because I ain't gonna lose out to no Knights." They shook on it with their secret Cobra shake. "It's good to have you back, bro," Chito said.

CHAPTER 33

Chase listened to Big Mike's transmission and then went upstairs to the Penthouse and played it for Giovanni and Angel. "If he wasn't on the up and up, he wouldn't have let us hear this conversation," Angel said.

"Perhaps," Giovanni stated, "but, just in case, you are not to leave the Towers." He then excused himself to go downstairs and meet with Carl.

"Big Mike also sent us Chito's phone number, which I'm running through the databases right now," Chase explained. "Sal seems to think we'll be able to unblock the call and get a number which will hopefully give us a name. Even if it's a crazy-ass fake name, we'll be able to find him. Just a matter of time," he said and clicked rapidly on his keyboard.

Andrew left to question his father and brothers and dig up anything he could on the Venturini that Big Mike had killed. They needed to know if this man had really been a traitor or if Big Mike and Trig were lying about what had happened in the field.

Tony left to track down an old friend who had a connection with the Knights to see if he could learn anything about the person who issued the hunting order.

In the meantime, Freddie and three of Giovanni's men took off toward the vacant air strip to find Vincent Carlachi and bring him in. Chase pulled up the air strip and hangar on satellite surveillance. "We should see our SUV's approaching within the next fifteen minutes," he announced.

Angel was pacing the floor between the dining room and the family room, gnawing on her index fingernail when Chase's cell phone rang and startled them both. Before answering the call, he looked at the incoming number and typed it into his computer, starting an immediate trace. "Chase here," he answered.

"It's the Snake," came the voice from the other end and Chase hit the speaker phone button.

"It's the Snake," he blurted to Angel.

Angel's mouth fell open from shock and her heart simultaneously leapt with excitement. "Sean!" She hollered as she rushed toward the phone.

"I'm live. Dropped at south side. Vacant hospital. Underground garage."

"We're on our way, Sean," Angel said. "Hang tight, we're on our way." The call disconnected and Angel shrieked with delight. "I knew he was alive! I could feel it."

"I don't mean to be the lame-ass bubble-buster here, but I don't know if that was really him," Chase said.

"What do you mean? It sounded just like him," she rebutted.

"His voice was choppy, like it had been recorded and spliced together to make us think it was him."

"Well, there's only one way to find out," Angel said. "Let's go."

"No way, uh-uh, not me," Chase twitched his head spastically back and forth. "I'm not taking you out of the Towers after Giovanni just pointed his finger at you and told you to stay."

"What are you, my babysitter?"

177

"Call me whatever you want, but I'm counting on staying alive today and I'm no mob-ass expert but I'm pretty sure the fastest way to die is to cross your grandfather," Chase explained as he raised his eyebrows and moved his head up and down like a bobble head.

"Fine," Angel huffed. "Then have Freddie and Giovanni's men stop by on their way back from the air strip and pick up the Snake."

"Right on, that I can do," Chase said and began clicking on his keypad. He had no sooner dialed Freddie, when the SUV's appeared on the surveillance screen. "Boss lady, we're live on video," he said over his shoulder and Angel slid into the chair next to him and watched as the two SUV's pulled passed the un-manned guard station and toward the hangar.

Angel shuddered in her seat. "Just seeing this place again gives me the heebie jeebies."

"Yeah, I'm having a wild-ass déjà vu right now."

The SUV's pulled toward the hangar and stopped. The two men in the back car stepped out and approached the hangar door, while Chase put his phone on speaker so Angel could hear.

"Freddie, I've got you on live feed," Chase said, "what do you see? Any sign of Carlachi?"

Before Freddie could answer, the hangar door slid open and a line of Brigatte Nero members opened fire on both vehicles. The two men that were out of their car were gunned down before they even knew what hit them. Angel gasped and came out of her seat as she stared at the screen. Freddie floored the gas while Giovanni's man in the passenger seat, grabbed his weapon, opened the window and fired back.

"Don't open the window!" Chase and Angel screamed almost in unison, but their words fell on deaf ears. Bullets soared through the opening, killing the passenger and hitting Freddie in the shoulder. The SUV swerved out of control as Freddie floored the gas pedal, skidded in a circle and screeched the tires, finally straightening the wheel and heading back toward the air strip entrance. The gate was now closed and two Brigatte Nero men stood armed at the guard station. Freddie saw them but didn't let up on the gas. The SUV barreled through the barrier taking Uzi fire, but got away.

Chase and Angel lost visual of Freddie the further he drove from the air strip and Chase yelled into the phone. "Freddie, man, you still with us?"

"Roger that," came a breathless voice. "I'm hit in the wing though, need to head to the hospital and gonna need someone to clean up."

"Right on, we'll send men to meet you at Northwestern Memorial," Chase said and disconnected the call.

Angel stared at the screen, stunned. "Why would he roll down the window?" She asked in a low whisper. "Everyone knows Giovanni's vehicles are bulletproof. Why would he do that? It was like committing suicide."

"It wasn't like it, it WAS it," Chase shrugged. "Some people don't handle pressure well. They freak out and do dumb-ass things." Chase excused himself to go downstairs and report what had happened to Giovanni. "Boy, is he gonna be pissed off," he said on his way out the door. "We just lost three guys and one SUV. It hasn't been a good week for him and expensive modes of transportation."

Angel sat quietly dumbfounded, mulling over what had happened. Chase was probably right. Rolling down the window was just a stupid mistake that cost him his life.   He probably panicked under pressure, she tried to tell herself, but something didn't set well in her gut. These were men that had been with Giovanni for a while. They were used to guns, used to killing, used to bullet proof glass. She shook her head as if to shake the thought from her mind, but it didn't work. It just didn't make any sense.

Angel looked back at the surveillance screen and watched as a black unmarked van drove toward the hangar and slowly pulled inside. She couldn't escape the nagging feeling that the person pulling the strings was in that van, and that somehow the Brigatte Nero were expecting them. She couldn't prove it, but her gut told her that the ambush was orchestrated. Angel leaned back and stared at the screen. "How did you know we were coming?" She mumbled aloud, unaware that Olga and Sophia had entered the room.

"Who's coming?" Sophia asked.

"Merciful Heavens," Olga exclaimed and threw her arms in the air. "If we're having visitors I've got to make some more ravioli and cannoli."

Angel giggled at Olga's drama. "No one's coming," she said. "I was talking to myself."

"She chews with her mouth open and talks to herself, humph, I don't think we need to worry about the whole husband thing," Olga teasingly said to Sophia, who rolled her eyes.

A loud banging on the door interrupted them and Olga waddled over to answer it. When she opened the door, Tony paraded passed her and made a beeline for Angel. "Babe, we need to talk," he said, taking her by the wrist and pulling her out of the dining room chair.

Olga slapped her hands together and grinned. "Ooh-wee, I love me a forceful man," she said, giving Sophia a wink. "Too bad she can't marry that one."

Tony dragged Angel out onto the rooftop terrace and around the corner out of plain view of the windows. Before she had a chance to ask him what this was all about, he pressed her against the side of the wall and kissed her; deeply and passionately. He kissed her in a way he hadn't done in a long, long time and Angel felt her body melt beneath his touch. His fingers wrapped around the back of her neck and weaved through her hair, as he pulled her close, using his other hand to guide her hips against his. She felt his wanting and wished for a moment she could make the world and all of time stand still so she and Tony could openly express the ignited desire trapped between them. His fingertips brushing gently over her breasts confirmed something she knew all along; her body still ached for him. Other men had come and gone but Tony knew her like no one else. They shared a history and nothing could change that nor take away that unspoken comfortable feeling. There was no awkward fumbling, no questions and no fear of embarrassment; Tony knew exactly what she liked. The truth was, despite her feelings for Andrew, she had missed Tony. They're relationship had ended so abruptly that her heart never truly learned to let him go.

Tony drew back from their kiss and took Angel's face in his hands. "Babe," he said and shook his head. "Don't marry anyone else."

Angel was startled, unaware that Tony had any idea about Giovanni pushing her to find a husband. "What makes you think I'm getting married?"

"I know how these things go down. I know Giovanni wants you to build the family and he'll push you to marry so you'll have an Under Boss..." his voice faded. "Please, just don't agree to marry anybody else."

"Tony..." Angel stopped. She didn't know what to say. Even if she were allowed to marry him, would she? *Yes!* There was a part of her that would and that desired nothing more, but that part of her was living in the past. That part of her was remembering life as Angel Martin, the University of Missouri Journalism School Graduate whose biggest concern in life was landing a job and deciding what she would have for dinner. She looked deeply into his eyes. "I don't know what to say," she whispered.

"Say you feel what I feel between us," Tony urged.

"I do. You know I do."

"Then say you won't marry anyone else." Tony moved a piece of hair from her face and tucked it behind her ear. "At least until I can have a fair shot at changing the rules."

Angel rolled her eyes. "You'll never change the rules. Families can't inter-marry. The last time we were engaged almost got you killed."

Tony couldn't refute that statement. When his family found out that his fiancée, Angel Martin, was really Michelangela Maratinzano, Tony was forced to call off the engagement and disappear from her life without explanation. It was an offer he couldn't refuse and remain alive.

He grunted frustration and then pulled Angel into another deep kiss. "I want you, Babe." He smiled and his brown eyes sparkled with desire. "I want you so badly I can't concentrate."

Angel knew the feeling. There was a part of her that wanted to push Tony into one of the patio chairs and climb on. The thought sent shivers of delight up her back and she wondered if he knew what she was imagining.

Tony placed his hands against the wall on either side of Angel and leaned in close enough to whisper in her ear. "Someday, Babe, I'm gonna bring you out here, when the night is clear and you can see a million stars stretched across the sky; and I'm gonna make-love to you."

Angel couldn't stop the smile from spreading across her face.

"I'm gonna touch you in ways no man has ever touched you," he whispered and she could feel the warmth of his breath against her ear. "I'm gonna bring you more pleasure than you ever dreamed possible," he said and then ran his tongue up her neck and fondled her ear lobe. Angel's body flushed with desire. "I know how to take you there," he said and Angel knew he wasn't bluffing. She remembered his magic fingers. "I'm going make you tremble and shake in my arms," he whispered and Angel felt like she was going to explode from the longing that was filling her entire being. He brought his lips close to hers. "Do you want that as much as I do?" He asked.

Yes! Omigod, yes, yes, yes! She didn't say it aloud, but gave a simple nod of her head. While she was hanging in the anticipation of another passionate kiss, Tony pulled back.

"I gotta go, Babe," he grinned, "but I'll be back to finish what we started."

He gave her a wink and left as fast as he had arrived. It took Angel several minutes to regain her composure and go back inside. She didn't want Olga and her mother to see her so flustered.

CHAPTER 34

The Snake had made the call and now there was nothing left to do but hope Chase was able to decode his message. Even if he could decode it in time, there was one thing the Snake wasn't sure he could fix, and that was the C4 vest that had been padlocked to his chest. He began to resolve himself to the fact that his chances of survival were slim to none.

Dropped by a concrete pole in the underground garage, the Snake slumped over in despair. Six Brigatte Nero members were in close proximity, though unseen to anyone entering the garage. They waited, armed and ready to take out Angel's men. It was the perfect ambush, that is, unless Chase could figure it out before they arrived. Waiting was the worst part. It gave him time to think of every awful scenario and the hundred ways this thing could go bad. It made him second guess his actions and fear that he had made a terrible mistake. Had he put more lives in danger? Had he inevitably placed Angel's life in danger? A pit formed in his stomach and he lowered his eyes to the pavement and prayed silently. "Our Father who art in Heaven, hallowed be Thine name, Thy kingdom come, Thy will be done on earth as it is in Heaven. Give us this day our daily bread and forgive us our trespasses as we forgive those who trespass against us. Lead us not into temptation, but deliver us from evil."

"I'd repeat that last part if I were you," came a whispering voice from behind him. The Snake jolted his eyes upward and glanced around. "Stop acting like someone is talking to you and sit still," the voice instructed.

"Who are you?" The Snake whispered.

"Right now, I'm your only hope, so I suggest you sit still and act normal."

"Did Angel send you?" The Snake asked but the voice didn't answer.

All of a sudden, the Snake heard the whoosh of a shot fired from a gun with a silencer. One shot, two shots, three, four, five. In between each shot was a barrage of voices, as Brigatte Nero members yelled, "Did you hear something?" Only to be silenced by another shot. After the sixth shot fired, the shooter appeared and stood before the Snake.

He put his hands to his lips to indicate the Snake should not speak and then lifted a Brigatte Nero radio to his lips and spoke with a heavy accent that sounded like a mix of Italian and Russian. "Maratinzano's men have been incapacitated. Taking prisoner to next location to pursue target."

A heavy accented voice replied through the radio. "Confirmed. Notify arrival at next location and when target is in reach."

"Confirmed," the man replied and then turned off the radio. "Now we can talk," he said, losing the thick accent. "Name's Big Mike." He outstretched his arm. "You must be the guy who threw Angel out of the jet. The Snake, right?"

The Snake was stunned, but reached up and took his hand, struggling to his feet and hobbling on one leg. "Guilty," he said. "Did Angel send you?"

"Nah, it's a long story. I'll fill you in on the way," Big Mike said.

"She's in danger," the Snake blurted.

"That's an understatement," Big Mike rebutted. "But looking at you, I'd say you're in the most imminent danger."

The Snake followed Big Mike's eyes down to the C4 vest and exhaled. "True."

Big Mike leaned closer to analyze the vest. "I gotta be honest, friend, I don't know much about explosives."

"It's a C4 device with a detonator switch," the Snake explained.

"I probably don't want to know who has the detonator," Big Mike commented. "We better get that off you fast."

"No," the Snake blurted. "If you remove it, it'll blow."

Big Mike narrowed his eyes and stared intently at the vest. The Snake tried to read his thoughts but couldn't. "I know a guy who might be able to help." He pulled out the phone Chase had given him and pressed the number one preset for speed dial.

"If Angel didn't send you, how did you find me?" The Snake asked as Big Mike helped him hobble toward his truck.

"I was tracking the Brigatte Nero," he said, hoisting the Snake into the front seat.

"Lucky for me," the Snake said.

Big Mike glanced down at the Snake's vest. "Let's hope we don't run out of luck."

CHAPTER 35

Chase got off the phone with Big Mike and immediately contacted Andrew, who agreed to meet them at the vacant strip mall where what Angel referred to as his "bat cave" was located.

"From the sounds of it, you're gonna need a full-on bomb squad," Chase told Andrew.

"I got it covered. I've worked with someone before and she's the best there is," Andrew explained.

When Chase filled Angel in on what was transpiring, Angel rushed to her room, threw on a pair of jeans and a black t-shirt, black tennis shoes and pulled her hair back into a low pony tail. She shoved her 9mm in the back of her jeans, threw on her sunglasses and met Chase in the foyer. "Let's go," she said.

Chase had thrown his lap top into a shoulder bag, along with several guns and slung it over his shoulder. "I'm just telling you, Boss Lady, this is a bad idea. Giovanni's gonna be wild-ass pissed when he finds out you're gone."

"He's always pissed," she shrugged. "And stop calling me Boss Lady."

She and Chase climbed into the black SUV, affectionately called the Tank because Giovanni had it outfitted with anti-ballistic, polycarbonate layers on all sides and bullet proof glass. Angel came to truly respect the vehicle after it had actually taken a hit from a grenade launcher and remained intact. It felt good to slide behind the wheel. Chase buckled up and gripped the handle above the passenger door.

Noticing his tight grip, Angel laughed. "We haven't even started moving yet."

"I know," he said, bouncing his knee up and down, "but I've seen the crazy-ass way you drive."

Angel rolled her eyes. She didn't drive crazy, though there did seem to be a pattern of destruction with her and vehicles; although most of it wasn't her fault. She couldn't control the fact that people had a tendency to shoot at her. Upon pulling out of the parking garage beneath the Towers, Angel took an immediate left and headed for the vacant strip mall.

Chase checked his watch. "It'll take us approximately nine minutes to get there and only about three minutes for Giovanni to be notified that you've left," he mumbled. "That means one of us should be getting a pissed-off call from him in five, four, three..."

Before he reached two, Angel's car phone rang and she hit the answer button on top of the steering wheel. "Michelangela!" Giovanni's voice was enraged. "You have directly disobeyed my order for you to remain in the Towers."

"I know, grandfather, and I'm sorry; but we found the Snake and he's wrapped in a bomb and we have to defuse it immediately," she justified.

"I do not understand," he bellowed. "You are to return to the Towers immediatamente. Immediatamente!" He hollered. Angel didn't need a translation for that word. It clearly meant RIGHT NOW!

It was always bad when Giovanni spoke in sentences that were inter-mixed with Italian and English. He usually spoke sentences in either Italian or English, but he mixed the two when he

was really upset. "I know you're angry, but the
Snake saved my life and I want to be there to
return the favor."

"What do you know of bombs? You are
putting yourself at great risk and for what
purpose? You must look at the bigger picture. We
have men to handle this. Your protection is of
utmost concern and you are to return
immediately."

"Maybe we should go back," Chase
whispered.

"Who is with you?" Giovanni questioned.
"Is that Chase?"

"Yes, Chase is with me so I'm not alone.
We're meeting Andrew and a bomb squad at the
vacant strip mall across town. I promise to return
as soon as the Snake is safe," Angel explained.

"The strip mall where you say Andrew has
a, what do you call it...." his voice tapered off.

"A cool-ass bat cave," Chase blurted.

"Si, a bat cave that is located in the heart of
Knights territory," Giovanni exhaled loudly and
then spoke in Italian, but Angel had no idea what
he said. She could hear Carl in the background
conversing with him in Italian. *I really need to
learn Italian,* she thought to herself. "I am sending
two men to assist you and to bring you back. Do
not resist them," Giovanni gritted into the phone
and before Angel could respond, the call
disconnected.

Chase's eyebrows were raised into the top
of his forehead. "Man, we are in some deep-ass
crap now," he said, shaking his spikey-haired head
back and forth. "Some deep-ass crap."

"We'll be fine," Angel sighed, but her
stomach was beginning to form nervous knots.
The truth was she hadn't done her homework on
the Cobra and Knights territories. She hadn't

realized that she was headed directly into the heart of Knights turf and she was now beginning to second guess her decision.

"It ain't too late to turn around," Chase said. "I mean..."

"We're not turning around," Angel blurted, cutting him off mid-sentence. She knew it was more logical and definitely safer to go back, but she also knew that she owed the Snake her life and if there was anything she could do to help him, she would be there to do it.

Chase's phone buzzed and he answered. After several seconds, he handed the phone to Angel. "It's for you," he smirked.

"Hello?" Angel said and barely got the salutation from her lips when Tony's irate voice filled her ears.

"Are you out of your frickin' mind, Babe?" He yelled. "What the hell are you doing? You're heading into Knights turf to sit next to somebody wearing a bomb!" Tony was panting in the phone and Angel could only imagine how red his face was. "I'm on my way to bring your ass back home and I'm telling you right here and right now that if you fight me, I will throw you over my shoulder and apply to your more logical side with several swats before throwing your butt in my car!" Before she could respond Tony hung up.

Chase chuckled and Angel tossed the phone at him. "Shut up," she said.

"Applying to your more logical side," Chase repeated. "That's wild-ass hot, right there."

"You heard that?" Angel gawked in amazement.

"Every word," Chase grinned. "These big ears aren't just decoration ya know."

Angel grunted and gripped the wheel tighter. Now she was just plain mad. She was the

Maratinzano family Boss. No one had the right to
tell her what to do or where to go. No one had the
right to remove her from a place she chose to be.
Who the hell does Tony think he is? The more the
anger boiled inside her, the heavier her right foot
fell on the gas pedal.

"Whoa," Chase expelled as she whipped
around a turn at forty miles per hour. "I'm pretty
sure even Bosses have to adhere to speed limits in
this town."

Angel didn't respond. *I dare someone to
pull me over!* She thought and then realized how
out of control her anger had become. She was
absolutely boiling mad. "He'll be lucky if I don't
shoot his ass!" She blurted aloud.

Gripping the handle above the door, Chase
grimaced. "Slow down, speed racer! You won't get
the chance to shoot anyone because you're gonna
kill us first." Angel's face was red hot, flushed
with anger. "Damn, Boss Lady, you gotta take a
breath. You're starting to look like your crazy-ass
grandfather."

Angel whipped the car into the back of the
vacant strip mall, hit the brakes and the Tank
skidded to a screeching halt. She threw it into
park, killed the ignition and jumped out, making a
beeline toward the Snake, Big Mike, Andrew and a
woman she didn't recognize.

They had angled two large dumpsters
toward the building, forming a triangle, so that
they were hidden from passersby. Big Mike stuck
his head out when he heard them approaching.
Once behind the dumpster, Angel dropped to her
knees in front of the Snake and kissed him on the
cheek. "I'm so glad to see you alive," she said.

"Likewise, Ms. Maratinzano," he grinned.
"And I'm hoping to stay that way."

Andrew stepped forward and reached for Angel's arm. "Angel, you need to get out of the way and more importantly, you need to get out of here."

"I wouldn't say that to her," Chase quipped. "It tends to generate a wild-ass angry reaction." Angel glared at Chase, who took two steps backward and held up his hands. "I'm jus' sayin'."

"This is Anya Grovashik. She's a bomb expert and she needs to get to work," Andrew explained, pulling Angel away from the Snake.

Angel looked at Anya and couldn't help but give her the mental size up. She stood about five feet, ten inches tall, had long dark hair with natural waves and auburn highlights. She was slender with the exception of a bust line that far exceeded Angel's, and she wore a form fitting, black, V-neck sweater which nicely showcased her cleavage. Her eyes were bright blue and her face could have graced the cover of Cosmo magazine. In fact, Angel was pretty sure that had she not chosen to be a bomb expert, super model would have been a viable career choice. A twinge of jealousy reared its ugly head as Andrew pulled Angel aside and placing his hand on the small of Anya's back, ushered her toward the Snake. She glanced at Chase, who was gawking at Anya like a drooling Chihuahua, and rolled her eyes.

The radio beeped and Big Mike motioned for everyone to be quiet, as he listened to the incoming transmission. "You have not left the garage location yet. Why?" The heavy-accented voice demanded.

Big Mike disguised his voice. "Taking longer than anticipated to clean up. Will be mobile shortly."

"Confirmed. Contact as soon as you are at the secondary location."

Big Mike met eyes with Andrew. "You better get this show on the road. As soon as they think something's wrong, they'll detonate that vest."

"How do they know that you haven't left the garage yet?" Angel asked.

"Probably a tracking device in their van," Big Mike answered. "I didn't think about checking it. I should have driven the van here instead of my truck," he berated himself.

"Even if you'd have driven their van, they'd still know you weren't at the secondary location," Chase added. "They'd be able to track your ass here, which I'm guessing wouldn't be good."

"The point is, we're running out of time," Big Mike said.

For the first time Angel saw fear in the Snake's eyes. She turned to Chase. "Do we know anyone else who can defuse a bomb?"

Chase shrugged. "I can contact Trig and see if he has any contacts in the area."

"What about Sal? Surely the FBI has resources for these situations," Angel suggested.

"It'll take too long to mobilize a bomb squad, Sweetheart," Andrew piped in.

"We don't' have that kind of time," said Big Mike.

"Anya's the best we have. She can do this. She has studied bombs her whole life and she has miracle fingers," Andrew explained.

"I bet she does!" Chase blurted.

"I've worked closely with her a number of times," Andrew continued.

"Lucky bastard," Chase mumbled under his breath and Angel shot him a dirty look.

"She's amazing. If anyone can defuse it, she can," Andrew said and that was the last straw

for Angel. She abruptly turned her back on
Andrew and stepped toward Chase.

"Not another word," she gritted at Chase.

Giovanni's two men arrived in a black SUV
with tinted windows and quickly approached the
dumpsters. "Ms. Maratinzano, Giovanni has
requested your presence at the Towers
immediately," said the man with the small, black,
triangular goatee.

"I'm aware," Angel responded. "I will return
with my men shortly."

Seconds later, Tony came screeching into
the lot in another black SUV, slammed it into park
and jumped out, racing toward the dumpsters. He
stopped dead in his tracks when he saw Anya, and
Angel watched as his eyes traversed the length of
her body, hesitating momentarily on her breasts.
Angel glared at him, jealousy building in her gut.

"Did you need something?" Angel blurted,
her tone quickly drawing Tony's eyes from Anya's
body to Angel's face.

"Yeah," he mumbled almost dazed, "we
need to go."

Angel crossed her arms. "I'm not leaving
until Sean is safe." Her jaw tensed as she spoke,
and she purposefully used his real name in a
feeble attempt to make Tony and Andrew jealous;
or at the very least plant a seed of doubt in their
minds. It was catty and manipulative but she
couldn't help it. Out of the corner of her eye, she
saw Andrew glance at her when she said Sean's
name; but she pretended not to notice.

"Ms. Maratinzano, we need to leave now,"
the goateed man hollered and pointed at several
rapidly approaching cars. They weren't mob cars
and they weren't Brigatte Nero vehicles. They were
Knights.

"Son of a..." Chase started but his voice tapered off as the cars turned sideways and the Knights began to climb out and take cover behind their vehicles.

"It's been a long time since I've been in a gang fight," Big Mike said, reaching behind his back and pulling a .45 from the waistband of his jeans.

"How'd they know she was here?" Chase asked, setting his black bag on the ground by the dumpster and retrieving a .38 and the Pistol Makrova given to him by the Shark. He held the .38 steady and stuck the PM in the back of his pants.

"Excellent question," Andrew added, pulling out his .45 and shooting Tony a dirty look.

Tony readied his .45 and returned Andrew's glare. "What the hell did I do?"

"I dunno, but their showing up right after you is too coincidental," Andrew retorted.

"Nobody followed me, Ace," Tony snapped.

Andrew looked down at the Snake and Anya, who was frantically trying to defuse the bomb or disconnect the vest. "How are we doing Anya?" Andrew asked.

"I need more time," she blurted.

"We're running out of time," Big Mike said.

"Unless you want all of us to blow up, you've got to buy me more time," Anya demanded and Andrew put his hand on her shoulder.

"It's okay, keep working, we'll figure something out," Andrew reassured her.

"I wish she was working on me," Chase raised his eyebrows and nudged Tony. "If you know what I mean."

"I got ya, Ace," Tony grinned.

Angel stepped in front of Tony and Chase, blocking their view of Anya. "Can we direct our attention to the Knights?" Both men whirled around and peered out from the behind the dumpsters.

"How many are there?" Chase asked.

"I count thirteen, but there could be more," Big Mike answered.

Andrew stepped out from behind the dumpster and held up his Chicago Detective badge. "I don't know what you're looking for," he hollered to the Knights, "but this is official police business and you need to get in your vehicles and drive away."

Noise of grumbling voices filled the air until finally one man from the Knights spoke. "We don't want no trouble from you, cop. We be here for Angel, that's all we want, brother. Give us Angel and we be gone."

"If you're referring to Angel Maratinzano, she isn't here. You've made a mistake," Andrew hollered back.

"Then why is her car here?" The Knight member yelled back and the grumblings grew louder.

"What do you want with a mafia Boss anyway?" Andrew asked.

"None of your business, cop," the Knight sneered.

Suddenly, Big Mike stepped forward and shot the Knight member through the forehead. "Anybody else want to be a wise ass?" Big Mike yelled and the grumbling exploded into a barrage of yelling voices.

Andrew rushed behind the dumpsters. "What the hell was that?" He yelled at Big Mike.

"He pissed me off," Big Mike shrugged. "Knights are disrespectful."

Chase's eyebrows shot high into his forehead. "I hope I never piss your crazy-ass off," he muttered.

"Nice shot, Ace," Tony said. "Now, you got a plan?"

"Yeah, we kill the Knights," Big Mike answered matter-of-factly.

Angel slid the 9mm from the back of her jeans, checked the clip and readied her weapon. She took a deep breath and felt Andrew's eyes on her. He grabbed her shoulders and spun her toward him, running his hands down her rib cage. "What are you doing?" She blurted, somewhat irritated and somewhat happy to see his hands on her instead of Anya. She secretly hoped Anya was taking notice.

"You're not wearing a vest?" Andrew said, as if he were shocked. "I've told you to wear a vest anytime you're outside of the Towers."

"I wasn't expecting to be in a gun fight," Angel argued.

"Sweetheart, you're the Capo di Tutti's granddaughter, you should always expect a gun fight."

The Knights had gathered into a posse and were collaborating behind their cars. "What are they doing?" Tony wondered aloud.

"Probably deciding what strategy to use," Big Mike said. "They don't know how many of us there are and they may not know for sure that Angel's here."

"So, are we just gonna sit here and wait for them to make a move, or you wanta start picking them off one by one?" Tony said, half serious, half joking.

"I got a better idea," Big Mike said, grabbing his phone and punching in a number.

"Who are you calling?" Chase asked.

197

"Back up," Big Mike replied and stepped toward the back of the wall where he could talk more privately.

"Ms. Maratinzano," the goateed man said, "I think we should get you into your vehicle where we can ensure your safety."

"That's a great idea," Andrew piped in. "Since you're not wearing a vest that would keep you from being hit by even a stray bullet."

"You just have to get that dig in don't you?" Angel smirked at Andrew.

"Yes, I do," Andrew grinned. "I figure that if I nag at you enough, one of these days you'll remember to wear a vest all on your own."

"Looking at these guys, I have a feeling there's gonna be a slew of wild-ass, stray bullets flying around," Chase added.

Andrew turned to Giovanni's men. "One of you needs to pull Angel's vehicle beside the dumpsters so that we can get her safely inside." He then turned back to Angel. "Once inside, crawl into the driver's seat and get the hell out of here."

"I'm not just driving away while you guys are in a gun fight," Angel protested. "I'll have Giovanni send more men."

Andrew's jaw tightened and he took her by the shoulders and stared into her eyes. "Stop being so damned stubborn. You're putting everyone in jeopardy if you stay here."

"Listen to him, Babe," Tony chimed in. "For once we agree."

"How am I putting you in jeopardy?" Angel asked, offended by the comment.

"Sweetheart, we've been down this road before. If we have to protect you, we can't take care of business, at least not as quickly," Andrew explained.

"I can protect myself," Angel argued.

"Babe," Tony blurted. "Get your ass in the car and get out of here."

The goateed man made a quick jaunt toward Angel's SUV and climbed inside. It wasn't until he turned on the ignition that the Knights took notice and started yelling obscenities and shooting at the vehicle. Big Mike angled himself between the dumpster and the wall of the strip mall, picking off a couple Knights. Tony took out three more and Chase took down one.

All of a sudden, cars came from every direction, lining up on both sides of the Knights.

"Here's your chance to get away," Big Mike said to Angel. "Make it quick."

"Who the hell are these guys?" Tony asked.

"My brothers," Big Mike replied with a sense of pride beaming on his face. "I told them the Knights had me cornered."

"Right on," Chase whooped. "That's one bad ass plan."

The Brigatte Nero radio beeped and a voice came through speaking Russian. They all froze; knowing their time to defuse the bomb was quickly coming to an end. "They're speaking Russian," Big Mike blurted. "They'll expect me to respond in Russian."

Anya stood up. "I speak Russian," she said.

"You're a woman. They're expecting a man to respond," Big Mike said.

"Tell them to repeat the message please," Anya said.

"How do I say that in Russian?" Big Mike's voice filled with panic.

Anya told him and Big Mike did his best to repeat it.

"Give me the radio," Chase blurted, trading his gun for Big Mike's radio. "If I can tweak the frequency, I can make Anya's voice sound lower, more like a man's." Chase went to work on the radio and within moments, he handed it back to Big Mike. "Anya can talk to them now."

Big Mike handed the radio to Anya. "Tell them we've encountered gun fire from a local gang called the Knights."

Anya repeated what Big Mike said in Russian and then translated their response into English. "They said to send the Snake over to the Knights and they will detonate the vest and wipe out the gang."

"How close are you to defusing the bomb?" Andrew asked Anya.

Her face grew stern. "I can't defuse it, but I think I can get the vest off and we'll have a few seconds to get it to a safe blast zone."

"How much time do you need to do that?" Big Mike asked.

"Two, maybe three minutes."

"Okay, Anya, tell them in Russian that we'll send the Snake over and we'll contact them when he's in position. Tell them it will be maybe four or five minutes," Big Mike instructed.

Big Mike set his watch. "Counting down from four minutes, just to be safe."

Anya shot Andrew a look that Angel couldn't interpret. Was it fear? Was it defeat? Was she quietly signaling Andrew that she couldn't finish the job? There was something in her eyes that Angel didn't understand. "Get everyone out of here," Anya said to Andrew. "Including you. If this thing blows we all die."

"I'm not leaving," Andrew said. "I brought you into this, I'm staying with you until the end."

Angel's jealousy transformed into a mixture of anger and sadness. There was obviously a meaningful relationship between Anya and

Andrew, one so strong that he was willing to give his life.

"I don't want to interrupt any special moments, but we got to get this show on the road," Chase said. "The Cobras and Knights aren't killing each other like we hoped."

"I think that plan backfired, Ace," Tony added. "It looks like they might be cutting a deal."

The goateed man pulled the Tank in front of the dumpsters and slid out the passenger side door, leaving it open for Angel to climb in. "Angel," Andrew barked. "You need to go NOW!" Angel felt completely conflicted. A part of her wanted to leave and knew she needed to leave but it felt cowardly to drive away and leave her men to fight for their lives. "Chase, go with her and make sure she gets back to the Towers safely," Andrew continued. "Make sure you're not followed."

"Right on," Chase said.

Angel bent down next to the Snake. Seeing the fear in his eyes choked her up. She wanted so badly to help him but she was powerless. "Go," he said to her. "Ms. Maratinzano, you need to go."

"Call me Angel," she said, forcing a smile.

He looked up at her, and for a brief moment she saw a sparkle replace the fear in his eyes. "Go, Angel," he whispered, over enunciating her name.

She put her hand on his cheek, lowered her face to his and planted a tender kiss on his lips. "I'll see you at the Towers, Sean," she said.

He gave a slight nod.

"Let's go, Babe," Tony said, pulling her to her feet. "We're running out of time."

"You and Big Mike are coming too, right?" Angel asked.

"We're right behind you," Tony said. "Now get out of here."

"Bad news," Big Mike blurted. "I just spoke with Chito, and the Cobras and the Knights have agreed to split the one-million-dollar bounty on Angel's head. If she gets in that car now, they're gonna follow her."

"Then we'll lead them away from here," Angel said excitedly.

Andrew instructed Giovanni's men to get into the other SUV and leave at the same time, heading straight to the Towers. "Angel, you and Chase take an alternate route to Tetterbaum's," Andrew said and then turned his attention to Tony. "You take a third route."

"All due respect, I think I'm better use to you here," Tony quipped.

Andrew pulled Tony aside. "If this blows you're dead too and then you're no use to anyone. Get the gangs out of here and get Angel home safe."

Tony agreed, and he and Giovanni's men made a quick dash to their vehicles, pulling both of them up to the dumpsters. They slid out so that the gang members had no idea which vehicle held Angel. Dark, tinted windows were one of the many benefits of mob cars.

"Big Mike," Andrew said and patted him on the back, "once they leave I need you to get to a safe location."

"Roger that," Big Mike replied. "We're down to two minutes."

The three black SUV's pulled out. Tony drove one. Angel drove the Tank with Chase in the passenger seat and the goateed man drove the other with Giovanni's man on board. Angel fought tears as she watched Andrew through the rear-view mirror. Her jaw clenched and she gripped the steering wheel tighter. Suddenly an idea popped

into her head and she whipped the wheel quickly
to the right and made an abrupt U-turn.

"What are you doing?" Chase gasped and
grabbed the handle above the passenger door.

"We're going back," Angel said matter-of-
factly.

"Why?"

"I'm not going to play cat and mouse with a
bunch of low life gang members, who just cut a
deal for my head," she hollered and pressed harder
on the gas. "Is your seatbelt on?"

"It's never good, when someone asks that
question," Chase mumbled, reaching over and
strapping himself in.

"Hold on!" Angel floored the gas pedal and
headed straight for the Cobras and the Knights.
Most of the members had jumped into their cars
upon seeing the SUV's pull out, but several
members were still standing in the parking lot.
Angel went for the cars first. She smashed into the
back of a lime green, rusted out Oldsmobile
carrying four gang members, spinning them
sideways. They opened fire on the Tank but Angel
didn't flinch. She knew better. She backed up,
straightened the wheel and then threw the car into
drive and floored the gas pedal again, this time
sidelining the Oldsmobile and smashing it into a
smaller, brown car that already looked like it
belonged in a junk yard.

"You are one crazy-ass demolition driver!"
Chase yelled, his eyes bulging and his spikey head
bouncing up and down.

Angel took out two more cars before Tony
finally caught wind of what she was doing and
joined her in creating wreckage. Tony took the left
side of the lot and Angel took the right. It didn't
take the Knights or Cobras long to retreat, and
Angel laughed out loud as she watched them

jumping into any car available and hightailing it out of the lot. She knew that they weren't gone for good, but for the moment, she felt great satisfaction. When she finally stopped, Tony pulled up next to her so that his driver's window was even with her passenger's window. Chase lowered the window and threw up his hands. "I had nothing to do with it, dude, she's a freaky-ass, out-of-control...."

Tony cut Chase off mid-sentence. "I know." He said, grinning from ear to ear. "I know."

Angel smiled.

The explosion wiped the smile from their faces. Angel saw Big Mike running from the right of the dumpsters and Andrew and Anya running from the left. All three of them were thrown to the pavement as the dumpster to the right lifted into the air and crashed landed several feet from its original position. Angel threw open her door and ran toward the dumpsters, but Tony caught her in motion and spun her around to face him. "No!" He yelled. "I can't let you go back there." Her breathing was erratic and her heart was pounding. Her eyes darted wildly, trying to assess what had happened. Tony gripped her face with both palms. "Angel," he spoke loudly in her face. "Get back in your car. I'll go look and come tell you."

Angel stepped backwards. Her hands trembled as she took a piece of her hair that had fallen from her pony tail, looped it behind her ear and nodded her head in agreement. If the Snake had been blown to pieces she didn't want to have that image burned into her memory forever. Angel watched closely as Tony disappeared into the thick dark smoke, while Big Mike scrambled to his feet and made his way toward Andrew and Anya. Aside from a few bruises and aching heads from the sheer impact of the explosion, they were all fine.

Big Mike helped steady Anya as they walked to where Angel stood, and Andrew staggered into the smoke after Tony. Angel chewed on her index fingernail, keeping her eyes glued on the cloud of smoke, waiting.

After several moments, silhouettes appeared in the smoke. Angel took two steps forward and squinted. How many were there? Two or Three? It was hard to tell. Tony and Andrew were moving slowly with the Snake dangling between them. He was unconscious but in one piece and Angel could think of nothing more beautiful in the entire world than the sight of the three of them emerging from the smoke alive. She rushed toward them, as did Big Mike, who helped Andrew and Tony lift the Snake into the back of Tony's SUV.

Angel approached Anya, who was leaning against the front of the Tank. "Thank you," she said, extending her right hand.

"I hope you don't expect me to kiss your hand or something ridiculous like that," Anya said, her eyes burning into Angel.

"No, I was going to shake your hand," Angel answered, confused by Anya's reaction.

"Let's get one thing clear," Anya said, standing up straight. "I'm not your friend and I don't work for you. I don't respect killers," Anya folded her arms across her body. "And there are no bigger killers than Mafia Bosses." Angel opened her mouth to speak, but Anya kept going. "Oh, I know you might not be the one who actually pulls the trigger, but you're the one who orders the hit, and that's just as bad. Maybe worse. If I had my way, I'd have let your mafia man explode. One less killer in the world." She took one step closer to Angel and lowered her voice. "The only reason I'm here today is because Andrew asked me for help. I did this for him. Not for you and not for your people." Before Angel could say a word, Anya paraded off and stood next to Andrew, who turned and gave her a long, tight hug. She glared at Angel over Andrew's shoulder and Angel climbed slowly back into the Tank.

"What was that all about?" Chase asked, but the lump in Angel's throat kept her from answering. She threw the SUV in drive and sped out of the lot.

CHAPTER 36

It was three in the morning when Angel sneaked quietly to the kitchen to make a cup of tea and raid the fridge for some left-over Cannoli. She carried the tea and plate of Cannoli to the dining room table and just started to sit down, when Giovanni's voice startled her.

"Anything over there for an old man to eat?" Giovanni asked from the shadow of his armed chair.

Angel jumped. "Don't do that! You almost gave me a heart attack."

"Oh, I wouldn't worry about that. We, Maratinzanos have strong hearts," he said.

Angel carried the Cannoli to Giovanni and then retrieved another one and another cup of tea from the kitchen. Then she took a seat on the couch by his chair. "What are you doing up so late?" She asked him, stuffing a bite of Cannoli in her mouth.

"I am up early, not late," he corrected. "Time is all in one's perspective." He sipped the tea. "I was thinking about you."

"What about me?"

"About your dangerous escapades this afternoon," his eyebrows narrowed. "About your courageous nature." His face became less stern. "About the depth of your heart for your men." His face grew concerned. "You have risked your well-being for your men, even against their urging. You have a very special heart, Michelangela."

Angel rolled her eyes. "No I don't. I'm just a killer like every other Mafia person."

"A killer?" Giovanni scoffed and appeared for a moment as if he were amused. "You are a lot of things, but killer is not one of them."

Angel felt that all-too-familiar lump rising into her throat. She didn't want to cry. She didn't want Giovanni to see her be emotional and weak.

"Who have you killed?" Giovanni asked and Angel couldn't escape the feeling that this wasn't a typical conversation that took place between most grandfathers and their granddaughters.

"I killed the Galante Boss," she shrugged.

"In self-defense," Giovanni added.

"I killed Denny," she said.

"To save your mother," Giovanni replied.

Giovanni was right. She wasn't a cold-blooded killer. Just because she had become desensitized to people being killed didn't mean that she had become a murderer. She'd never ordered a hit on anyone. If anything, she had fought to keep people alive. She fought for Tony's life and Andrew's life and Stefano's life. The lump in her throat started to dissipate and Angel smiled at her grandfather.

"Men who kill without reason are killers," Giovanni said. Admittedly, it was a philosophy that was a bit warped, but in the light of this lifestyle it made perfect sense.

"You're right," Angel said. "I'm not a killer."

"Why would you ever think you were?"

Angel sighed. "Just something somebody said." They took a moment of silence to bite their Cannolis and sip their tea. Then Angel noticed that faraway look forming in Giovanni's eyes again. "Grandfather, is something wrong?"

Placing his tea cup on the coffee table, Giovanni leaned back in his chair and ran his hands over his jowls, as if he were trying to decide how or where to begin. "I am an old man," he began slowly, "a man that has had many years of experience with people. Reading people. Few were more skilled at reading the motives of men than I."

"I've heard that you used to be called the lie detector," Angel interjected and Giovanni's face lit up with surprise.

"Did your aunt tell you that?" He asked and Angel smiled and nodded. "That was a very long time ago. I fear my skills are weakening with age."

Angel moved closer, placing her hand atop his on the arm rest. "Your skills aren't weakening, times are changing."

"A good leader changes with the times," Giovanni replied. "In my day, we did not have the technology of computers and satellites and tracking devices. We had only our instincts and our guns. Men who looked guilty were guilty. There was no tracing phone calls and framing others. Our world was more dignified than that. Good was good and bad was bad. A hit was made in public in the middle of a restaurant, only the target was hit and everyone knew who had made the hit and why. We set no traps and we told no lies." Giovanni squeezed Angel's fingers. "The world you have to live in is one death trap after another, and I fear I do not have the wisdom to bestow on you for this age."

Angel slid to her knees next to his chair and kissed Giovanni's hand. "You have given me more wisdom than you know. You, Salvatore, my mother and my father have made me who I am. Don't be afraid for me."

"You must have strength and wisdom surrounding you…" he began but Angel interrupted him.

"I know." She slid back onto the couch. "I know this is why you want me to marry and have a Compare and an Under Boss. I understand your reasons." She leaned back on the couch and stared up at the ceiling. "That's why I'm not sleeping right now. How do I choose a husband when I can't even select from the ones I love most?"

Giovanni cleared his throat. "Who would you choose, if there were no restrictions?"

Angel sighed deeply and felt a hollow aching in her heart. "I don't know." Tears formed in her eyes. "I was going to marry Tony before I knew who I was, and I still love him very much; but then there is Andrew and..." she stopped talking and exhaled.

"And?" Giovanni prompted her to continue.

"I don't think he feels the same way," she sighed. "I thought he did, but, something's different now."

"Ah," Giovanni nodded. "Another woman?"

Angel's eyes widened. How could he know that? She hadn't told anyone what Anya had said to her, and no one knew that seeing Andrew with Anya had made her feel jealous. Had someone else noticed the interaction between them and said something about it to Giovanni? Or maybe she wasn't as good at hiding her feelings as she had thought? Angel shrugged. "I'm not sure. Maybe."

"I am not skilled at giving advice in the matters of love, but perhaps you should forget about Tony and Andrew for now, and focus your attention on Salvo Cusanelli and Sean Shepherd?" Giovanni rose from his chair and gave her a wink. "They might be very good husband candidates, but how can you see if you are unwilling to even take a look." He walked slowly across the room.

"Why didn't you ever remarry?" Angel blurted out of the blue, although it had been a question she always wanted to ask and never found the right time. It stopped Giovanni in his tracks and he turned to face her. "Was it because you were afraid you would lose her again?"

Giovanni slumbered back into the arm chair. "Si," he said. "Your grandmother was the love of my life. L'amore della mia vita," he repeated in Italian. I vowed never to love another and I have kept that vow."

"What was she like?" Angel asked.

Giovanni leaned back in the chair and his eyes sparkled as he began to tell stories about Angel's grandmother. "She had the biggest heart and the meanest temper I'd ever seen packaged in one tiny woman," he chuckled. "One time she threw a shoe at me and the heel whizzed by my face and wedged into the drywall." Giovanni chuckled aloud and his face glowed as he relived precious memories. "She was a spitfire."

"How did you know she was the one for you?" Angel asked.

"The moment I saw her I couldn't take my eyes away. She was walking out of a bakery with a loaf of freshly baked bread. She was the most beautiful girl I had ever seen and I leaned over and told my buddy, that's the one for me." His eyes lit up when he spoke and he shook his finger in the air. "I told him, that's the girl for me."

Angel smiled. "I wish I could be so sure of myself."

"Your world is different. What we held sacred, your generation throws away. Young people today give themselves away too easily and too often and then they wonder why their heart is confused." Giovanni rose from the chair. "This old man is going to lie back down and rest now," he said, kissing the top of her head and then heading for the door. "Sweet dreams, Michelangela."

"Sweet dreams, grandfather," she said and then flopped over on the couch. Maybe Giovanni was right. Maybe she needed to give Salvo and the Snake a chance, though who was to say if they even wanted a chance. Salvo was probably being coerced by Giovanni and Carl, and Sean, well, Sean had never given her any indication of interest.

Giovanni poked his head around the foyer wall. "Michelangela, you are the spitting image of your grandmother. I do not doubt that she looks down from Heaven and smiles on you." He gave her a wink and left.

CHAPTER 37

Vladmir approached the black van with a certain sense of hesitancy, knowing what had happened to Johan when he failed. He stepped inside and closed the door.

"You idiot!" The man in the back of the van spewed. "You lost our prisoner, a prisoner that would have drawn Angel out and made her an easier target."

"We are not certain what transpired," Vladmir said. "But I will find out."

"You had a detonator. Why didn't you use it?" He seethed.

"It would have killed our people too," he replied.

"We cannot afford more errors."

213

CHAPTER 38

Upon opening the penthouse door, Angel was immediately stopped by Freddie, who stood guard with his arm in a sling. "Why don't you take some time off?" Angel asked, glancing at the sling.

"I'm okay Ms. Maratinzano. The bullet went right through," Freddie said.

He followed Angel to the elevator. "You don't need to help me," she said, "I'm just going downstairs to talk to Chase."

"I'll escort you."

"Really, I'm fine," Angel argued, but Freddie insisted and stepped into the elevator with her.

Once inside, Freddie stood staunch and faced the front, while Angel couldn't help but stare at him out of the corner of her eye. Somehow, he was different from Giovanni's other body guards, though she couldn't put her finger on it.

"I've been instructed to remind you not to leave the building," Freddie said with his jaw sternly set.

"What makes you think I was going to leave the building?"

"Your keys are in your left jacket pocket, your cell phone and license are in your right pocket, your 9mm is in the back of your pants and you're wearing a bullet proof vest," he said without turning his head away from the elevator doors. Angel's mouth fell wide open. "That, and the fact that I've been instructed to give you this." He retrieved a small, white envelope from inside his sling and handed it to her.

Angel opened the envelope and pulled out a notecard that read: "Meet me at Tetterbaum's alone. We need to talk." It was signed, "Andrew."

"Did you read this?" Angel asked.

"Yes, ma'am," Freddie nodded.

"And you think I should go?"

"No, ma'am. I can't advise you to go against Giovanni's orders," he said.

"But...?" Angel asked, as his tone clearly indicated there was a but to follow.

"But I know you're not going to listen to him or to me," he said, finally making eye contact with her. "So, I will escort you."

Angel smiled. She knew there was something she liked about Freddie.

As she and Freddie entered the lobby, Giovanni's men were escorting Trig inside. "Ms. Maratinzano," one of the guards spoke, "he says it's urgent that he speak with you."

"What is it Trig?" Angel asked. "I'm on my way out."

"I need to talk to you in private," Trig mumbled, his eyes darting between Giovanni's men, as if he didn't trust them. Angel assumed that he was naturally jumpy because of the way he was treated the last time he was in the Towers. After all, being taped to a chair and held at gun point isn't exactly a trust builder in any relationship.

"I can't right now," Angel answered flatly and then turned to the guards. "Take him upstairs to see Chase."

"But, Angel, give a brother a second," Trig blurted.

"Chase will help you with whatever you need," she said and hurried with Freddie toward the garage entrance. She had one thing on her mind, meeting Andrew.

Angel pulled the Tank into the alley and parked behind Tetterbaum's Pub, adjacent to the backdoor. It had been several weeks since she was inside the pub. In fact, the last time she was there was the night that she met Scotrovi, and the Vamloskaya massacred her patrons and staff. She and Chase had narrowly escaped by hiding in the secret passageway between the kitchen and the bar, where Mr. Tetterbaum had once hidden his infamous tapes. She closed Tetterbaum's prior to leaving on her trip to Italy and hadn't yet reopened it.

While inserting the key into the backdoor, Angel discovered that the door was already unlocked and assumed that Andrew was already inside. Besides, the hall light was on. She turned to Freddie. "Would you mind waiting outside the door?"

"No, ma'am," Freddie said.

Angel walked down the hall, making a mental note that the air inside was damp and stale, and for the first time, the pub felt lifeless. She stopped momentarily at the wooden desk, which sat against the wall just in front of the hallway leading to the bathrooms. She flipped on the kitchen lights, made her way to the bar and turned on the tiny yellow lights that lined it. It cast a yellow hue throughout the main dining area and brought a flood of familiar warmth. There was a time when she had loved working at Tetterbaum's Pub, and she now understood that a big part of her affection for the pub was linked to her feelings for Andrew. When she met Andrew, he was working undercover as a bartender, trying to locate Tetterbaum's tapes. They spent almost every evening together behind the bar and Angel missed those nights. Even after she had purchased the pub, Andrew stayed on and worked alongside her.

Angel walked around the outside of the bar, running her fingertips along the top. It felt smooth and clean. She was surprised Andrew wasn't standing behind the bar but shrugged it off. He was probably in the restroom. Ducking beneath the serving arm to reach the main dining room light switch, Angel suddenly felt her boots give way to something slippery on the floor. She glanced down and gasped at the shadowy figure of a young woman, gagged and bound with a knife driven into her abdomen. Angel backed up and screamed, and then reached into her pocket, retrieved her phone and dialed 9-1-1. She slid back under the serving arm and backed away from the bar just as two men, wearing ski masks ran from the bathrooms straight down the hallway and out the back door. Angel drew her gun and held it in front of her as she raced down the hallway, towards the back door. She called out for Freddie, but he didn't respond. Pushing the back door open, she headed for the Tank, running straight into Salvo, almost knocking them both down.

"Whoa!" Salvo gripped her arms to steady her. "Why are you in such a hurry?"

Angel's eyes were wide with panic and her hands were trembling. "Salvo?" She gasped. "What are you doing here?"

"I knew you owned the pub and I wanted to see it, so when Olga said you were here I thought I'd drop by," he explained. "Is it a bad time?"

Angel nodded. "You need to get out of here before the police get here," Angel said. "There's a dead girl behind my bar and..."

Salvo gasped. "Did you kill her?"

"No!" Angel blurted. "Just go back to the Towers and I'll meet you there after I talk to the police."

Salvo nodded. "Are you sure you're okay?"

She convinced him that she was fine and prodded him to leave. The last thing she needed now was to try to explain to Carl that his grandson had been arrested on suspicion of murder.

Two police officers and an ambulance arrived and Angel escorted them inside. Moments later, Andrew entered briskly through the backdoor. Two strides behind him was Anya. Angel explained to the police how she had found the body and as soon as she was finished giving her statement, Andrew took her by the arm and pulled her into the kitchen.

"What the hell are you doing here?" He demanded. "You're not supposed to leave the Towers and especially alone!"

"I came to meet you," she seethed. "And I wasn't alone. Freddie was with me."

"What?" Andrew stared at her as if he had no idea what she was talking about.

"I got your note saying to meet you here, so I came right away and I brought Freddie with me. I didn't realize you were busy with Miss Magic Fingers," she pushed by Andrew and headed down the hall toward the backdoor.

"Where are you going? You can't just leave a homicide scene," he said, following her down the hall.

She whirled around and pointed her gun in his face. "Watch me," she spat, her eyes narrowed with anger.

"Don't do this. I need to know what happened."

Angel's eyes welled up and she struggled to hide her emotion. "I came to meet you and I found a body behind my bar. That's what happened."

"Sweetheart," he said and reached for her, but Angel stepped back and held her aim.

"Don't sweetheart me," she said. "This is over."

"What's over?"

"Whatever we had or didn't have. Everything between us is over." She stormed out the back door, with Andrew on her heels.

He grabbed her by the arm, spun her around and pushed her back against the Tank. "What's this really about?" He yelled. "You're throwing a fit because you're jealous? Is that what all of this is about?" Angel didn't answer. She felt too embarrassed and too upset to even speak. "Sweetheart, there is nothing between me and Anya. We work together every now and then. That's it."

"Maybe you should tell her that, because she made it very clear that you were hers," Angel said, pushing Andrew back, turning around and pulling the driver's door open.

"What?" Andrew said with a genuine shock in his voice.

"Why did you tell me to meet you here and then bring her?" Angel said with disdain. "Did you just want to rub it in my face?"

Andrew stared at her, as if he didn't know what else to say. "Sweetheart, I didn't..."

"We're done," she cut him off. "You just keep her as far away from me as possible because the next time she calls me a killer, I'll prove her right." Angel climbed in the Tank, slammed the door and drove off. She didn't know what happened to Freddie or who had killed that poor, young woman behind the bar, and at the moment she didn't care. All she knew was her heart was breaking and she'd lost Andrew forever.

She was almost at the Towers when her cell phone rang. It was Chase calling with more bad news. "Where are you?" He blurted into the phone.

"I'm almost home. I'll talk to you when I get there," she said, trying to mask the fact that she had been crying.

"You're not at the pub, are you?"

"I just left there, why?"

"Oh, thank God," Chase exhaled loudly and Angel was beginning to hear panic in his voice.

"What's going on?" She asked.

"There's been an explosion at the pub. I don't have all the details, but according to Trig the Cobras and Knights had a plan to make it look like they blew you up so they could get the payout."

Angel's mind was racing almost as fast as her heart. "Oh my G...." Angel's voice cut short. "Chase," she gasped. "Andrew was inside."

"What the hell was he doing at the pub?"

Angel's hands were trembling. "I don't know. He was coming to meet me to talk, I think. I don't know. There was a dead woman behind the bar and then I turned around and called the police and Freddie was gone and...." Her voice cut off mid-sentence as what Chase told her about the Cobras and Knights plan sunk in. "They killed that woman and then blew up the place so they could pass her off as me."

"That's what Trig said their crazy-ass plan was," Chase acknowledged.

"What about Andrew? And Anya was there too and there were two paramedics and two police officers," Angel ranted. "And Freddie, what about Freddie? He just vanished."

"Just get back here now and meet me in the penthouse," Chase blurted. "Hurry and try not to let anyone see you."

Angel pulled into the garage at the Towers and made a beeline for the elevator. She passed two of Giovanni's men that were guarding the front doors. When she reached the penthouse, Chase was already there and so were Trig and Tony. Chase had his computer on the dining room table and was clicking wildly at the keys.

"Have we heard from Andrew?" Angel blurted as she came through the door.

"Andrew and Anya left before the explosion," Tony said, "but the paramedics didn't make it."

Relief flooded her. Being angry at Andrew was one thing, but she didn't want him dead. "What about the two cops?" Angel asked.

"I'm pulling up the feed from the security cameras now," Chase said.

"The surveillance is running even when the pub is shut down?" Angel asked.

"I've always got the cameras rolling," Chase said. "Olga eavesdrops and I videotape, it's our God given talents."

"Babe," Tony pulled her close to him, "you okay?"

Angel nodded, but she was lying. She wasn't okay. She could have been blown up. As weird as it sounded, that wasn't what was really bothering her. It was Andrew. Her heart was broken over Andrew, but she could hardly explain that to Tony.

"What about Freddie?" Angel asked. "Was he in the explosion?"

Chase's fingers flew across the keyboard at warp speed. "Uh-uh, at least not according to the initial police report. Just the two paramedics and

221

a dead Jane Doe." Chase brought up the security camera just before the explosion. "See, it looks like right when the paramedics go to move the body, the bomb goes off."

"Yo bro, I told you that was the plan. Kill somebody that looks like Angel, put the body in the pub, smoke the pub and then when the police retrieve the burnt unidentifiable body, they assume it's Angel and the Cobras and Knights split the one mil," Trig explained.

"That's the stupidest plan I've ever heard," Angel sneered. "What about finger prints?"

"Burned 'em off after they killed her," Trig quipped.

"What about dental records, Ace?" Tony chimed in and Trig's face dropped.

"I don't think they thought of no dental records," Trig said. "We ain't exactly high tech, bro."

Chase stopped typing and turned to face them. "I have an idea," he said, twirling a pen spastically in between his fingers. "I say we help the Cobras and Knights with their plan. Let everyone think it really was Angel killed in the pub, and then we follow the money trail to the real man calling the shots."

Angel stared at Chase, mulling over the idea and trying to find any cracks that would shatter the plan. She could tell by Tony's expression that he was doing the same. "How many people saw you alive after the explosion?" Tony asked.

"You guys and two of Giovanni's men guarding the front doors."

"That's it?" Chase asked.

"Well, Andrew saw me drive away from the pub, and maybe Anya," Angel said. "The two cops, if they're alive, know that I wasn't the dead woman

222

behind the bar," she added as she began to pace across the room.

"Still containable," Chase said. "If Angel stays out of sight."

Olga peeked her head around the kitchen wall and into the dining room. "You want me to Taser her? One good zap will keep her down for a while."

Angel pursed her lips and crossed her arms, giving Olga a look that said she wasn't amused.

"That's not a bad idea," Tony replied with a grin.

"Shut up," Angel retorted. "I won't leave the building."

"You left it twice already," Chase said.

"Yeah, Babe, what were you doing at the pub anyway?" Tony asked.

Angel didn't feel like going through the whole story, so she pulled the white envelope from her jacket pocket and handed it to Tony, who read the card aloud.

"Why wouldn't Andrew just come here to meet with you?" Chase asked. "And why would he show up with Anya, if he was telling you to come alone?"

Tony wadded up the note and threw it across the room. "That son of a bitch almost got you killed!" He seethed.

"Weird that he shows up with a bomb expert and then a bomb goes off. That's funky-ass ironic right there," Chase quipped.

"I'm telling you I don't trust him," Tony spewed.

"Yes you do," Angel argued. "You don't like him but deep down you trust him; otherwise you would have killed him when Giovanni ordered you to kill him." Tony grunted, but the look in his eyes said she was right.

"Freddie's the one whose motives are in question. He's the one who gave me the note to begin with," Angel explained. "And Salvo showing up."

"Salvo?" Chase blurted. "Salvo Cusanelli was there?"

"Yes, but only for a minute and he never went inside. I ran into him when I was coming out the back door."

Olga peeked her head back into the dining room. "I can help with that one," she said, waddling in while wiping her hands on her bright yellow apron. "I might have told him that I thought you might be at the pub and might have recommended he drop by to see you." She had a guilty grimace on her face.

"How would you know I was going to the pub?" Angel asked.

"Merciful Heavens, I was only trying to help," Olga wailed, throwing her hands into the air.

Angel winced within. Every time Olga tried to help with her love life it turned out ugly and Angel had a distinct feeling this time was no different. "Exactly how did you try to help?" Angel asked.

"I might have overhead your conversation with Giovanni and might have thought I would help by giving you a little shove in the right direction," Olga explained. "There's no harm in an old aunt nudging her niece on the road toward happiness, is there?"

"Go on," Angel mumbled.

"I suppose I might have jotted down a note and then given it to Freddie and then I might have made him swear he would go with you so you would be safe."

"You wrote the note?" Angel yelled.

"That is one cunning-ass old lady, right there," Chase chuckled. "Woo-hoo! I did not see that coming."

"And you said it was from Andrew?" Angel wailed.

"Merciful Heavens, can you blame me? I knew you'd rush off to meet him and then Salvo would be there to console you when Andrew didn't show up."

"Sounds like you had it all planned out," Tony remarked and Angel shot him a dirty look, as if to say, "don't encourage her."

"Well, now, how am I supposed to know some street gangs were going to kill someone who looked like Angel and then blow up the pub?" Olga put her hands on her rounded hips. "I'm not a mind-reader you know."

Angel was ready to pull out her own hair. Not only had her pub been blown to smithereens, but she had humiliated herself in front of Andrew, probably placed Freddie in some type of danger and God only knows what kind of lunatic Salvo probably thinks she is; and all because her eavesdropping, meddlesome aunt couldn't keep her nose out of her love life.

"Let me guess," Angel began, "my mother was a part of this big charade too, right?"

"Merciful Heavens, no, child, your mother would never come up with a plan so perfectly orchestrated. She's just not that sneaky," Olga gloated.

"Perfectly orchestrated?" Angel repeated. "Is that your perspective of what went down today?"

"I can't be held responsible for some gangs mucking it all up. My plan was perfect," Olga argued and threw her hands in the air.

"Where is my mother?" Angel asked, exasperated.

"She might be out on a date with Miguel Cusanelli, showing him all of Chicago," Olga grinned.

"You set my mother up with Miguel?" Angel gawked.

"I was just trying to help," Olga argued. "Giovanni's not going to let her marry Joseph Venturini anymore than he'll let you marry Tony or Andrew, so I thought that you marrying Salvo and her marrying Miguel looked like a nice little packaged deal." She threw her arms into the air and stormed off toward the kitchen. "Curse the old woman for trying to make everyone happy," she moaned and then followed it up with several Italian phrases that Angel didn't understand.

Chase's eyes were bugging from his head. "She is one wild-ass woman right there. If I were older I wouldn't mind ...."

"Chase!" Angel interrupted. "I don't need that visual in my head."

"Nobody needs that visual," Tony added.

"True dat, man," Trig said. "What the hell's wrong with you, bro?"

"I like a woman with a devious plan," Chase chuckled.

A call from Sal, Andrew's long-time FBI contact, beeped on Chase's computer and he answered with video conferencing. "Sal, any news?" Chase asked.

"Yes, but I fear it is not the news you were hoping to receive."

"Lay it on me," Chase said.

"The telephone numbers are not registered to any names within our current or past database, which indicates one of two things; either we are dealing with professionals with very good aliases or we are dealing with brand new criminal minds," Sal explained.

"Damn," Chase grunted. "Thanks Sal." Chase disconnected the call.

Angel paced around the family room. "Before Giovanni finds out what has happened, I need to know if Salvo has returned to the Towers," she said. "If he hasn't, I need someone to find him."

"Yeah, 'cuz he saw you alive and knows you ain't the dead chick in the pub," Trig stated the obvious.

"I also need to know what happened to Freddie," Angel said. "I can't go to Giovanni with inaccurate information or a bunch of guesses. He's already going to hit the roof because I left the Towers."

"I'm on it, Boss Lady," Chase said and started clicking away at his keyboard, pulling up surveillance feed from the cameras both inside and outside of the pub.

Turning to Tony she said, "I need you to contact the Snake and Big Mike and tell them to come here right away."

"Got it, Babe," Tony said, pulling out his phone.

"We need all the information we can get before I go to Giovanni," she reiterated, pacing and chewing on her index fingernail.

"What about Andrew and Anya?" Chase asked. "You want me to call them in too?"

Angel paused. She hated the fact that Anya had seen her alive and therefore needed to be brought into the Towers before she talked to anyone. She didn't trust her and she certainly didn't like her, but if their plan was going to work, they had to secure anyone who knew Angel didn't die in the explosion. "I'll handle them," Angel mumbled, pulling out her cell and stepping onto the patio where she could talk in private.

CHAPTER 39

The two bodyguards, who had seen Angel alive, were taken to the secret meeting room, and two new guards were placed at the front doors. Tony, Chase, Big Mike, Trig and the Snake, who despite having a broken leg, was now coherent, hydrated and looking much better, joined them.

Andrew arrived with Anya, but upon entering the building, Anya was immediately separated from him and escorted by Giovanni's men to a holding room just below the penthouse. Andrew was instructed to join the group in the secret meeting room.

Angel entered the meeting room and asked everyone to sit down around the long mahogany table. She took Giovanni's regular place at the head, folded her hands on the table and waited until they were all seated. The moment her eyes met Andrew's, she could tell he was irritated by the fact that she had had Anya escorted from him; but in that moment she didn't care.

"Giovanni and Carl are out for the afternoon so we need to work quickly. Before they come back and join us, I want a plan of action in place." She stood up and began to pace around the table. "Anyone not in this room is not a part of this plan and should not be trusted." She couldn't help but tighten her jaw and glare at Andrew when she spoke. "Does anyone have a problem with this?" No one said a word. "If someone from outside this group is brought in, they will be detained until such a time as they are proven trustworthy."

"Guilty until proven innocent," Andrew mumbled under his breath. "Sounds like someone else I know."

"Back off, Ace," Tony said, and shot Andrew a glare that Angel thought just might have had the power to blow his head right off.

Angel motioned for Chase to begin and he tapped on his keyboard, pulling up Tetterbaum's surveillance video feed on the big screen so they could all see. "If you look closely you can see that the bomb went off as soon as the paramedics tried to move the body."

"So, the EMT's didn't stand a chance," Andrew interjected.

"No," Chase agreed. "They didn't even know what hit 'em. Now the cops are over here by the front door, and they got out alive." They all watched the two police officers run through the front door on the surveillance feed. Chase clicked some keys and the feed switched to the surveillance camera outside Tetterbaum's front door. "See, the cops leave the pub, but then look. They don't get in a cop car or go across the street and call it in. A black van pulls up and they both climb in."

"Where did the van come from?" Andrew asked.

Chase shrugged. "I don't know. The whole thing just looked to be timed a little too perfectly if you ask me."

"Agreed," Tony said.

"What about Freddie?" Angel asked. "Any sign of him?"

"Yeah, but it don't look good," Chase said, altering the video feed to show the outside surveillance camera angle at the pub's back door. "Angel walks in, says something to Freddie..."

"I asked him to wait outside," she interjected.

"Then a few minutes later Freddie walks down the alley and disappears around the corner," Chase explained. "It's the damnedest thing."

"Maybe he had to take a leak and didn't want to do it right by the back door so he went around the corner?" Trig posed.

"He could've taken a leak inside," Andrew said.

"It looks like something caught his attention and drew him away," Chase said. "See how he suddenly looks up and to the right and then starts walking in that direction."

"Can you pull up a camera angle showing where he went exactly?" Andrew asked.

"Nope." Chase threw his hands in the air. "It's as if he knew that down that alley was the only spot I couldn't see."

"You thinkin' what I'm thinkin', Ace?" Tony said to Andrew. "That Freddie's the one driving the black van?"

"It crossed my mind," Andrew said.

"Here's another strange happening," Chase said and switched to the inside camera near the pub's back door. "We see Angel and Andrew conversing, Angel pulls a gun on Andrew, not sure what all that was about," Chase began.

"You two care to elaborate on that?" Tony asked.

"No," Angel and Andrew said in unison.

"Angel walks outside, Andrew follows her and look what we have here," Chase said. They all watched as Anya walked down the hall, pushed the back door open a crack and leaned out.

"She was listening to our conversation?" Angel blurted.

"Seems she has the same gift as Olga," Chase teased. "But that's not the part that bothers me."

"Well, it bothers me!" Angel spat.

"No, what I mean is, why is she so interested in what you're saying? Is it because she's hot for Andrew or jealous of Angel or maybe she's reporting information back to someone?" Chase explained.

"Eavesdropping isn't a crime," Andrew said.

"No, but I agree that we need to take a look at the motive behind it," the Snake added.

Andrew shook his head and stared down at the table. "I've worked with her on and off for over ten years. She's one of the good guys."

"Sometimes good guys make bad choices," Angel said matter-of-factly and stunned herself at how much she sounded like Giovanni.

"Let's jump to the phone records. This is where it gets really good," Chase said and fidgeted in his seat, twirling a pen between his fingers. "I checked the incoming numbers on Mr. Clean's phone, Chito's phone and cross-referenced them with both incoming and outgoing numbers on Vincent Carlachi's phone. I'm also running a trace on Anya Grovashik's phone." Andrew's eyes widened with surprise and the anger he was feeling was evident in the tensing of his jaw.

"This is bullsh..." Andrew began and Angel cut him off.

"We need to hear this," she said. "Chase, continue."

"Remember we had isolated three cell numbers from Mr. Clean's phone, one with a New York area code, one with a Chicago area code and one from Iowa. Our Brigatte Nero visitor gave us

Vincent Carlachi as a contact name that he
claimed to recognize, but we now know this was
only to throw us off course."

"What?" Angel blurted with surprise. "You
mean Carlachi isn't behind this?"

"No," Chase said. "Vincent Carlachi's cell
phone was taken from him when we held him
captive here at the Towers several weeks ago,
before you left for Italy. His phone was never
returned to him." Chase pulled a manila folder
from his black bag which sat on the floor next to
his chair leg and slid it to Andrew. "If you check
the police report from the day he was found here,
taped to a chair and taken into custody, there is no
cell phone mentioned in his list of belongings."

"So, what does this mean, Ace?" Tony
asked.

"There are two crazy-ass possibilities, and
neither one bodes well. First, it could mean that
someone from inside our own organization took
Carlachi's cell phone and used it to make the call
to Mr. Clean. This would mean that he would have
had prior knowledge of Giovanni's pilot's murder
and instructed Mr. Clean to brand the Brigatte
Nero emblem into his chest." Chase took a deep
breath. "Or, option number two, Carlachi's cell
phone was indeed confiscated by the police, but
was intentionally left off of the list of belongings so
that it could later be used to frame Carlachi and
keep us from finding out the name of the man or
woman behind the entire scheme."

"Either way, Vincent Carlachi is innocent,"
Angel said.

"Well, I wouldn't go that far, but he sure
ain't guilty of what we're dealing with today,"
Chase replied.

"I put a trace on Carlachi's cell phone
number, and anyone want to guess where it was

last used?" Chase smiled and let his eyeballs dart around the table.

"Just tell us," the Snake said.

"Chicago, more specifically, two blocks up from Tetterbaum's Pub, a mere ten minutes after the bomb went off." Chase was beaming and Angel could tell that he was totally in his element. "You want to know who they called?" Chase asked, and let his fingers glide across the keyboard and the New York number appeared on the screen.

"I see it's a New York number, but is the phone currently in New York?" Big Mike asked.

"Nope," Chase said. "It's right here in Chi Town." Chase clicked a few more keys and brought up a satellite map. "Right here at our favorite Russian hotspot."

Angel stared at the screen and winced when she saw the hangar and the airstrip. "Not again," she mumbled.

"What does this have to do with Anya?" Andrew piped in. "Do you think she was the one using Carlachi's phone? Is that why you're holding her?"

"No," Chase answered. "Though that is a viable option. I'm tracing her phone because she was within that vicinity when the call was made. I'm tracing your phone too." Andrew's eyes widened.

"We're holding her for now because she knows I didn't explode at the pub," Angel said. "And we're only holding her until the plan comes to fruition and we find whoever is calling the shots. After that, Anya, if she's not involved, will be free to leave."

"What is your plan?" Andrew asked.

Angel defaulted to Chase who explained the plan in full detail. He told them a statement would be released to the press indicating that confirmation had been received that Mafia Boss, Michelangela Maratinzano had been murdered in a bombing that took place at Tetterbaum's Pub. "The report will state that the Capo di Tutti is grieving, yada, yada, yada, and a memorial service announcement will follow in the next several days," Chase explained. "Chito will undoubtedly contact whoever ordered the hit and make arrangements for payment," Chase said.

"Hold on," Big Mike interrupted. "Chito told me there was no contact number and his instructions were to bring the body to the hangar."

"That's a problem," Tony said.

"Why not send Trig or Big Mike back to the Cobra's with a tracking device?" Andrew posed. "Then they can go along to pick up the money, get a visual of the person and record what is said."

"Oh, no, you ain't puttin' another one of them devices inside me, man," Trig spurted. "No way, man."

"We'll work out the details, the point is, we follow the Cobras and Knights to the rendezvous location and find out who's behind the whole operation," Chase explained.

"Sounds weak," the Snake said, drawing everyone's eyes.

"You got a better plan?" Chase defensively asked.

The Snake, whose broken leg was propped up in the chair next to him, grimaced as he shifted in his seat. "I think I do." He cleared his throat. "While we were behind the dumpsters I couldn't help but notice that Anya spoke to the Brigatte Nero in Russian."

"She's originally from Moscow," Andrew interjected.

"Do any of you know Russian?" The Snake asked and everyone shook their heads to indicate no.

"Do you?" Andrew asked.

"No, but I can't get passed the fact that she had a conversation in Russian with some of the Brigatte Nero and none of us know exactly what was said," the Snake explained. "She conversed with some of the most ruthless killers in the world and appeared comfortable. That doesn't sit right with me."

I knew I didn't like her, Angel thought.

"She's a bomb expert," Andrew said. "She's very good under pressure."

I'm sure she is, Angel's mind raged, though she remained outwardly expressionless. *Under pressure, under the covers, whatever!*

"What's your plan?" Chase asked.

"Since we have her here, we use her to communicate with them again, only this time we set it up to be interpreted," the Snake explained.

"If none of us know Russian, man, how do we interpret it?" Trig asked.

"I can link into an audible translation site, without her knowing," Chase uttered and then shoved the pen behind his ear and started clicking on his keyboard.

Andrew shook his head. "First, she's not guilty of working with the Brigatte Nero, but let's pretend for the sake of argument that she is. If you pull her in here and ask her to make a call, she'll know it's a set up and she'll say exactly what you want her to say." Andrew shook his head. "She is a highly trained expert in her field. She will see through what you're proposing."

"Not if we seem desperate," Angel added, raising her eyebrows. "If we make it appear that we are desperate for her help, wouldn't she be inclined to help us? I mean, you're the one that says she's one of the good guys." Angel glared at Andrew and he licked his lips and shook his head. "And if she isn't a good guy, wouldn't she take this opportunity to manipulate the call to her advantage?"

"Fine. What would you tell her to say to the Brigatte Nero?" Andrew asked.

"We set up a meeting," the Snake replied. "The man in charge is named Vladmir. Whoever is running the show rides around in a black, unmarked van and never leaves the van. I'm guessing its bullet proof. Vladmir's afraid of him, and I would be too after he gunned down the previous commander, a man named Johan Bernardelli, simply because Angel made it back to Chicago alive."

"Bernardelli," Tony narrowed his brow and looked at Andrew. "Why do I know that name?"

Andrew shrugged. "Doesn't ring a bell."

"Anyway," the Snake continued, "we can assume that since I'm free and Angel is still alive that Vladmir is in deep trouble and desperate. We set up a meeting to turn the tables on whoever is in the van."

"You mean side with the Brigatte Nero?" Big Mike blurted with disgust.

"The way I see it, the Brigatte Nero isn't the real enemy," the Snake said and Big Mike came out of his chair.

"They're my real enemy!" He spat.

"I get that," the Snake said calmly, "and you'll have your revenge."

Big Mike's jaw clenched tighter. "They publically killed my father, beat and murdered my mother and then killed the only family I had left. I will not side with them even for one second!" Big

Mike's face was fire, red as he spoke and his hands clenched into fists.

Angel felt compassion for him. She knew what it was like to have your father murdered in cold blood. She knew the helplessness of having someone you love violently taken from you. She gazed up at Big Mike with eyes of understanding. "I promise we will help you avenge your parent's death and the Nelson's murders. You have my word that the Brigatte Nero will pay for their crimes against your family, and they will pay with their lives." Angel's jaw was set. "You have my word." Big Mike nodded and slid back down into his seat. Angel turned her attention back to the Snake. "Please continue," she said.

"I think we have to assume that the Brigatte Nero are working for the man behind the scenes with the promise of one of two things, money and power," the Snake explained.

"Which means whoever this is has a crap-load of both," Chase added.

"Right," the Snake agreed.

Andrew leaned forward, resting his elbows on the table and Angel could see the wheels spinning in his head. "Or stands to gain a lot of power," Andrew said, almost more to himself than to the rest of the room.

"What'd you say, Ace?" Tony asked. Andrew didn't answer. His brow was narrowed and a sudden seriousness had come over his face. He looked at Angel and then his eyes darted to Chase, the Snake, Big Mike and back to Angel. Tony snapped his fingers in front of Andrew. "You got something you want to share with the class?" Tony quipped.

Andrew held up his index finger to indicate that he needed another minute to process his thoughts, and then he rose from the table and walked over to where Chase was sitting. "Pull up the surveillance video from the main dining room at Tetterbaum's, the one where the two cops are standing near the front door."

"Right on," Chase said and clicked on his keyboard. Seconds later the feed was up on the larger screen across the room.

Andrew walked toward the screen and pointed to the cop standing to the right. "This is officer Bernardelli," he said. "We call him Bernie."

Tony snapped his fingers. "That's how I knew that name. Bernie's the go-to guy when we need to remove evidence from a crime scene."

"Which family does he work for?" Trig asked.

"All of them. Anyone who needs something in the evidence department to magically vanish goes to Bernie," Tony explained.

"Or have it stricken from the list of belongings," Andrew added.

"Like Carlachi's cell phone," Angel said with an ah-ha tone.

"Do you know the other cop?" The Snake asked.

"No, he's a newbie on the force," Andrew replied.

"So, he's either in on it or dead," Tony said and Andrew nodded in agreement.

Trig put his hands to his ears and closed his eyes. "La,la,la,la,la," he sing-songed aloud and the whole table stared at him.

"What the hell are you doing?" Chase hit his shoulder, causing Trig to open one eye.

"I know how this goes down, and this brother don't wanta know or see too much, 'cuz when you know too much, man, that's when you end up in the bottom of the lake," he stuttered.

"I don't think anyone's ever accused you of knowing too much," Big Mike teased.

"Yeah, man up," Chase blurted. "You're embarrassing."

Angel smiled at Trig. "We never kill anyone for knowing too much."

"Yeah, Ace, it's the dumbasses we get rid of," Tony chuckled.

Andrew was still staring at the video surveillance up on the screen. "Chase, can you pull up the feed from the street cameras in front of the pub? I want to get a look at the van again."

"That's the van I saw at the hanger," the Snake blurted. "Whoever is in that van is the person calling all the shots."

"I say we notify our brothers and have the Cobras find that van," Big Mike interjected with a sudden enthusiasm.

"Wait a second," Andrew said and held up his palm. "We need to make sure we're connecting all the dots." He paced around the room.

"Oh, no," Tony whined. "Here he goes with his cop-titude."

"Yo, bro, what's cop-titude?" Trig asked.

"It's that investigative attitude cops have. I call it cop-titude," Tony explained.

Chase laughed out loud. "That's a cool-ass word."

Ignoring their banter, Andrew continued, "We know the Cobras and Knights joined forces to kill Angel and split the one-million-dollar bounty, right?" Everyone nodded. "We know the Cobras and Knights killed the woman behind the bar so they could claim to have killed Angel and get the money."

"Right on," Chase said.

"We're dealing with street gangs here, and a street gang mentality is not to stage a killing. They kill all the time and for way less than a million dollars. Something doesn't feel right," Andrew ran his hand through his hair and exhaled.

Clearing his throat and standing up slowly, Big Mike swallowed hard. "I had something to do with that," he confessed. "I convinced Chito that the Maratinzano family would back him up in taking out the Knights if he staged Angel's death in the meantime and helped lead us to the Brigatte Nero who gave the hunting order."

"Now, that makes more sense," Andrew said and Big Mike slid back into his seat. "My second question is, why did Salvo show up at the pub?"

"I can answer that one," Angel said. "It seems Aunt Olga in her meddlesome, matchmaking ways tried to arrange a spontaneous date for me."

"With Salvo Cusanelli?" Andrew gawked as if completely surprised.

Tony laughed at Andrew's expression. "I know, Ace, he is totally not her type."

"Not at all," Chase added.

"What can I say?" Angel threw her hands up and forced a grin. "He's on the potential husbands list." She rolled her eyes, pushed her chair out from the table and walked toward the windows.

"So, Olga wrote the note that you thought was from me, which is why you thought you were meeting me at the pub," Andrew mumbled to himself as he walked closer to Angel. She looked at him and it was evident in the softness of his eyes that he now understood why she was so upset when he showed up with Anya. "I'm sorry," he mouthed to her.

The Snake, who had been scribbling down notes on a piece of paper, chimed in. "Wait a minute; did you say there's a husband list?"

"Yes." Angel sighed with embarrassment. "Giovanni is pressing me to marry, take on a Compare and an Under Boss and strengthen the family here in Chicago."

"Holy Mary Mother of..." Tony stopped himself and pound his fist on the table. "Babe, we gotta see that list."

"No!" Angel blurted. "It's private."

Tony and Andrew stared at each other, as if they were exchanging silent thoughts, then they both made a beeline toward Angel, while Chase slipped out the door unnoticed. Andrew was closer and got to Angel first. "Sweetheart," he began, "the man who marries you stands to gain a lot of power."

"A helluva lot of power," Tony added.

"Not just the man who marries her," the Snake chimed in. "Her Compare, the Under Boss or her husband could easily be the one to take over the family in the event of her demise."

"Would that person be able to give power to the Brigatte Nero in the city?" Big Mike asked.

"No," Angel answered. "The other Bosses wouldn't allow it. Look what happened to Galante when he sided with the Russian Vamloskaya. The Bosses rallied against him."

"She's right," Tony said, "one boss alone wouldn't have that much power."

The Snake turned his body as much as he could to face the windows where Angel, Tony and Andrew stood. "But the Capo di Tutti Capi would."

Chase slipped back in the door, carrying the spreadsheet with the list of candidates.

"The Capo di Tutti Capi?" Angel repeated and scrunched up her face. "You think my grandfather is working with the Brigatte Nero?"

"No," the Snake said. "But the man who marries you or becomes your Under Boss steps into a unique position."

"He's right," Andrew uttered, almost shocked by the thought. "He stands closer than anyone else to become the next Capo di Tutti Capi."

"Whoa!" Chase blurted, "I did not see that crazy-ass angle coming."

Trig plugged his ears again and sang, "La-la-la-la. I hear nothing.' I see nothing.' I know nothing.'"

"I didn't think the Capo position was just handed down to the next generation within a family, like a King," Big Mike uttered.

"It's not," Andrew said. "But if a Capo from a particular family is a highly respected and well-liked individual, the propensity becomes greater that their bloodline will be selected again. Several Venturini's served as Capo di Tutti Capi long before Giovanni was elected."

"Now's not the time to brag about your bloodline," Tony quipped.

"How many Andriachinis have been Capo?" Andrew remarked with sarcasm, indicating that none of the Andriachinis had ever held the position.

"Babe, we need that list," Tony urged.

"Right here, boys," Chase gloated and held it up.

"Where did you get that?" Angel demanded.

"While you guys were bickering, I went up and asked Olga for the list. She knew right where to find it."

"Of course she did," Angel said, crossing her arms and shaking her head.

They placed it flat on the table in front of the Snake so he could see and they all huddled around it. "Looks like you didn't make the cut, Ace," Tony said, smacking Andrew's arm.

"I don't see your name on it either," Andrew rebutted.

"She's forbidden to marry anyone from the other four families," the Snake explained. "These are a list of candidates who have proven themselves worthy with their loyalty and service to Giovanni. It doesn't mean she loves or even knows any of them."

Angel couldn't help but feel as if somehow the Snake was defending the fact that his name had been handwritten onto the list, as if he were justifying it to the other men. She studied his face, but he met her eyes only once and then only briefly, before returning his attention to the spreadsheet.

"I have a question," Big Mike interrupted. "If only the man who marries her, or becomes Under Boss stands to gain this power, why did the Brigatte Nero try to kill her before she has a husband or Under Boss?"

"Excellent question," Chase belted and then looked to Tony, Andrew and the Snake for the answer.

Angel thought deeply. "That's right," she said. "They'd only gain an advantage if they killed me after I had those key positions filled."

The Snake's eyes suddenly grew distant, as if he were trying to recall a memory. "When I was in the barracks in Iowa, talking to Johan Bernardelli, he was angry and said that I had forced them into Plan B."

"What was Plan A?" Andrew asked.

"I don't know," the Snake replied. "But when Angel made it back to Chicago alive, Plan A was dead."

Angel began to pace across the room and chew on her fingernail. "If I died prior to instating an Under Boss or husband, who would take over the family?" She asked.

"Giovanni would appoint a new Boss," Andrew answered and his eyes lit with a spark of understanding. "Chase, can you get that list up on the large screen."

"Sure thing, just need to scan it in," Chase said and went immediately to work.

When the list appeared on the screen, Angel sank into her chair. It was humiliating to say the least. Andrew stood close to the screen, scanning the list of names. "Chase, can you cross reference these names in every database with the Brigatte Nero, Johan Bernardelli and Anya Grovashik?"

"I thought you swore by Anya's innocence," Angel said.

"Just because something looks good doesn't mean it is good," Andrew replied without taking his eyes from the large screen.

"And damn that girl looks good. I mean she is crazy-ass hot," Chase said.

"Stacked," Tony grinned.

"And when she started speaking in Russian," Chase fidgeted in his chair, "I was like, come over her you Russian mama and let me show you my..."

"Chase!" Angel interrupted him, her eyes wide with shock.

"What?" He grinned. "I was just gonna say my guns."

Trig burst out laughing. "You ain't got no guns, white boy," he teased. "A smokin' chick like that needs a brother with a long, hard missile." Trig made a thrusting motion in his chair and Chase chuckled.

Boys and their toys! "Are you two done?" Angel asked, raising her eyebrows to show she wasn't amused.

"Sorry, Boss Lady," Chase said, grinning ear to ear.

By the time Giovanni and Carl returned to the Towers, Angel and her team had come up with a plan, though it still had some holes. Anya's motives were unclear, they still didn't know what happened to Freddie, Salvo hadn't returned to the Towers as of yet, and Officer Bernie and his partner never filed a report about the body, or the explosion and worse yet, never returned to the precinct. Angel knew that the first part of the plan was going to be the most difficult. They were going to have to tell Carl that his grandson, Salvo, was missing.

CHAPTER 40

The guard from the air strip radioed Vladmir, who was in the hangar, and informed him that several carloads of Cobra and Knight members were waiting at the gate, professing to have murdered Angel Maratinzano.

Vladmir grinned as he held the radio close to his yellow, crooked teeth. "Did they bring the body?"

"No sir," the guard responded. "They said the police arrived and the paramedics took the body, or what was left of it."

"What do you mean, what was left of it?" Vladmir asked, narrowing his eyes.

"They said the pub, where they put the body, blew up," the guard relayed what he had been told. "They're getting unruly, sir, and are requesting to meet with you in person."

"Tell them they will not be paid until I see the body," Vladmir seethed into the radio.

"They're not going to like that news, sir. There's only two of us and about twenty of them."

"I will send more guards to assist you. Sit tight." Vladmir tossed the radio onto a table and ordered six of his men to go to the guard station immediately.

"What are our orders, sir," one of the Brigatte Nero men asked.

"Kill them." Vladmir seethed. "Kill all of them."

CHAPTER 41

Angel met privately with Giovanni and Carl Cusanelli in the penthouse family room. Giovanni sat in his armed chair, Carl on the couch and Angel paced in front of them. As soon as she told them about the explosion at Tetterbaum's, Giovanni came unglued. "Another death trap!" He hollered, his face burning bright red. "You had no business leaving the Towers," he shook his finger at her. "I forbid you to leave this building! Do you understand me, Michelangela?" Giovanni was breathing so hard that Angel was concerned that he might have a coronary or hyperventilate.

"Yes, I understand," she said.

"These people are luring you into their traps!" He threw his hands into the air. "I cannot protect you, if you do not obey my rules!" He was so loud and so gruff that it made Angel tremble inside.

"I'm sorry, grandfather," she uttered. "I won't leave again."

When Carl heard that Olga had tried to set Salvo and Angel up and now Salvo was missing, he leapt from the couch enraged, sputtering Italian phrases that Angel did not understand.

"La vostra sorella meddlesome!" He yelled. "Questa volta è andato troppo lontano!"

"Calma voi stessi," Giovanni said, and Angel guessed he was trying to tell Carl to calm down, but it didn't seem to do much good. Carl continued to rant.

Out of the corner of her eye, Angel saw Olga peak around the corner, her eyes widened with fear. She excused herself and pulled Olga down the hallway and into Olga's bedroom.

"Merciful Heavens, that man hates me," Olga said.

"What did he say?"

"He said I was meddlesome and that I'd gone too far." Olga put her hands on her hips. "Meddlesome. Humph. I'm not meddlesome. Am I meddlesome?"

Angel gave herself a mental head slap. *Yes!* But she stifled the urge to say it. "Is my mother back yet?"

"Not yet," Olga said with a sneaky grin that swept across her entire face. "That probably means she and Miguel are really hitting it off." She rubbed her hands together. "I can't wait to hear all about it. I have a feeling you and Salvo would hit it off too."

Angel rolled her eyes. "NOW, you're being meddlesome," she said and Olga frowned at her.

"Well, forgive an old woman for trying to help."

As soon as Angel left, Olga slammed her bedroom door, mumbling in Italian. Angel exhaled loudly. She loved Olga, but Olga was exhausting.

Back in the family room, Carl paced the floor, trying to reach his son, Miguel. "I keep getting his voicemail," he complained.

"I will send my men out to search for Salvo," Giovanni assured him. "We will find him."

Carl grunted angrily and sat down on the couch, burying his face in his palms. "I shouldn't have brought him here," he said. "He isn't ready for this life. He doesn't have the street smarts to survive in this world."

Angel joined Carl on the couch. "Don't underestimate your grandson. The last time we saw Salvo, he was alive. He never entered the Pub and he's probably sightseeing. Until we hear otherwise, we're going to assume he's alive and well. We'll find him." Angel turned her attention to Giovanni. "Grandfather, I need to know if any of the people on this list knew for certain that they were destined to take over the family if I died." She handed a copy of the spreadsheet to Giovanni.

"No, Michelangela, those decisions had not been formalized," he said.

"Were they discussed with anyone else?" She asked. "Anyone at all?"

"No, those are private matters of family, discussed only between myself and my Compare." He motioned toward Carl.

Angel rose from the couch. "I'm going to talk with Chase and prepare to set things in motion," she said and then addressed Carl. "Does Salvo carry a cell phone with him?"

"Si, yes, of course," Carl answered.

Angel rushed to the kitchen drawer, pulled out a piece of scrap paper and a pen, and then hurried back to the family room. "Can you give me that number?"

Carl jotted down Salvo's cell number and handed the paper back to Angel. "There's a chance Chase will be able to track his whereabouts using the signal from his phone," she explained.

"Very good," Carl uttered.

"Michelangela," Giovanni said, "can Chase track Miguel's cell phone as well?"

"I think he can track any cell signal, given that it's in use and he knows what he's looking for," she shrugged.

Giovanni looked at Carl. "Write down Miguel's number and if his location can be determined, I will send men to bring him and Sophia safely back."

"Grazie," Carl said and jotted down the number.

"I've got to head downstairs now. Are you ready to make a statement to the press confirming my death?" She asked Carl.

"Si," he uttered. "I am ready."

CHAPTER 42

Chase blasted Carl Cusanelli's statement to every major network in the Chicago area and it was quickly picked up and broadcast as Breaking News in Chicago, New York and around the globe. Angel watched a live feed and couldn't escape how surreal it felt to see her picture on television and to be thought dead by millions of people.

Within minutes of the Breaking News release, and despite the time difference, Salvatore called from Sicily, his voice filled with grief and panic. Olga took his call and relished in the fact that she was the one who got to tell him the truth and fill him in on their plan to bring down the Brigatte Nero.

Upon hearing that Angel was indeed alive and that she had found Mike Maletta, aka Big Mike, the son of his best friend, whom he had looked after all those years ago, Salvatore couldn't hide the excitement in his voice. "I will be aboard the next flight," he told Olga, and she came waddling out of the kitchen shrieking with delight.

Everything was going according to plan, with one exception, no one had heard from Sophia or Miguel, and Salvo still hadn't returned. Angel was deeply concerned that her mother would see the news and think it were true. She didn't want to put her through that type of heartache again.

In the meeting room, Chase had set up surveillance equipment and multiple screens so he would be able to track each member as they went out on their assignments. Giovanni's two guards

that knew Angel was alive were sent to kill the
Brigatte Nero captive and deliver his body to the
security gates of the air strip with a note attached
which read: "Angel is dead, that's the truth. You'll
all be dead soon, here's your proof." Chase had
written the note and was pretty proud of himself,
claiming not everyone could write a threatening
note with a "cool-ass rhyme."

Andrew was to use every resource at his
disposal on the Chicago police force to locate
officer Bernardelli, the newbie and hopefully, find
Salvo alive.

Big Mike and Trig set out to rendezvous
with Chito and the rest of the Cobras and set up a
time and place to negotiate the promised one
million dollars. They were unaware that many of
the gang members had been massacred by the
Brigatte Nero at the airstrip.

Tony's assignment was to locate Freddie,
dead or alive, and find out how he fit into the
picture. He took two of his men with him.

Chase, Angel and the Snake sat in the
secret meeting room, watching surveillance screens
and running phone numbers through multiple
databases.

"This can't be right," Chase blurted,
clicking the computer keys. "I must have screwed
something up when I entered the numbers."

"What's wrong?" Angel asked, scooting
closer so she could see his computer screen.

"See this number," he pointed at the
screen. "This is Miguel Cusanelli's cell phone
number."

"Okay?" Angel uttered, unsure of the
relevance.

"And this number is Anya Grovashik's cell,"
he pointed to a number with a Chicago area code.

"Okay…" Angel's voice tapered off to indicate she wasn't following his train of thought.

He clicked around and pulled up another screen. "Why has Anya been talking to Miguel?" Chase bounced his knee up and down spastically. "Do they know each other? Are they friends?"

Angel stood up. "No. I mean, I don't know. How would they know each other?"

"Seems a little too coincidental if you ask me," the Snake interjected.

"Now, I know this isn't right," Chase said, staring at the screen. "See this number; this is Carlachi's cell phone." It was easy to see because it was an Iowa area code so it stood out from the Chicago and New York area codes. "The last place I tracked it was within a few blocks of the pub, right after the bomb went off. Now, look, it's in the building."

"What building?" Angel asked.

"This building. Carlachi's phone is in the Towers and it's in use right now," Chase blurted excitedly.

"How is that possible?" Angel searched his face. "Who are they talking to?"

Chase's fingers flew across the keyboard and screens changed rapid fire before her eyes. "Carlachi's phone dialed the New York number, the unregistered number we found in Mr. Clean's incoming phone log."

"Can you trace the New York number?" The Snake asked.

"I'm trying. As long as it stays in use long enough I can get a satellite link," Chase said, wiggling his fingers over the top of the keyboard while waiting for the screens to catch up to the data he had just input. "C'mon, c'mon," Chase spoke to his equipment. "Find that freaky-ass number," he muttered.

Angel dialed Giovanni and told him to order his men to lock down the building. "No one in or out," she told him.

"Michelangela, what is wrong?" Giovanni questioned.

"Nothing," Angel lied. "We're in no imminent danger, and I'll explain the details later, but I need the Towers locked down."

"Consider it done," Giovanni said and disconnected.

Angel turned her attention back to Chase. "Can you pinpoint the floor that Carlachi's cell phone is transmitting from?"

"I can only do one wild-ass trace at a time," Chase barked and Angel apologized. It felt like it was taking forever, and then finally Chase yelped, "Gotcha!"

"Where is it?" Angel and the Snake said in unison.

"The old boat docks down on the south side of the lake," Chase said.

Angel dialed Andrew. "Whoever has Carlachi's phone is currently speaking to our mystery New York number. We've traced their locations and I need you to go to the old boat docks down on the south side of the lake," she said. "Do you know where that is?"

"Sweetheart, everybody knows where that is," Andrew teased. "It's the hottest make-out spot in the city. Has no man ever taken you to the old boat docks?"

Angel was stunned silent by the question and then a little bit humiliated by the answer. No one had ever taken her parking at the old boat docks. Now she couldn't help but wonder why. "Of course I've been there," she lied. "I just didn't know if you had been there."

He chuckled into the phone. "You're a terrible liar."

After they hung up, Angel dialed Tony and asked him to meet Andrew at the old boat docks. "First time I'll be meeting another man there," Tony joked.

"Oh, been there often, have you?" Angel sarcastically quipped, which made Tony him and haw around.

"No, just a couple times in high school. You know, kid stuff, Babe," he said.

"Uh-huh." Angel rolled her eyes. "Chase will pull up live satellite of the area if he can, but contact us the minute you find anything."

Moments later Big Mike called in and Chase put the call on speaker. He informed them of the killings that took place at the guard station by the airstrip. "We're gathering up the men left and then we're going in and we're gonna kill as many Brigatte Nero as we can," Big Mike said and Angel could hear the rage in his voice.

"Hold off," Angel begged him. "Give us some time to find the man behind this whole thing and then we will help you take down the Brigatte Nero."

"They murdered our brothers," Big Mike seethed. "We're not waiting."

"Listen, man, it's a crazy-ass suicide mission if you go in alone," Chase told him.

"He's right," the Snake added. "I've been inside. They probably outnumber you, they have the protection of the hangar and they're weapons are greater. Stand down until we can back you up."

Big Mike hesitated to answer and Angel could only guess what was going through his mind. The Brigatte Nero were so close and ripe for his revenge. She knew he wanted it so badly he could taste it. "How long before you can send help?"

Angel looked to Chase for an answer. "Give us one hour," Chase said. "One hour and then you'll have a chopper and vehicles they can't shoot through."

"One hour," Big Mike repeated. "If we don't hear from you in one hour, we're going in with or without your help." He disconnected the call.

Chase dialed Sal and placed the call on video conferencing mode on his computer. "Sal, we have a situation developing at the boat docks south of town and at the vacant air strip. I'm sending you the exact coordinates now," Chase explained.

"Yes, I see them," Sal replied.

"I need live satellite feed with no delay. Can you do that for me?" Chase asked.

"I'll see what I can do," Sal said and disconnected.

"Can't you tap into the satellite by yourself?" Angel asked.

"Yeah, but the FBI has better equipment and I've got a feeling we're gonna need a freaky-ass up-to-the-millisecond visual."

The Snake sat quiet with an expression that told Angel he was mulling over all the facts in his brain. "Have you run a trace on Miguel, Salvo or Sophia's cell phone's yet?" He asked.

"No," Chase threw his hands in the air. "I'm just one guy, here people. I can't do everything all at the same time." Angel had never seen Chase so edgy and agitated. "What do want done first?" He blurted.

"Find Miguel and my mom so we can ensure that they get back safely before everything blows up," Angel said. "Then we'll trace Salvo and lastly we'll get the exact location of the person in the building with Carlachi's phone." It seemed logical to wait on that one, as the building was now in lock down and whoever it was, wasn't going to be able to escape.

Chase's fingers flew across the keyboard and various data images appeared on his screen. While they waited, Angel went to the bar across the room and opened two bottles of Goose Island Pale Ale, giving one to Chase and one to the Snake. "We could all use something to take the edge off," she said with a sincere smile.

"Holy..." Chase blurted but didn't finish the phrase. "Angel, are you sure Sophia is with Miguel."

"That's what Olga said," Angel replied.

"Well, I can't get a trace on Miguel's cell phone, but your mom's cell is at the old boat docks," Chase grinned and raised his brows. "You don't think she's getting some action?"

"Gross!" Angel gasped. "No, I don't think that." Angel tried to shake the image of her mother and Miguel together. "If they're at the docks, I'm sure it's just because it's a quiet place to talk."

"Yeah, if you're speaking the universal language of love," Chase teased and made body gestures which Angel deemed inappropriate, since he was speaking about her mother.

"My mother has more class than to get it on in the back of a car at the boat docks," Angel stammered.

"Boom-chicka-wow-wow," Chase teased and the Snake bit his lip to hide his smirk.

Angel exhaled and rolled her eyes. *Men!* "Can you pinpoint her exact location because she hasn't responded to my texts or calls and I'd like to have Andrew or Tony bring her back before everything goes down out there."

"I would not like to get that assignment," the Snake moaned.

"No kidding," Chase chuckled. "If the car is a rockin' don't bother knockin'."

Chase and the Snake laughed out loud and Angel couldn't help but turn her back and crack a smile. It was a disturbing mental image, but also the tension relief they all needed at the moment. Chase took a swig of his beer and went back to stroking his keyboard. "Sophia's near pier four," he told Angel and she immediately called Andrew and Tony.

While she was on the phone with Tony, Chase interrupted her. "We got a problem," he said, the color draining from his face. "A big problem."

"What?" Angel asked.

"I ran another trace on the mystery New York number, to make sure it wasn't moving, and it's in the exact same location as your mom."

"What?" Angel exclaimed. "How close to her?"

The Snake leaned in toward Chase's computer and they exchanged a glance that told Angel something was terribly wrong. "The same coordinates," Chase uttered.

Panic was beginning to fill her as she relayed the message to Tony. "Find my mom," she told him. "Please, Tony, get to her before anyone else does."

"I'm on it, Babe," Tony replied. "I'm almost there. Don't worry."

Angel disconnected the call and paced in front of the windows overlooking the city. She tried to wrap her mind around what was happening. Was the mystery New York number the man behind everything? If so, he had to be someone close enough to the family to know about Vincent

Carlachi, to know the police had removed him from the Towers after the last attack by the Shark, to know that using Carlachi's phone would be a believable distraction to throw them off course. It had to be someone close enough to be considered for a replacement head of the family if Angel were killed. It had to be someone trusted by Giovanni. Angel spun around. "I need to see the spreadsheet of candidates again," she blurted and Chase dug through a file folder and handed her a copy. She stared at the paper, trying to connect the dots in her mind. "Chase, can you call up Sal for me?"

"Now?" He asked. "'Cuz I'm sort of in the middle of a trace on Salvo's phone."

"Please," she said as a demand more than a request.

When Sal's face appeared on the screen, Angel jumped over the usual salutation and dove right into business. "I need you to cross-reference some names for me, and I need any information you have on these people."

"I will see what I can do," Sal said.

Angel rambled off names. "Salvo Cusanelli, Miguel Cusanelli, Mike Malleta, Vincent Carlachi, Johan Bernardelli, Don Venturini, Anya Grovashik and Carl Cusanelli."

"That's a lot of people," Sal said with a sigh.

"I know and I need it right away," Angel acknowledged. "Please."

"Give me a few minutes and I'll call you back," Sal replied and then the screen went blank.

"That's a crazy-ass lot of names," Chase said.

"I know," Angel answered as she hurried for the door. "See if you can pull up the satellite surveillance on the boat docks. I'll be back down in a minute."

Angel made a dash up to the penthouse and found Giovanni, Carl and Olga sitting around the dining room table, sipping tea and eating homemade Cannoli and crumb cake.

"Have you located Salvo?" Carl asked, rising immediately to his feet.

"No," Angel grimaced, "but we're still trying to trace his phone. I'll let you know as soon as we find him." Carl sank down into his chair, lines of stress beginning to show on his face.

"Olga, can I borrow your Taser?" Angel asked and Olga's face lit with excitement.

"Absolutely!" She blurted, clapping her hands together and then raising from the table and waddling swiftly down the hall to her bedroom.

Giovanni raised an eyebrow. "Do I need to be concerned?"

"No." She kissed his cheek and whispered in his ear. "It's not for you this time."

He grunted as a sign of disapproval for her comment.

"Merciful Heavens, you're going to love using it," Olga said as she came back into the dining room, handing the Taser to Angel. "Be careful, though," she warned. "Don't accidentally zap yourself. It hurts like the dickens." Olga shook her head.

Angel wanted to ask, as there was obviously a story to be told about Olga zapping herself, but there wasn't time. She made a mental note to revisit the conversation later.

On her way back to the secret meeting room, Angel stopped on the floor where Anya was being held and addressed the bodyguard outside her door.

"Ms. Maratinzano," he said and dipped his head down as a sign of respect.

"What is your name?" Angel asked.

"Alberto," he said. "Alberto Basilio."

Angel gave Alberto a quick once over. He looked like your typical mob body guard, dressed in black pants, black t-shirt and black boots. He had tattoos down both arms and one going up the back of his neck. His dark brown hair was cut short and spiked up in the front and Angel surmised that he probably used a powerful hair gel every morning to get it to stay that way. His eyes were light brown and he had a crooked smile which somehow added to his cuteness.

"Did you collect all of Anya Grovashik's personal belongings when she came in?" Angel asked.

"No ma'am. I wasn't instructed to do so."

"Good," Angel smiled. "I need you to do me a personal favor. I need you to go inside and Taser Anya." She handed the Taser to Alberto.

"What setting ma'am?"

Angel wasn't aware of the settings. "I want her incapacitated long enough for us to search her, her belongings and the entire apartment if necessary."

"What are we looking for ma'am?" Alberto asked.

"A cell phone. Actually, two cell phones," Angel said.

CHAPTER 43

Andrew, Tony and two of the Andriachini bogata boys met up at the second dock. "This is gonna be like finding a needle in a haystack," Andrew said, staring out at the five vacant, run-down piers. Several had dilapidated shacks near the end, where, in its prime, people could pull in and pay to valet park their boats. A concrete walkway connected each pier, and old, abandoned restaurants lined the walkway opposite.

"Especially since we don't really know who we're looking for," Tony added.

"Let's check pier four first, since that's where Chase said the signal was coming from," Andrew said.

Tony told his men to follow behind and do a quick search of piers one, two and three. "Meet us at four," he said.

Andrew's phone buzzed and simultaneously, so did Tony's. They both answered and heard Chase on the other line. "I've conferenced us all together," he said. "So, if you split up you can hear each other and I'll be able to see and hear both of you. Just keep your phones on."

"Roger that, Ace," Tony said.

"I've got you guys on Sal's FBI satellite feed so I can see everything live. I'm going to check out the piers and let you know if there's something you need to investigate. Hang tight."

Andrew reached over and patted Tony on the stomach.

"What the hell?" Tony belted. "Keep your hands to yourself, you fruitcake."

Andrew smirked. "Don't flatter yourself. I was checking to see if you were wearing a vest."

"You could've just asked me," Tony remarked. "I would've told you the truth."

Andrew shook his head. "You should have a vest on."

"I hate to break this to you, but all of us aren't cops, in fact, most of us aren't cops."

"Who's us?" Andrew asked.

"Bogata brothers. That's who us is. Most of us aren't cops," Tony said. "We don't run around with bullet proof vests and conduct an analysis of every crime scene. Most of the time we get in, make our mark and get the hell out."

"You gotta problem with me being a cop?" Andrew asked.

"Yeah, as a matter of fact I do. I got a big problem with it," Tony sneered.

"Why?"

"It makes you untrustworthy, Ace." Tony shrugged. "Your loyalty is divided and that makes you say one thing and do another. I don't trust people like that."

"My loyalty has never been divided," Andrew commented. "And if I recall, I've saved your ass a couple of times."

"You wanta go there?" Tony quipped. "Because if memory serves me, I was supposed to put a bullet in your brain several weeks ago."

"Then why didn't you?" Andrew seethed as he stopped walking and glared at Tony.

"We all make mistakes," Tony said and kept walking.

"Guys?" Chase interrupted. "I've got a black, unmarked van sitting between pier four and five on your right-hand side. It looks to be hidden between two buildings."

"We see it," Andrew quietly commented, and both Tony and Andrew readied their weapons.

"You got a plan, Ace?" Tony asked Andrew.

"Yeah, I'll go first since I'm wearing a vest," Andrew quipped. "Just make sure you cover my ass."

"I always do," Tony said.

CHAPTER 44

Alberto opened the door to where Anya was being held and Angel followed him inside. As soon as she heard the door, Anya, who was standing by the window, spun around to face them, holding the phone to her ear. Her eyes grew wide but before she could say anything Alberto zapped her. Anya's body fell forward like a limp rag doll and Angel stepped over it. *If I were a killer, I would have shot you instead of zapping you,* Angel sarcastically retorted in the quiet of her mind.

Alberto retrieved the phone still clutched in Anya's hand and handed it to Angel, who dug through Anya's purse and found another cell phone, tucked neatly in the side pocket. Angel instructed Alberto to tape Anya's wrists, legs and mouth.

"Notify me when she awakens," Angel ordered and then left to take the phones to Chase, who began running an immediate scan.

"The one she was talking on is Carlachi's phone," Chase confirmed. "This one, from her purse is her own personal cell phone, the one she used to call Miguel Cusanelli."

While Chase analyzed the phones, the Snake filled Angel in on what was happening at the boat docks. Angel watched on the surveillance screens as Tony and Andrew approached the black van. Her heart was thumping violently and she prayed this was not another trap.

Tony reached for the sliding door, while Andrew flanked to the side ready to turn and shoot inside the van if needed. On the count of three, Tony yanked the door open and Andrew spun toward the door, stopping abruptly and cursing aloud.

"What is it?" Angel gasped.

"We can't see inside the van. You're gonna have to verbalize it for us," Chase said.

"It's Officer Bernardelli," Tony responded. "He's dead."

"How'd they kill him?" The Snake asked.

"Knife to the gut," Tony answered.

The Snake looked at Chase. "I want a picture of that knife," he said.

Andrew reported the body to the police and then he and Tony continued searching pier four and five. Chase kept insisting that Sophia's phone was near pier four and Andrew and Tony kept arguing that Sophia was nowhere to be found. Angel was beginning to have that sick feeling in the pit of her stomach. The one that told her something was very wrong. By the time Big Mike telephoned to inform them that an hour had gone by and the Cobras were going to storm the air strip with or without help, everyone was at their wit's end.

Just then Alberto entered, carrying Anya and following Angel's instructions, he set her down in a chair at the end of the table. Anya glared at Angel and Angel returned her stare with equal fervor. Without taking her eyes from Anya, Angel spoke into the phone and addressed Big Mike. "We've got a new play here, so give me thirty more minutes; then you'll have all the back-up you need."

Big Mike wasn't happy but he agreed to wait the extra time.

Angel approached Anya. "I'd like to know about your relationship with Miguel Cusanelli," she said pointedly and then reached down and ripped the duct tape from Anya's mouth.

Anya winced and glared up at Angel. "My personal relationships are none of your business."

"I disagree," Angel said flatly, "but we can move on. Tell me about your relationship with Officer Bernardelli."

"I work with him on occasion, that is all."

"Did he give you Vincent Carlachi's cell phone?" Angel asked.

"I don't know what you're talking about," Anya spat.

Angel retrieved Carlachi's phone from the table. "This phone belongs to Vincent Carlachi. Why did you have it?"

Anya stared at the phone but didn't speak.

"Who were you talking to when Alberto Tasered you?" Angel asked.

"That is none of your business," Anya seethed.

Angel motioned for Alberto, who was standing guard by the door, to come closer. "Zap her again," Angel said matter-of-factly and turned her back as Alberto hit Anya with another jolt and Anya's body twitched and she lost consciousness.

Chase winced. "Damn, that hurts just watching."

"When she wakes up, zap her again," Angel said to Alberto, who stood next to Anya with the Taser ready in hand.

"Damn, Boss Lady, I hope I never piss your crazy-ass off," Chase grimaced.

Angel felt the Snake's eyes on her and saw a look of concern sweep over his face. "Ms. Maratinzano," he cleared his throat, "several jolts in a row like that can kill someone, particularly someone of her size and stature."

"What would you like me to do? I need her to talk." Angel replied.

"I gotta back the Snake here on this one," Chase added. "Crazy-ass thing about dead people is they can't talk."

Angel grunted frustration. She needed information and she knew Anya had it. She could sense it.

Giovanni and Carl entered the meeting room, with six bodyguards. "Michelangela, I am sending these men out in search of Salvo. Are there areas your men have already covered?"

Angel looped her arm in Giovanni's and escorted him to the bar in the far corner. She didn't want to talk in front of Carl as her suspicions that Salvo, Miguel and her mother were in some sort of danger had increased. She filled him in on all that was occurring and watched as sadness filled his eyes. "I'm sorry," she whispered. "Tony and Andrew haven't found Salvo, my mother or Miguel yet."

"Carry on with your operation. I will have my men search the area around Tetterbaum's for Freddie and Salvo." He made the sign of the cross over his body. "God willing, may we find them alive." Giovanni gave his men instructions and then went behind the bar, filled two glasses with scotch and took one to Carl. "Let us sit, friend, there is much to discuss," he said and led Carl to the round mahogany table in the far corner by the windows.

Just as they sat down, Angel approached Carl, leaning on the table with both palms and facing him so she could not be heard by the rest of the room. "Do you know the woman sitting over there?"

"No," Carl answered without hesitation. "Should I?"

"Is it possible that she and Miguel are romantically involved?" Angel asked and was surprised by the shock on Carl's face.

"Miguel is widowed. God rest her soul." Carl and Giovanni each made the sign of the cross over their bodies and then Carl kissed his fingertips and threw the kiss into the air. "He has not taken an interest in another woman since his beloved died."

"Why do you ask?" Giovanni asked Angel.

"There are several calls to and from Miguel on her cell phone. I simply wondered how they might know one another," Angel defended.

"Does she live here in the city?" Carl asked.

"I think so," Angel said with a nod.

"Then I can assure you Miguel has not been carrying on with her, as he has not left New York in years," Carl said confidently.

"She could have flown to see him in New York," Angel proposed.

"Miguel spends time only with me and Salvo," Carl rebutted. "I would bet my life on the fact that they are not romantically involved."

Tony and Andrew arrived back at the Towers, never having located Sophia or her phone, and Angel grew more concerned. Why would her cell phone be at the docks, if she wasn't there?

"Could someone be re-directing her cell phone signal to lure us somewhere?" Angel asked.

"No," Chase said, "I'd catch it bouncing and know. But even if they were, we went to where the signal was and she isn't there."

"Maybe they wanted us to find Officer Bernie's body?" Tony said.

"Who's body?" Anya groggily asked.

"Officer Bernardelli," Chase replied. "We found him stabbed to death in the back of black van."

Chase moved the airstrip surveillance feed to the large screen in the room and spewed obscenities. Angel looked at the screen and couldn't believe her eyes. She blinked several times, trying to get her brain to process what her eyes were seeing. There on her knees on the airstrip, with her hands tied behind her back and duct tape over her mouth, was Sophia. "Mom!" Angel gasped. Right then, Carlachi's phone rang.

Chase grabbed the phone, hit speaker and began trying to trace the incoming number. "Turn on your surveillance and look who I've got," the voice taunted.

"That's Vladmir," the Snake whispered.

"Say goodbye to mommy," Vladmir laughed in the phone, and then the surveillance feed went dead.

"What happened to the picture?" Angel blurted, staring at the blank screen, tears forming in her eyes.

Tony rushed to Angel, while Andrew made a beeline for Chase's computer.

"Don't panic, Babe," Tony said, squeezing Angel's shoulder and pulling her into his chest.

"What happened?" Andrew hollered to Chase.

Chase's fingers flew over the keyboard, panic showing on his face and his eyes bulging. "They killed the satellite feed or somehow blocked it," he mumbled and then cursed aloud. "I can't get it back," he said, typing frantically.

"Call Sal," Andrew barked.

Chase brought Sal up on video. "We're trying to work around it now," Sal explained. "Somehow they rerouted the coordinates so that we can't get a visual on that particular location. We should have it decoded and recoded in a few minutes. Hang tight."

Angel's stomach went hollow and she suddenly felt light headed. "How did they get my mom?" She uttered more to herself than anyone.

The Snake locked eyes with Anya. "Vladmir called Carlachi's phone, the same phone you had in your possession," he said to Anya. "How would he know that phone was here unless you spoke with him earlier and told him you were at the Towers?"

Anya didn't say anything.

Giovanni and Carl joined the rest of them at the long table just as Alberto reached over to Taser Anya again, but this time Angel stopped him. She leaned down and starred Anya in the eyes. "Were you talking to the Brigatte Nero when we came into your room?"

Anya's face was red and her eyes glassed over. She said nothing.

"How many times do you think we can zap you before you have a massive stroke or a heart attack?" Angel yelled in her face. "How many times?" She snatched the Taser from Alberto's hand and held it up, ready to jolt Anya again. "Three? Four?"

Andrew started to move toward Anya and Angel but the Snake reached up and grabbed his arm, pulling him down into a bent position so he could speak into Andrew's ear. He told him what they knew of Anya's calls to Miguel Cusanelli and that they had found Carlachi's phone in her possession. It was the phone that had been used to make calls to the mysterious New York number, and also the same one used to order the clean-up job on Giovanni's pilot. Angel glanced at Andrew and saw the utter surprise on his face. She could tell in an instant that he was genuinely shocked that Anya was in any way involved.

272

The satellite feed came back live and momentarily drew Angel's attention away from Anya. Sophia was no longer on the airstrip. "Where is she?" Angel demanded. "Chase, find her!"

"I'm working on it," Chase's fingers flew over the keyboard, broadening the scope of the surveillance.

"They could have moved her inside the hangar," Tony said.

"What about Miguel and Salvo?" Carl interjected. "Can you trace their cell phones? Last we knew Miguel and Sophia were together."

Everyone in the room knew this didn't look good for Miguel, but no one said it out loud. If Miguel and Sophia were together and Sophia had fallen into the hands of the Brigatte Nero, which she obviously had, it most assuredly meant Miguel had been killed.

"I can't get a trace on Miguel's phone because it's not in use or even turned on," Chase explained. "I haven't run Salvo's phone through yet, because I keep getting assigned other tasks." He exhaled. "I'm running it now."

Andrew walked to the back of the room and called his father, Joseph Venturini. Everyone knew of Venturini's feelings for Sophia and Angel suspected that Andrew wanted to prepare his father for the worst, though Angel refused to accept the worst as even a remote possibility. *We are going to find Sophia and she is going to be okay,* Angel told herself.

"Inform Giovanni that I am on my way to the Towers and am requesting permission to attend this meeting," Joseph Venturini told Andrew. "You have our men and resources at your disposal, son. Find my Sophia."

When Giovanni's men arrived back at the Towers it was with more bad news. Salvo's cell phone had been located in a dumpster in the back alley behind Tetterbaum's Pub with Freddie's body and the body of Officer Bernie's newbie partner on the force; both had been stabbed. There was no sign of Salvo.

"Trap after trap after trap," Giovanni seethed.

Carl sank lower in his chair. "Presa di morte," he uttered and Angel looked to Tony for an interpretation.

"It means death trap, Babe," Tony whispered.

Sal video conferenced in and Chase put him on the big screen so everyone could see and hear what he had to report. "I ran the list of names you gave me earlier. There are many discrepancies, but here are my findings." The information he rattled off about Mike Malleta, aka Big Mike, checked out and the background information on Carl Cusanelli was accurate as well.

"You ran an FBI check on me?" Carl interrupted, his face showing both shock and offense.

"Just because you hold Giovanni's trust doesn't mean you hold mine. I'm not taking any chances," Angel responded.

The information on everyone else proved interesting. "Johan Bernardelli has a brother on the Chicago police force..."

"Officer Bernie," Andrew interrupted.

"He also has a daughter in Chicago, who goes by her married name of Anya Grovashik," Sal explained and Angel glared at Anya. *I knew she was trouble from the first moment I saw her!* She didn't say it out loud, but it shown on her face.

274

When Sal had finished and Chase disconnected the call, Angel grabbed Anya by her long dark hair and pulled her head back. "You want to start talking now or do you need a few more volts of electricity to help you think?"

Anya stared down at the floor. "I will not betray my father and my uncle no matter what you do to me," she uttered.

"Your father's dead," the Snake belted. "I watched him die."

Anya raised her chin and stared at the Snake. "Liar," she spewed. "I should have let you die with that bomb!"

"I'm not lying." The Snake shifted in his chair, trying to lower his casted leg from the chair to the floor. "Whoever was in the black van killed your father, gunned him down on the airstrip and Vladmir took over after him."

Angel watched as Anya studied the Snake's face. "I do not believe you," she said in an emotionless tone. "You are trying to trick me."

Chase hit his keyboard with rapid motion, bouncing up and down in his seat. "What day and time was that?" He asked the Snake who thought back and then answered with an approximate hour. "Give me a sec," Chase said. "If it was on the airstrip, I should be able to tap into the archived feed and pull it up." A few more clicks and Chase blurted, "Whalah! I love me some wild-ass technology!"

Anya turned and faced the large screen and watched as Johan emerged from the black van and was gunned down on the pavement. Tears filled her eyes and for a brief moment Angel felt compassion tug at her heart.

"I'm sorry for your loss," Angel said, "but if you help us find the man in that van you can avenge your father's death."

275

"You will only kill me," Anya whispered as if all the strength had left her body. "Even if I help you, you will kill me, because that's what you people do." Anya broke into sobs.

"There you go calling me a killer again," Angel spewed sarcastically. "If I were going to kill you, you'd already be dead."

"Your people murdered my husband," Anya wailed. "You murdered my husband!"

Angel was stunned. She looked to Giovanni for an answer, but he, too, was clearly unaware of what Anya was talking about. "Ms. Grovashik," Giovanni began, "who was your husband and under what circumstances did he die?"

Anya's head hung low and she labored with every word. "He was a good man," she said. "He came to Chicago to start a new life, a life away from the mafia."

"Of what family was he a member?" Giovanni asked.

"He was never Made. He served for the Cullatos in New York for many years but wanted out of the lifestyle and came here. He wanted to be a policeman and fight against the crimes he had seen among your families. He wanted to protect the innocent and you gunned him down."

"I do not recall ordering a hit on any man named Grovashik," Giovanni replied.

"It was at a small grocers on Rush Street. Your men came in demanding piso and my Hank stood up to them, told them they had no right to demand money from the store owner," Anya's voice shook with anger. "Your men shot him, right through his heart." She wept.

"When did this incident occur?" Giovanni asked.

"Six years ago," Anya cried.

Angel dropped her chin to her chest and exhaled. She wanted to hate Anya but the more she spoke the more empathetic Angel became. First, her husband was killed, now her father and her uncle. "That wasn't us. That was Venito Barone, posing as my father's Compare for many years and acting out his violence in the name of the Maratinzano family. We only discovered what he was doing a few months ago and now he is dead." Angel could see Anya swallow hard. "Get her some water," she ordered one of Giovanni's men, "and un-tape her hands."

"Michelangela, she is still working against us," Giovanni huffed.

"She thought she was avenging her husband's death. She has killed no one, and if she helps us find the man in the black van, then she will have earned the right to live," Angel said, turning her attention back to Anya. "Who were you talking with before you were Tasered? Who is the man with the unlisted New York number?"

"Miguel Cusanelli," Anya said sheepishly.

Carl rose from his chair and drew his gun in one fast, fluid motion. The Snake hit his arm upward, causing the bullet to soar mere inches above Anya's head. "Bugiardo!" Carl yelled, firing off another shot, which flew between Anya and Angel, brushing Angel's shoulder just enough to tear through her blouse and cause a little bleeding, before Andrew and the Snake wrestled him to the ground. Andrew confiscated Carl's weapon and patted him down to be sure he wasn't carrying another piece, while the Snake rolled over, trying to maneuver his casted leg off Carl and pull himself up.

Carl was ranting in Italian and Angel couldn't understand a word. Giovanni tightened his jaw and kept his eyes forward as he instructed his men to escort Carl to a holding room just below the penthouse. "Bugiardo!" Carl yelled as he was being dragged from the meeting room. "Bugiardo!"

"What does that mean?" Angel asked.

"Liar," Giovanni replied.

Turning his attention to Anya, Giovanni asked, "What is the nature of your relationship with Miguel?"

"Our relationship was business," she answered. "If I retrieved Carlachi's phone and kept an eye on Special Detective Venturini, he assured me that he would make you pay for what you did to my husband."

"Why did he want you keeping an eye on me?" Andrew asked.

"He said that he needed your eyes off Angel and onto someone else," Anya explained.

"How was he going to make us pay for what happened to your husband?" Angel asked.

"His original plan was to have you killed and then he would take over the family."

"That's ridiculous," Angel blurted. "What made him think that he would even be eligible to take over as head of the family?"

Giovanni folded his hands on the table and cleared his throat. "Because of my long history with his father, I was considering Miguel for your Compare and in such need, to take over as head of the Maratinzanos."

"And you told him this?" Angel questioned.

"I discussed it with Carl. I was not aware of Carl sharing any of this with his son," Giovanni explained.

"So, how did the Brigatte Nero get involved?" The Snake chimed in.

"I needed Uncle Bernie's help to get Carlachi's phone from the evidence room and have it stripped from the record. When I told him about the plan, he talked with my father, Johan and they wanted in," Anya explained.

"What were they going to gain by helping Miguel?" Andrew questioned.

"Revenge, money and positioning in the city," Anya muttered. "At first Miguel didn't want them involved, but when he found out that Angel would be flying on Giovanni's jet from New York to Chicago, he decided to utilize my father and the Brigatte Nero."

"He sent the order to the Brigatte Nero through you to Johan and then he used Carlachi's phone to order the clean up," Andrew repeated the details aloud.

"And he had Mr. Clean brand the Brigatte Nero emblem into the pilot's chest to make sure our focus remained on them," Tony added.

"Yes," Anya nodded. "Except something happened on the plane that threw everything off course."

"I think I figured that part out," the Snake chimed in. "I believe the co-pilot got suspicious when the pilot flew off course. He probably started to contact ground control so the pilot killed him. By the time I realized something was wrong and started banging on the cockpit door, the pilot must have been in a panic." The Snake stared at the table as if he were deep in thought and forcing a memory. "I'm still uncertain as to why he pushed the co-pilot's body out of the cockpit."

"Good thing he did though, 'cuz that was the crazy-ass move that saved your lives, right?" Chase asked. "I mean, it wasn't until you saw the Brigatte Nero emblem on the knife that you realized you had to throw Angel off the plane and take a wild-ass ride in the sky."

"True," the Snake said.

"So, who blew up the plane? The Brigatte Nero or Miguel?" Angel asked.

"Miguel," Anya answered without hesitation. "He didn't trust the Brigatte Nero because of their history of taking hostages and their past squabbles with Salvatore."

"How do you know that?" Andrew asked her.

"Because he had me install a bomb on the plane," she exhaled. "A bomb that he could detonate from the ground at any time."

Angel couldn't believe her ears and when she looked at Andrew, she could tell that he was riddled with the same disbelief.

Tony pulled his .45 from the back of his black jeans and took aim at Anya's head. "Say the word, Babe," he said to Angel. "I'd be my honor to take out this trash."

"No," Giovanni answered before Angel could speak. "There is more we need to learn from her." Tony tightened his jaw and lowered his gun.

"Where did Miguel take my mother?" Angel asked Anya, but Anya only shook her head back and forth slowly.

"I don't know," she uttered. "This was not part of the plan."

"What wasn't part of the plan?" Andrew seethed. "You getting caught or Miguel kidnapping Sophia?"

"None of it," Anya cried. "Angel was supposed to die in the explosion. That was Miguel's plan. But my father..." Anya's voice faded and her hands trembled. "My father had another plan. He instructed the pilot to land the plane in Iowa where they had a compound. He was going to kill the pilot and everyone on board, except Angel, and use her as leverage to get revenge on Salvatore."

"Right on, a cool-ass double cross," Chase nodded and bounced his knee up and down.

"He didn't plan on Angel escaping from him," Anya continued. "No one did."

Angel looked across the table at the Snake and he grinned and gave her a wink, acknowledging that they were both thinking the same thing. If he hadn't forced her out of the plane, they'd both be dead. Angel also knew that weren't it for Big Mike she would have been found by the Brigatte Nero and would probably have been tortured and killed by now.

"I hate to interrupt all the crazy-ass action, but we got movement on the airstrip," Chase interjected excitedly, putting the satellite feed on the large screen.

"Oh no," Angel gasped. "I forgot about Big Mike and the Cobras."

"They'll get slaughtered, if they go in there alone," the Snake said.

Chase dialed Big Mike and Angel took the phone from him. She explained about her mother and asked him to hold off.

"Tell him he'll have all the Venturini's to help if he just waits," Andrew added.

"The Andriachini's too," Tony piped in.

"Please Big Mike, I don't want my mother caught in the cross-fire," Angel begged.

Chase took the phone from Angel. "Where are you? I'm not picking you up at the airstrip gates."

"I'm hidden, just down from the guard station, trying to see who, if anyone, we can pick off from a distance," Big Mike answered.

"You got high powered rifles with scopes?" Chase asked excitedly.

"Yep, M24 sniper rifles," Big Mike said.

"Damn, I'd like to hold that baby in my hands," Chase said.

"Remain on task," Giovanni reprimanded and Chase immediately steered the conversation back on course.

"Keep us updated on your progress," Chase said and disconnected.

Angel paced anxiously. How were they going to get her mother back? Her phone buzzed in her pocket and startled her. She pulled it out and immediately handed it to Chase, who started a trace. "Hello?" Angel answered when Chase gave her the go ahead.

"I have something you want and you have something I want," Vladmir's voice filled the room. "Give me Anya and I'll give you back your mother."

"What makes you think I have Anya?" Angel asked.

"Do you take me for a fool?" Vladmir's voice dripped disdain. "I know everything happening in that secret little room of yours."

Angel looked around, scanning the faces of everyone in the room. Was someone a traitor? Was someone reporting to Vladmir? "Why do you want Anya?" Angel asked. "What use is she to you?"

"Bring her to the boat docks, pier four or you will never see your mother again." The line went dead.

Angel's hands shook as she pulled out her 9mm and aimed it at Anya. "How does he know you're in a secret meeting room?"

"I don't know," she wailed. "I swear I don't know."

Tony pulled his gun back out and pointed it at Anya. "Let me do it, Babe, I got this one," he said.

"Wait!" Andrew belted. "Was Miguel Cusanelli ever in this room?"

"Yes, during the meeting where we went over the spreadsheet," Angel answered.

"Si," Giovanni interjected. "That was the only time."

"Where did he sit?" Andrew asked.

Angel pointed to the chair and Andrew quickly crawled under the table, running his hands across the bottom and retrieving a tiny bug that had been stuck to the underside of the table.

"Kiss my white ass and call me stupid," Chase barked. "They've been one step ahead of us the whole time."

Andrew took the bug, set it on the bar and smashed it with the butt of his gun. "Damnit," he blurted.

Angel studied all the faces in the room, and they all looked grim. "What do we do now?" She asked. "How do we get my mother back?"

A heavy silence filled the room.

Finally Chase broke the silence. "I say we follow his instructions and trade Anya for Sophia," he said. "What other choice is there?"

"No!" Anya wailed. "If he killed my father then he only wants to kill me, too."

"How do you know that?" Andrew asked.

"Why else would he want me?" She sobbed. "Please don't give me to that man."

Angel swallowed hard and tightened her lips. "I'm sorry Anya, but it's the only way to save my mother."

CHAPTER 45

Angel hurried to her bedroom where she changed into her boots, in which she could conceal a gun and put on a blouse that would easily fit over a Kevlar vest. Andrew joined her a few moments later and slid the wire under her blouse, taping it to her skin in the back. "Remember, with this wire we'll be able to hear you but you won't be able to hear us." He then adjusted her vest and slid a .22 in her left boot. "Practice reaching down with your right hand and quickly retrieving the gun," he told her. She tried a few times but it was easier said than done. It kept getting caught on the lining of her boot.

When she was all wired and ready, Andrew put his hands on the outside of her shoulders and exhaled. "I wish I could go in your place," he said.

"You can't. I have to do this."

"I know," he mumbled, "but I don't have to like it."

"That makes two of us," she teased, trying to lighten the moment and distract herself from the fear that was rising in her gut.

"Sweetheart," he said, walking passed her and closing the bedroom door. "You said that whatever this is that we share is over."

Angel wasn't expecting him to bring it up, especially not right now. She closed her eyes and sighed. "I was just upset..."

"No. You were right. I was involved with Anya once, a couple of years ago," he confessed. She knew she had seen something between them, something in his eyes, but she had dismissed it as a manifestation of her own jealousy.

"Oh," was the only word she could muster.

"It was brief and it's been over for a long time," he continued.

"You don't owe me an explanation," Angel said. "It's not like we're committed to each other. I mean, everyone has a past and let's face it, we don't have a future so..." She tried to act aloof and scoot by him, but even she wasn't buying her cool act, so she felt certain that he wasn't either.

He stepped in front of her, blocking her path. "Don't do that," he said, his jaw tensing and his stare piercing through her.

"What?" She crossed her arms.

"Don't act like you don't care, when I know you do and you know I do and if you weren't so damn stubborn..." his voice cut off mid-sentence and Angel could only guess at what he was about to say. He threw his hands up in the air. "You know what, forget it. Just go." He moved out of her way and sat down on the edge of the bed, leaning his elbows on his knees.

Angel stood still. A part of her wanted to storm out of the room just to prove that she was independent and powerful enough to do it. The other part wanted to stay and never leave. Turning to face him, she looked down and emotion poured from her. "Okay, I was jealous," she admitted. "I saw how tender you were with her and when you touched her, it made me want to kill her." Angel's voice shook and Andrew looked up. "I know it isn't fair and I know you have every right to see other women and it shouldn't bother me, but it does. It hurts." Tears filled her eyes and Angel rolled them in disgust. "I didn't want to get all girly and emotional."

Andrew stood up and took her hands. "I don't want to hurt you. You know that."

"I do," she whispered.

He raised her chin so he could look directly into her eyes. "If it were up to me there would only be one name in the husband list on Giovanni's spreadsheet." He wiped away a single tear that had escaped and was trickling down her cheek.

"I don't want to hurt you either," she sighed. "It just gets overwhelming sometimes."

He pulled her against him, letting her head rest on his chest. "I know, Sweetheart."

"There's a part of me that wants to run away from all of this, buy a little house with a yard, get married, have babies..."

"A dog," Andrew added.

"Or cats," Angel said.

"Or a dog," Andrew reiterated and embraced her tighter.

She exhaled and felt her body sink into his. She didn't want to leave his embrace. She wanted to close her eyes and have the whole world disappear just for a moment, just so she could breathe and clear her mind. "I'm scared," she whispered and felt his arms wrap tighter around her.

He kissed the top of her head and ran his fingers through her hair. "Me too, Sweetheart, me too."

Chase banging on the door brought their tender moment to an abrupt halt. "Yo, Boss Lady, we gotta roll," he hollered through the door.

"I'll be right there," she yelled back and then looked up at Andrew and forced a smile. "I guess it's show time."

He leaned down and kissed her lips tenderly. "You'll be fine. Just stick to the plan," he said.

CHAPTER 46

The plan seemed simple enough on paper, but Angel already knew that the execution was always the hard part. She had walked into these situations before, the difference this time was that she knew she could pull the trigger without hesitation if needed. Alberto drove Angel's SUV, aka the Tank, and another of Giovanni's men rode in the passenger seat. Angel sat in the back with Andrew on one side and Chase on the other. Anya was in the SUV behind them with four more of Giovanni's men.

"Let's walk through it one more time," Andrew said and Angel gave herself a mental head slap. They'd been through it a hundred times already. Angel was supposed to walk to the base of pier four and wait for Vladmir. When Vladmir showed up, she was to ask to see her mother in person. At that time, she would signal Giovanni's men to bring Anya to Vladmir and they would make the exchange.

"We're not going to let him take Anya though, right?" Angel asked. "You've got a plan to save her too, right?" Andrew and Chase exchanged a glance that made Angel feel suddenly uncomfortable. "What aren't you telling me?"

"Sweetheart, we're going to do the best we can to save Anya, but you and your mother are our priorities here," Andrew explained.

Chase fidgeted in the seat and bounced his leg rapidly up and down. "There's gonna be some sweet-ass fire power out there," he said while

287

looking out the window like a little kid on a road trip.

"Remember," Andrew continued, "do not walk to the end of the pier."

Angel nodded. She'd heard this lecture already and knew that walking to the end of the pier increased the danger.

"We can't get to you quickly if you're at the end of the pier," Andrew reminded her. "The docks will be crawling with the Brigatte Nero, as well as our people."

"Though I think Big Mike and the Cobras have picked off a lot of the Brigatte Nero," Chase said with a grin.

"You might not see all our guys, but they're there. If things start to head south, signal for help," Andrew said

"Got it," Angel uttered, her nerves increasing.

"Do you remember the signal?"

Angel nodded. "Yes, I make the sign of the cross over my body."

"The Snake has the chopper in close range," Chase added, "in case we need him."

"He can fly it with his broken leg?" Angel asked.

"You don't use your legs to fly," Chase teased, "but you should have seen us trying to cram his crazy-ass cast into the cockpit." Chase laughed out loud. "He wasn't happy."

As they approached the abandoned docks, Angel stomach launched into nervous spasms. She took a deep breath and exhaled slowly, trying to calm herself. Andrew squeezed her fingertips. "There's a chance they want to be done with this, to take Anya and go."

"Are you smoking some kind of funky-ass weed over there?" Chase said to Andrew. "They came here for a fight."

Andrew stared at Chase, his eyes clearly telling him to shut up, and then directed his attention back to Angel. "Miguel's plan is dead. Even if he were to kill you, he wouldn't take over the family, so there is no longer a logical reason to attack you. And because he won't be taking over the family he cannot offer the Brigatte Nero power or position in Chicago, which renders him useless to them."

"What about the Brigatte Nero wanting Angel for the purpose of revenge against Salvatore?" Chase blurted and Andrew reached around the back of Angel and smacked Chase in the head.

"You're not helping," Andrew gritted.

Chase raised his palms in the air. "Sorry for trying to make sure we cover all the crazy-ass bases. I thought we might not want to go traipsing into this completely in the dark."

Their bickering wasn't helping her nerves. Angel licked her lips and could already feel her mouth going dry. There was no hiding it, she was scared. "Do we have enough manpower if the Brigatte Nero attack?"

"Don't worry about that, Sweetheart, I'll handle that part," Andrew said. "We've got Giovanni's men, the Andriachini's, the Venturini's and a few cops who are pissed off about Officer Bernie and his partner being murdered in cold blood."

"What about the Cobras and the Knights?" Angel asked.

"Big Mike's gonna clean out the hangar and air strip and then join us here," Chase reiterated.

The SUV rolled to a stop near pier four. "This is it," Angel mumbled.

Andrew stepped out of the Tank and surveyed the area before Angel slid out. "Remember, you're not alone even if it feels that way. You've got an army on your side, just stick to the plan. Meet, make the exchange and get the hell out of here."

Two of Giovanni's men climbed out from the SUV behind them and escorted Angel to the base of the pier.

As Andrew climbed back in the Tank, Chase opened his laptop and uploaded the satellite link Sal sent him of the area. Red shadows on the screen indicated an increase in temperature most likely due to body heat. Andrew peaked at the screen. "Sure is a lot of red out there," he remarked.

"Yeah, let's hope most of it is our guys," Chase quipped. "Otherwise we're in some deep shitake."

Angel and her bodyguards walked slowly toward the base of pier four, where two of the Venturini men joined them, one in front of Angel and one to the rear. She was boxed in for protection. She recognized the layout of the docks from watching the surveillance video when Tony and Andrew found Officer Bernie dead in the black van. The van was no longer there but the yellow, crime tape still marked the area. Angel shivered as she passed it. Taking two steps onto the pier, she stopped and waited. "I don't see anyone," she whispered, knowing Andrew and Chase could hear her through the wire. The fact that she saw no one was twisting her stomach into nervous knots. *Is this another trap?* She wondered.

Pier four had a small shack on the very end that was falling apart and Angel tried to take a few steps to the right and then to the left to see around the shack; but it was impossible from a distance. "Do you think my mother could be in that shack?" Angel asked her bodyguards.

"Do you want us to check it out ma'am?" One of them asked.

It was obvious that the only way to see if someone was on the other side or even inside was to walk toward it. Angel took a few steps closer, as did her bodyguards, and she replayed Andrew's warning in her mind. Under no circumstances was she to walk to the end of the pier, he had told her. She knew it was dangerous, but she couldn't stop wondering if her mother was in that shack. As she started to inch her way along the pier, Andrew opened the SUV door to step out, but a shot ricocheted off the door next to his hand and sent him diving back into the seat.

"Somebody doesn't want you out of the vehicle," Chase said.

Two more shots fired and the bodyguards to her left and right fell over. Angel instinctively hit the ground, as did the Venturini men. She was frozen with fear.

"Find those snipers!" Andrew yelled to Chase, whose fingers flew rapidly over the keypad.

One of the Venturini men rose to his feet but was gunned down the moment he stood erect. Angel screamed and covered her head as his body fell inches from her. "Andrew," Angel shrieked into the wire. "They're going to kill us."

Andrew opened his door again and shots pummeled the vehicle, sending him back inside. He cursed and grabbed his phone, dialing Tony. "I can't get to her! They've got snipers on us! I can't get out of the car."

"I'm working on it, Ace, but we're taking fire too," Tony yelled back.

Angel reached her hand to the Venturini man that was still alive. "What's your name?" She asked.

"Devin, ma'am, Devin Potola," he answered, breathless with fear.

"Okay, Devin, I have a hunch they're going to kill you if you move, so don't," Angel said and Devin gave no argument. Then she spoke into the wire. "Andrew, I've instructed Devin to lay still and I'm going to stand up slowly."

"What the hell is she thinking?" Chase blurted to Andrew.

"She's thinking they want her to walk to the end of the pier alone," Andrew said and then punched the seat in front of him and cursed.

"But you told her not to go to the end of the pier," Chase said.

"I know," Andrew hunched over.

"If they wanted to take her ass out, they could have done it already," Chase added, bouncing his knee spastically up and down.

"Andrew," Angel uttered his name almost breathlessly, as fear engulfed her. "Pray with me." Angel slid into a kneeling position. "Il nostro padre, che l'arte nel cielo, hallowed è nome di thine."

"When did she learn to pray in Italian?" Chase blurted and Andrew smiled with tears forming in his eyes.

"I taught her," he said quietly.

"Il tuo regno prossimo. Tuo sarà fatto su terra come è nel cielo," Angel continued and rose from her knees to a squatting position.

"Man, don't get all emotional on me," Chase blurted. "If I see your ass cry then I'm gonna cry and that just ain't cool."

Andrew swallowed hard and didn't take his eyes off Angel.

"Diaci questo giorno il nostro pane quotidiano e perdonici le nostre trasgressioni," Angel prayed as she slowly rose to a standing position with her hands held in the air. "Come perdoniamo coloro che trasgredice a contro di noi."

Andrew prayed aloud in the car with her and Chase joined in with the English version of the Lord's Prayer.

"Conducali non nella tentazione ma trasportili dalla malvagità," Andrew and Angel prayed simultaneously.

"And deliver our asses from evil," Chase added.

And they all three said, "Amen," as Angel took two steps around the body in front of her and inched her way slowly toward the end of the pier.

"Andrew," Angel spoke into the wire, "I'm going to turn around and see if they'll let me walk back." Angel took one step back, and as she anticipated, a shot fired within inches of her footing. She instinctively ducked and then slowly turned to face the end of the pier again. It was obvious Vladmir wanted Angel to walk the pier unescorted. As long as she kept moving forward, the shooting stopped. Fearing for her life kept her from being consumed by anger at the moment, but she could feel her blood boiling. She didn't like being a pawn in Vladmir's game or being lead into a potential trap with the dangling hope of finding her mother. If she lived through this, Vladmir would pay.

Half way down the pier, Angel called out. "Vladmir? I'm here, just as you said." No one responded. "Show me my mother and I'll give you Anya," she hollered, but there was no response.

293

"What do they want her to do now?" Chase blurted.

Andrew shook his head and peered out the window, his eyes surveying the area around her.

By the time Angel reached the dilapidated shack at the end of the pier, she could hear a noise that sounded like a muffled cry. "Mom?" She called out, pulling her 9mm from her waistband and reaching toward the wooden door.

Andrew lowered the window and screamed, "Angel, NO!" She turned her face toward the sound of his voice, but as soon as her fingers brushed the door handle, the shack exploded, blowing Angel's body upward off the end of the pier and into the lake below.

"Holy shi...." Chase yelled but he never finished his sentence, as a barrage of bullets hit the SUV and he instinctively ducked, forgetting that they couldn't penetrate the polycarbonate layers.

Andrew hit speed dial on his phone and called Tony again. "Get Angel!" He yelled into the phone. "I'm trapped in the car and she went off the end of the pier. She's wearing a vest!"

Chase's eyes grew wider, "she'll sink like a big-ass rock," he said.

Tony threw his phone down and took off in a dead sprint toward the pier. When he got to the end there was no sign of Angel. The weight of the vest had pulled her to the bottom. Tony jumped into the water and opened his eyes, but the lake water was murky. He came up for air and dove back down, feeling his way along the bottom until he found her. He gripped her by the vest and pulled her to the surface, wrapping his arm under hers and pulling her head back against his chest. Dragging her to the shore, he handed her off to several of the Andriachini men who lifted her over

the retaining wall and onto the shore. Two officers
dashed to assist, maneuvering the heavy vest off
and administering CPR. Within moments Angel
spit up the water that had entered her lungs and
regained consciousness. She didn't remember
anything after reaching for the handle.

Giovanni's men, the Andriachini's and the
Venturini's took out the Brigatte Nero who had
opened fire on Angel's SUV. When Andrew was
finally able to get out of the car, he yelled to Tony,
who gave him a thumb's up, indicating Angel was
alive. He then made a beeline to the SUV where
Anya sat. Pulling open the door, Andrew pushed
his .45 against her temple. "You knew about that
bomb and you didn't tell us," he barked, digging
the barrel in harder against her head.

Anya sat stoic.

"You set that bomb, didn't you?" He
seethed. "Didn't you?"

"No. It may have been one I built but I
didn't set it."

"How many other bombs are there?" He
demanded.

Her hands began to tremble. "I don't know.
None of this was supposed to happen."

He cocked his gun and dug it into her skin.
"Give me one reason not to put a bullet in your
head, right here, right now!"

Anya cried, "Because I love you."

Chase radioed for the Snake to bring the
chopper and take Angel back to the Towers. She
was fighting to stay conscious as they loaded her
into the chopper, but the magnitude of the bomb
left her head pounding and her vision blurred.
"Find my mom," she uttered to Tony as he kissed
her fingertips.

"I'm on it, Babe," Tony said and then yelled to the Snake. "Get her home safe."

"Will do," the Snake hollered back and lifted the chopper.

Chase opened his door and hollered for Andrew and Tony. "Big Mike phoned. We got a problem at the hangar."

"What's the problem?" Andrew asked.

"The good news is they've taken out the rest of the Brigatte Nero," Chase said and then paused. "The bad news is they found Sophia."

"Dead?" Tony asked.

"No, but she's wired to blow," Chase said.

"Son of a bitch!" Andrew cursed and paced back and forth by the car. "Tell Big Mike to stay there, but to keep a safe distance, and we're on our way," he told Chase and then turned to Tony. "Get our families together and meet us there."

"On it," Tony said and hurried off.

Andrew rushed to one of the officers and ordered him to call in a bomb squad to meet them at the hangar. Then he retrieved Anya from the SUV and dragged her to Angel's vehicle, shoving her into the back seat.

"Get out," he said to Chase who gawked at him awkwardly. "Take the other car back to the Towers and run surveillance from there. I need you and Sal keeping us up to date on anything or anyone headed our way."

"I can do that from right here, man," Chase argued and Andrew's lip tightened.

"Angel's going to wake up and not have any visual of what's happening with Sophia," he explained. "She needs you there so she can see."

"Right on," Chase said and grabbed his laptop, hopped out of the SUV and ran up to the next one.

Andrew tapped Alberto on the shoulder. "Get us to the airstrip as fast as you can," he said and then turned toward Anya. "You better pray you can defuse Sophia's bomb because it's your only chance of staying alive."

CHAPTER 47

Chase set up his equipment in the meeting room and placed the live feed on the large screen. The Snake had already briefed Giovanni on what went down at the boat docks, and Chase filled him in on what was currently happening at the hangar. Giovanni ordered Carl to be brought to the meeting room. Joseph Venturini, who had arrived at the Towers while everyone was at the boat docks, now joined them in the meeting room. He was visibly upset, ringing his hands together and muttering quiet prayers.

Chase's fingers flew rapidly across the keyboard. "Sophia must be in the hangar," he said aloud, "and I can't see inside." He dialed Big Mike's phone. When Big Mike answered, Chase blurted, "Yo, I need you to be my eyes in the hangar."

"Andrew ordered everyone out," he said. "Sophia's wearing a wired vest, sort of like the one the Snake had on, but this one has a timer."

"How much time we got?" Chase asked.

"Sixteen minutes."

"Is the bomb squad there yet?"

"Nah, just Andrew and Anya. It don't look good man."

Chase hung up the phone and relayed the conversation to Giovanni, Carl and Joseph Venturini. "May God help us," Giovanni uttered and crossed his body, head to chest and shoulder to shoulder.

Three minutes later, Olga escorted a wobbly Angel through the door and to the table.

"Michelangela, you should be in bed," Giovanni said.

"Nonsense," Olga blurted. "It's her mother out there. The child's not going to rest at a time like this."

"E' una presa di morte," Carl uttered beneath his breath.

"Death trap," Angel said softly, translating the gist of his sentence.

Giovanni gazed up at her, surprised. "You understood what he said," Giovanni grinned. "I am proud of you."

Angel didn't smile. It hurt too much to move any part of her body. Fear for her mother left her emotionless as she stared at the surveillance feed, unable to imagine what Sophia was going through. She prayed silently in her heart.

Joseph Venturini paced near the windows and Angel could see the agony on his face. His son and the woman he had secretly loved and cherished for years were in danger and he was powerless to help them. Angel slowly walked toward Don Venturini, stopping to grip the edge of the table until the room stopped tilting and the dizziness calmed enough for her to continue walking. She reached her hands out to Joseph Venturini and he guided her toward the window. "You should sit down," he told her.

She shook her head and squeezed his fingers. "I'm joining you in prayer for the people we love," Angel spoke softly.

"Grazie," he said and they stood together in silence.

Carl slumped forward in his chair as if the weight of the world were pushing him into the ground. His eyes were red and swollen and Angel could only imagine what he was going through, the shock of discovering that his own son was a traitor, the fear that his grandson was dead and the guilt of knowing that had he not confided in Miguel, none of this would be happening. Compassion for him tugged at Angel's heart. "Chase," she said weakly, "is there any sign of Miguel or Salvo?"

Carl immediately looked up and Angel met his stare. The sadness in his eyes was almost more than she could bear.

"No," Chase answered.

Olga pulled out the chair between Carl and Giovanni and plunked her rounded hips into it. She then reached over and took each of their hands. "No sense in placing blame where blame isn't due," she said, giving both their hands a squeeze. "We can't control our children. Why, we can barely control ourselves," she said. "We need to stand together now and pray for our Sophia." Olga's lip quivered slightly as she spoke but she fought back the emotion.

"How much time do we have left?" Angel asked.

"Six minutes," Chase said.

CHAPTER 48

Andrew stood with the .45 aimed at Anya. "Defuse it," he ordered.

"I'm trying," Anya cried.

"Don't give me your sob story," he barked. "You built all of these bombs for them."

"Not all of them," she wailed.

"If you can build it, you can defuse it," he seethed.

She turned and looked up at him. "I didn't build this one. I swear."

Tears streamed down Sophia's cheeks as she sat on the pavement in the middle of the empty hangar. Andrew paced beside her. "Can you tell me where Vladmir and Miguel went?"

Sophia sniveled. "I don't know. I haven't seen Miguel since the pier."

"What happened at the pier?" Andrew asked.

"Miguel got a phone call to meet someone at the old boat docks so he asked if I would mind stopping there for a moment," Sophia explained. "I said it was fine, but when we got there Miguel was jumped by these men and I was dragged from the car and brought here."

"You haven't seen Miguel since?"

"No," Sophia's voice shook. "I assumed they had killed him."

Andrew bent down so he was face to face with her. "Sophia, this is important. What did the men who jumped Miguel look like?"

"Two of them were African American and one was white," she answered confidently.

"Were they wearing military camouflage?"

"No, just regular street clothes," she said.

The timer changed to three minutes and Anya looked up at Andrew. "I cannot defuse it," she said. "I can try and buy us a second to get the vest off before it blows, but there is no guarantee."

"If she dies, you die," Andrew said, his jaw set.

Anya went back to work on the vest. "I think we can get it off but we won't have time to get out of the hangar and I don't know the intensity of the bomb."

"We're running out of time," Andrew barked.

"Okay," Anya spoke quickly, "as soon as I tell you, you slide it off her right arm and I'll slide it off her left, then we each pull her up and run for the entrance."

"On the count of three," Andrew instructed. "One....two...three!"

They pulled the vest off and Andrew gripped Sophia's arm, managing only a few steps before the explosion hurled them through the air and across the pavement. Big Mike, Tony and Giovanni's men rushed toward them just as the hangar exploded, knocking everyone backwards.

Inside the meeting room, they shrieked when they caught a brief glimpse of Andrew and Sophia and then went silent as they watched a second explosion engulf the hangar and surrounding area in flames. Chase dialed Big Mike. "C'mon, answer," Chase blurted aloud. "Answer!"

When Big Mike finally answered, he was disoriented. He stumbled over to where Sophia and Andrew lay and grabbed Sophia's wrist. "She's alive," he mumbled in the phone and then checked Andrew's pulse. "They're both alive. Get an ambulance."

Cheers rang out in the meeting room and Joseph Venturini embraced Angel. Even Carl breathed a sigh of relief, though sadness still hung heavy upon him.

"Wait!" Chase exclaimed, "I've got movement behind the hangar." Chase clicked across the keyboard, showing the surveillance from a different angle. "There's a black van leaving the area!"

"Where did it come from?" Giovanni asked.

"It must have been behind the hangar the whole time," Chase said. "I didn't see it, but I wasn't really looking for it."

Chase dialed Tony's cell and yelled into the phone when he answered. "There's a black van leaving the area, can you follow it?"

"We'll try, Ace, but everybody's moving a little slow here, shell-shocked I think."

"Damn!" Chase blurted, disconnecting the call and dancing his fingers wildly across the keys. "Maybe Sal can track where it goes," he said to himself, but loud enough for everyone to hear. Chase dialed Sal on the computer and he agreed to try and follow the van via satellite but reminded Chase that unless there was a device on the van to track, he would most assuredly lose it.

Chase disconnected the call. "It's a long shot and it'll be dumb-ass luck if we're able to follow it, but we'll see. Crazier things have happened."

As they began to disperse Andrew phoned in, speaking slowly and laboring over every word. Chase put the call on speaker and Angel could hear sirens in the background. Chase switched the surveillance feed back to the front of the hangar revealing several fire trucks, police cars and ambulances around the air strip. "There are no bodies inside the hangar," Andrew said. "No sign of Miguel or Salvo."

"What about Anya?" Angel asked.

"She's gone too," Andrew said, "though I don't know how."

Chase told him about the black van in the back of the hangar and surmised that she must have gotten into it.

"I don't see how that's possible," Andrew replied. "There's no way she could have lived through both explosions."

CHAPTER 49

Giovanni allowed Big Mike to stay the night in one of the apartments next to Chase, while the Snake took an apartment across the hall from Giovanni and Carl stayed in the apartment next to Giovanni. Salvatore, who arrived at the Towers only minutes after Sophia and everyone had returned, stayed in the apartment below Giovanni's with two of his bodyguards. Giovanni ordered everyone, Sophia and Olga included, to attend a meeting the next morning at 9:00am sharp.

Angel took three more ibuprofen and crawled into bed next to Midnight and Mo. She laid on her right side, flipped to her left and finally flopped onto her back, staring at the ceiling. Her body ached, physically and her heart, emotionally. She couldn't get past the sadness in Carl's eyes, but that wasn't the only thing haunting her. Her mind kept drifting back to one simple question, if Anya was one of the bad guys, why would she save the Snake and Sophia? Why wouldn't she have allowed them to blow up? It felt as if there were still many unconnected dots. Knowing sleep wasn't anywhere in her near future, Angel got up, threw on her satin robe and went to the kitchen to make tea and raid the fridge. Pulling out a knife from the drawer, she sliced a Cannoli in half and had an epiphany. The knife. When Officer Bernie was found dead, the Snake asked to see a picture of the knife. Why? What information could the knife possibly have given him?

She opened the junk drawer and pulled out a piece of paper and a pen. *Maybe if I jot everything down it will help me connect the dots,* she hoped, but it didn't. In the end she was left with a full page of questions and few answers. Who was the Venturini that Big Mike killed in the chopper? Was he really a traitor and if so, was he working with Miguel or with the Brigatte Nero?

After finishing her tea and placing her plate and cup in the sink, Angel took her piece of paper and headed downstairs to the Snake's apartment. She knocked several times before she finally heard him hobbling toward the door.

"Ms. Maratinzano," he said with genuine surprise in his tone. "Do you need help with something?"

"For heaven's sake, Sean, call me Angel," she said, striding passed him and taking a seat at the glass top kitchen table by the window.

He closed the door and limped to where she sat. "You do realize it's midnight, right?" He asked.

"Yes. I'm sorry I woke you, but..."

"I wasn't sleeping," he interrupted. "Too much going on in my brain."

"Me too," she said.

"What's on the paper?" He asked, lowering himself into the chair next to her.

"Some of the unconnected dots."

He pointed to her notation about the knife. "This one's been bothering me too."

"That's why I came here," Angel confessed. "You commented that you wanted to see the knife used to stab Officer Bernie. Why?"

The Snake scratched his head and leaned back. "The Brigatte Nero are rich in tradition and known for several things: Taking hostages, demanding ridiculously high ransoms and authentic military grade weapons." He shook his

306

head. "A Brigatte Nero wouldn't kill by stabbing and leave a random knife to be found. It's inconsistent with their history. It just isn't who they are. If they were going to stab someone and leave the knife, the knife would have the BN emblem on it." The Snake shook his head. "The Brigatte Nero claim responsibility for their killings. They take pride in their work. When they do something, it is never one random act."

"So you think whoever killed Officer Bernie wasn't a Brigatte Nero member?"

"Definitely not," he answered with a sigh. "I also think whoever stabbed Officer Bernie, also stabbed Freddie and the other Officer and I think it was someone they all knew."

"Why?" Angel puzzled.

"Because to stab someone, you've got to get close to them," he explained. "So either our killer sneaked up quietly on them, or he approached easily because they were acquaintances or friends."

"So who would know Officer Bernie, the young officer and Freddie?" Angel asked.

"Andrew and Tony and probably Anya," the Snake said, with a shrug and a raised eyebrow.

By the time Angel crept back into the penthouse it was after 1:00am and she found Sophia and Olga sitting up at the dining room table; both sipping tea and eating Cannoli.

"Did you go on a secret rendezvous?" Olga asked with raised eyebrows.

"How did you know I was gone?"

"We saw your dishes in the sink and checked your room," Sophia responded.

"Want some more Cannoli?" Olga asked, lifting the plate toward Angel, who couldn't resist helping herself to one more.

Angel took a big bite and then spoke. "Mom, what did you think of Miguel?"

"Merciful Heavens, child, Emily Post is rolling in her grave," Olga ranted and then looked to Sophia. "Elsa down at the hair salon says her grandkids chew with their mouths open too. It must be this generation." Angel tapped Olga on the forearm and when Olga turned her head to look, Angel opened her mouth and proudly displayed the mashed-up Cannoli on her tongue.

"Angel May!" Sophia gasped.

"You're like a three-year-old," Olga sputtered, throwing her hands in the air as a gesture of giving up. "I don't know where you learned such nonsense."

Angel grinned ear to ear. She didn't know why it felt good to taunt Olga, but sometimes it just did. "Back to my question," Angel said after swallowing her Cannoli. "What did you think of Miguel Cusanelli?"

Sophia shrugged. "He was a very polite man, with few interests other than his father and his son. In fact, all he really talked about at lunch was Salvo."

"What about Salvo?" Angel asked.

"The usual stuff parents brag on, like how intelligent he is, how quickly he had acquired a reputation and social standing within the high-tech community in New York and around the world, how Miguel was concerned that he didn't have romantic relationships..."

"Why? Does he think he's a homo?" Olga interrupted.

"No," Sophia grimaced. "He thinks he works too much and has little time for girlfriends or even friendships."

"Did you talk about anything else?" Angel asked.

"Not really," Sophia shrugged. "We had a nice lunch together and then he got a call from someone and asked if I would mind stopping at the boat docks for a moment."

"I bet he faked the call and just wanted to take you there for some action," Olga blurted.

"Olga!" Angel scolded. "You're as bad as the guys."

"Elsa says the old boat docks are responsible for all the teen pregnancies in the city," Olga said.

"Oh, well, if Elsa says it, it must be true," Angel teased and rolled her eyes.

"Don't sass your old aunt." Olga shook her finger in Angel's face. "Nobody has more information on the pulse of a city than hair dressers and priests."

Angel nibbled another bite of Cannoli and tried to sort through her thoughts. Something still didn't fit but she couldn't put her finger on it. All of a sudden, it came to her. "Mom," she blurted, "you said Miguel received a phone call while you were at lunch?"

"Yes." Sophia nodded.

"That means his cell phone must have been turned on."

"Nice work Sherlock," Olga teased and giggled to herself.

Angel smirked sideways at her. "Chase couldn't trace Miguel's phone because it wasn't on, but if he took a call it had to have been on." Angel didn't like where this was heading. Was Chase lying? Was there a reason he was purposefully not checking Miguel's phone?

"Do you know what number he was trying to trace?" Sophia asked. "Because I know Miguel was using a temporary phone."

"How do you know that?" Angel belted excitedly.

"Because he complained about not liking the temporary phone and said he was hoping to find his old one."

Angel was on her feet and pacing. Anya lied. She wasn't talking to Miguel, she was talking to the person who stole Miguel's phone. Or, it was possible that Anya didn't lie and really believed that she was talking to Miguel; but that didn't fit as easily as the first option. In any case, that meant Miguel was probably innocent. Angel dialed Andrew. "I need you right now," she said when he answered.

"Sweetheart, it's the middle of the night and your mother and Olga are right down the hall. I'd be more comfortable if we came back to my place."

Angel paused. It took her a moment to process what he thought she was talking about and then she grunted silently. *Men! Do they always have sex on the brain?* "No. I need your logical, investigative skills."

"Oh," he said sheepishly. "I thought you..."

"I know what you thought," Angel interrupted, "and as good as that sounds, I just need your brain." She hung up the phone and dialed Chase, whom she instructed to call Big Mike, and then she called Tony.

"Babe," Tony answered. "I was just thinking about you."

"I need you to come over right away," Angel said and then quickly added, "for a meeting."

"Is it your body meeting my body," Tony teased.

Angel gave herself a mental head slap. *They really do have a one track mind.* "No, it's your brain working with my brain."

"On my way, Babe."

"Merciful Heavens, you're calling a meeting in the middle of the night?" Olga grunted. "People aren't going to be happy about this, especially your grandfather." She shook her head. "On second thought, wake the old coot up, he doesn't deserve a good night's sleep," she snorted and chuckled to herself.

"Mom, I want you to join us in the meeting room and Olga, we're all going to need coffee."

"Coffee and snacks, coming right up," she said, smacking her hands together and waddling to the kitchen. There was nothing Olga enjoyed more than preparing snacks, even if it was the middle of the night.

Angel then went downstairs and woke up the Snake and Giovanni. Then she rushed back to the Penthouse to change out of her pajamas. After she brushed her teeth and hair, threw on a little lip gloss, eyeliner and a dab of blush, she went to the kitchen where Olga was busy preparing food. There was one last thing she needed to understand before she could solidify her theory. "I have a question," Angel said to Olga as she entered the kitchen.

"I hope I have an answer," Olga quipped without looking up.

"Remember when you told me that you wrote the note from Andrew, saying I should meet him at Tetterbaum's? And then you said you sent Salvo there, hoping we would hit it off?"

"Merciful Heavens, I said I was sorry. Meddling and matchmaking is what I do," Olga defended.

"It's okay. I just need to know where you got the idea."

Olga stopped futzing around the kitchen and turned toward Angel, a spark of understanding gleaming in her eyes. "Salvo asked me how he might be able to get you alone so he could get to know you better, him being on the husband list and all. He said he didn't feel comfortable talking to you around here with bodyguards and everyone listening. He suggested you two meet at the pub, since he had been wanting to get a look at it and it was closed. I made sure Freddie would go with you and gave him the note," Olga explained.

"That's what I thought," Angel said. "That's exactly what I thought."

"So, you're not still upset with me?"

Angel kissed Olga on the forehead. "You're still meddlesome, but I love you anyway."

By the time everyone arrived, Angel and Chase had already run through Angel's theory, rapidly connecting the dots. They also searched the meeting room for additional bugs but didn't find any. *Better to be safe than sorry*, Angel thought. It was imperative that the information that was about to be shared did not leave the meeting room. Olga brought in coffee and raspberry Danish, Cannoli and bagels with cream cheese and lined the bar with the snacks, plates, cups, sugar and creamer and napkins. Once everyone made a plate and sat down, Angel began.

"Thank you all for coming. I realize it's the middle of the night and I will make this as brief as possible. Miguel Cusanelli is not the man in the black van and the one pulling the strings." A murmur of disbelief filled the room and Angel paused for a moment until everyone quieted down. "I thought at first that Carl was behind the whole thing, but it isn't him either." Angel took a deep breath and exhaled. "The mastermind behind this whole thing is Salvo."

"What information do you have to back this up?" Giovanni asked.

Angel gave Chase a nod and a picture of Salvo appeared on the large screen. "As soon as Sophia told me that Miguel was bragging about his son's reputation and good standing in the high tech industry in New York and around the globe, I started to think that it might be possible for him to conduct business under another name." Angel paced as she spoke. "A lot of people have aliases, so I contacted Chase and Sal."

Angel gave Chase a nod and he took over the explanation. "Salvo Cusanelli is renowned for his work in weapons design, particularly in the area of explosives," Chase explained. "This didn't come up in the initial background check we ran because he uses an alias for his work, Salvo Genio."

Andrew and Tony exchanged amused glances and Giovanni huffed, but Angel didn't understand why. "Is something wrong?" She asked.

"Genio in Italian means genius," Giovanni explained and then nodded his head for Chase to continue.

"Under his arrogant-ass alias," Chase mocked, which made everyone around the table chuckle, "he's created some of the most powerful and deadly weapons' technology on the planet and is particularly well-respected in Moscow."

"Which is where we believe he met Anya Grovashik," Angel interjected and Chase clicked his computer to show a picture of Anya on the screen. "Andrew mentioned that Anya was a bomb expert, originally from Moscow."

"That's right," Andrew said.

"Evidentially, she travels to Moscow on a regular basis to keep her skills updated. Our guess is that Salvo and Anya met there and

313

continued their relationship upon returning to the States."

"According to Sal's records, Anya has an apartment in New York and one here in Chicago," Chase added.

"So, everything Anya told us was a lie?" Tony asked.

"Not everything," Angel replied. "She was married once and her husband was gunned down."

"Which gives her a clear motive for revenge against the Maratinzano family," Andrew said.

"She really is the daughter of Brigatte Nero member, Johan Bernardelli, and the niece of Officer Bernie. All of that is true," Angel explained.

Chase piped in. "We believe things didn't just accidentally happen in the crazy-ass way she pretended. We think Salvo and Anya developed their plan with the Brigatte Nero from the very beginning."

"What makes you believe this?" Giovanni questioned.

Angel took a deep breath. "Anya told us that Miguel's motive was to kill me so that he could take over the family. This was a lie. Based on everything we've learned of Miguel, he was a private man, completely absorbed with his son and his father. According to Carl, he had no life outside of his family and never left New York. I don't believe he had any desire to move to Chicago and become head of our family."

"That's not evidence, that's hearsay," Andrew said.

"The evidence is in the fact that Miguel's cell phone was stolen and we believe Salvo is the one who stole it so that it could be used to make calls to and from Anya. That way if anything went wrong, his father would take the fall," Angel replied.

"It's true that he was using a temporary phone," Sophia chimed in. "He complained about it at lunch."

"So, then we have to ask, who knew Miguel's temporary phone number?" Chase said.

"Carl didn't have it," Angel responded, "because when I had him write down both Salvo and Miguel's numbers he wrote down Miguel's old number."

"And we couldn't trace Miguel's old number because Salvo kept the phone off, except for his sporadic calls to Anya," Chase added.

"If Salvo and Anya orchestrated this entire thing, what was their motive?" Tony asked.

Chase wiggled in his seat. "This is where it gets really good." He grinned and twirled a pen between his fingers. "Salvo owns a high-tech company in New York, but it's really a front for dealing weapons. I'm not talking about low-end street guns. I'm talking premium, high-grade missiles, bombs and some scary-ass new explosive technology that's still in the testing phase overseas."

"To whom does he sell these weapons?" Giovanni asked.

"Terrorist groups mainly and other militant groups like the Brigatte Nero, who just happen to be one of Salvo's top paying customers," Chase beamed.

"We believe Salvo didn't go to the Brigatte Nero with his plan, they came to him using Anya," Angel suggested and she could feel all eyes on her as she paced back and forth. "The Brigatte Nero already hated Salvatore..."

"Yeah, why is that again?" Tony interrupted.

Angel looked to Big Mike, who took the cue and told them the story about the Brigatte Nero

murdering his father, Salvatore taking him and his
mother in, and ordering his men to enact revenge
on the Brigatte Nero. "It was the only time in
Italy's history that the police and the mob joined
forces to annihilate a group," Big Mike explained.

"How many men were killed?" Tony asked.

"I don't remember, but it was well over one
hundred," Big Mike said.

"After that massacre, the Brigatte Nero
disappeared for a long time, obviously regrouping
elsewhere," Angel added.

"Yeah, right here in the States," Big Mike
said.

"During the massacre in Italy, the head
commander of the Brigatte Nero was murdered.
His name was Antionne Bernardelli, father to
Johan Bernardelli," Chase explained and a joint
exhale of understanding filled the room. Angel
could see by their expressions that they were all
making the connection now. "There's more," Chase
said excitedly, and clicked on his keyboard to
display another image on the large screen.

"That's Vladmir," the Snake said as soon as
he saw the image.

"Correct," Chase replied. "His name is
Vladmir Grovashik, father to Hank Grovashik,
Anya's husband who was murdered."

Tony threw his hands in the air. "Wow!"

Chase bounced spastically in his chair. "I
know, I didn't see that coming either," he blurted.
"It's one crazy-ass wow, for sure!"

"Here we have Johan Bernardelli seeking
revenge against Salvatore Buscetta for his father's
death, and we have Vladmir Grovashik seeking
revenge against the Maratinzano family for his
son's death," Angel explained, stopping only to
draw in a deep breath and continue. "In steps
Salvo, the grandson of the Compare to the Capo di

Tutti Capi, who happens to be a Maratinzano with a granddaughter who is both Buscetta and Maratinzano...."

"And it's the perfect matching to enact revenge on both families at the same time," Giovanni sighed.

"So, Salvo didn't promise the Brigatte Nero positioning and power in the city, it was Salvo who stood to gain from the whole thing," Angel said.

"What does he gain?" Tony asked.

"Money. A crazy-ass amount of money, not to mention the power that comes with the reputation of being the greatest designer of weapons technology of all times," Chase said and Angel could see him almost salivate when he talked about weapons.

"Salvo probably thought that if I were out of the picture, his father, Miguel, might actually become head of the Maratinzano family," Angel added.

"Which he could certainly use for his own benefit down the road," Giovanni noted and they all nodded.

Angel glanced at Andrew and watched his logical brain churning the facts. "In the beginning, on the plane, was the pilot ever supposed to land like Anya implied?"

"We don't think so," Chase said. "We think the plane was intentionally rigged to blow over that particular Iowa area so that the Brigatte Nero would be right there to ensure that there were no survivors."

"When the plane blew up and for a period of time afterwards, everyone probably thought the mission was a success," Angel said.

"That is until Andrew phoned Giovanni with our suspicion that something or someone had come out of the plane just before the explosion," Chase said.

"It was after that call that Anya, Salvo and the Brigatte Nero had to put another plan into action," Angel explained.

Giovanni rubbed his hands over his jowls. "Si, I took the call and immediately reported the information to Carl and we began making preparations to come to Chicago."

"We know Carl informed his sons of what was happening because Miguel and Salvo accompanied him here," Angel added. "We can assume Salvo told Johan there was a chance I was alive, which was later confirmed when the Brigatte Nero found the Snake."

"After that your men flew in with choppers and the Brigatte Nero took them out," Big Mike added.

"Except for the one Venturini in the co-pilot seat who Big Mike killed before he could kill Trig," Chase said. "His name was James Serci, brother to Michael Serci, who worked for the Cullatos out of New York and just happened to be recently murdered."

"Si," Giovanni uttered, "Carl killed him in my home."

"We ran a trace on James, cross-referencing him with our key players and it turns out that both Michael and James Serci worked for Salvo dealing weapons in New York, prior to James coming to Chicago and hooking up with the Venturini family."

"That explains why the Brigatte Nero didn't kill him in the chopper," Andrew said.

"Yep, we can assume Salvo called in a favor and James made sure he got assigned to help find Angel," Chase said. "That way, if she was found alive, he could kill her."

"Then, when Trig brought me home, Salvo must have notified the Brigatte Nero that they had failed..." Angel began but the Snake interrupted.

"That was the phone call I overhead," he said and snapped his fingers. "Johan was very upset. He got off the phone and ordered his men to find and kill anyone who helped Angel escape. That was right before they transported everyone to Chicago."

"That's probably when the Brigatte Nero came into my house and killed the Nelsons," Big Mike said.

Giovanni's jaw tightened. "Li ha usati per regolare la sua presa della morte!"

Sophia reached over and patted Giovanni's hand. "Non riuscirà. Lo arresteremo," she said.

"Do you guys think we could chit chat in English, so nobody feels left out?" Angel's tone dripped both humor and sarcasm. "I mean, it's late and, call my crazy, but I think if we speak the same language we might get done faster."

"E' aggressive," Giovanni whispered to Sophia, rolling his eyes.

"Si, molto aggressive." Sophia nodded.

"Moving on," Angel blurted. "Once the Brigatte Nero knew I made it home alive, they had to make other plans, so Salvo issued the hunting order to the Cobras and the Knights and put a one-million-dollar bounty on my head."

Chase fidgeted in his seat. "This is where Salvo started to lose control."

"Explain," Giovanni uttered.

"Something changed and we think whatever it was made Salvo panic," Angel said.

"I think I know what it was," the Snake said. "I think this is around the time that Salvo killed Johan and put Vladmir in charge."

Chase snapped his fingers in an a-ha fashion. "It would stand to reason that maybe killing Johan was a mistake and Vladmir wasn't as easy to work with."

"Vladmir definitely has more rage and ego than Johan did," the Snake said.

"If Salvo killed Johan, that would surely put a damper on his relationship with Anya," Angel said, pacing back and forth, "which is maybe why Anya didn't let the Snake explode after all?" She posed. "Maybe letting him live was her own little way of sticking it to Salvo?"

"But when she was sitting here, she seemed genuinely surprised to learn Johan had been killed," the Snake said.

"Yes, she did," Angel acknowledged, "but that could have been an act."

"In either case, we believe it was Salvo who phoned Miguel while he was at lunch with Sophia, lured him to the boat docks and kidnapped them both," Angel said.

"Why would he do that?" Tony asked.

"To take Sophia," Angel replied. "See, he hired some thugs to kidnap them both, deliver Sophia to Vladmir and then we can assume they were supposed to set Miguel free."

"But Anya had other plans," Chase said, exchanging a quick glance with Angel. "We think Anya paid those thugs to tie Miguel up and position him to be killed."

"Why would she want to kill Miguel?" Andrew asked.

"Because Salvo killed her father," Angel explained.

"Do you have proof Miguel is dead?" Giovanni asked.

"Not yet, sir," Chase answered, "but I expect confirmation any time now."

"When I approached the shack on the pier, I reached for the door because I heard something, something that sounded like a muffled cry. I was worried it was my mom, but now we believe it was probably Miguel," Angel explained.

"At this point, I had called everyone to the Towers and thanks to the bug Salvo planted under the table, Vladmir knew that we had Anya and he called to make the trade. Anya for Sophia," Angel explained.

"Salvo planted the bug," Tony mumbled more to himself than to anyone else.

"We think so," Angel said. "He was sitting right next to Miguel so it would have been easy to place the bug closer to Miguel's seat than his own."

"How can a son frame his own father?" Sophia shook her head in disgust.

"Vladmir called to arrange the trade, but they were obviously never going to make a trade at the docks. That was all a setup, hoping to blow me and Miguel up at the same time."

"If they wanted you dead, Babe, why not just plant a bullet in your head while you were wide open on the pier?" Tony posed.

"The Brigatte Nero don't work that way," the Snake answered. "They thrive on power and control. Shooting her wouldn't have been nearly as fulfilling to Vladmir as having her play along with his little game and then blowing her up."

Big Mike nodded in agreement. "That's exactly right."

Angel shivered. "When I survived, Anya panicked because now she was not only returning to Vladmir having failed, but she would have to face Salvo's rage once he learned that she had killed his father."

"So, all Anya's begging and crying was an act?" Andrew asked.

"She's good," Tony quipped.

"There's a lot of holes in this story," Andrew said.

"Give her some credit, Ace, it's the middle of the night and she's sure as hell connected more dots than the rest of us," Tony sneered.

"Amen to that," Big Mike grinned.

"Okay, then why didn't Anya let Sophia blow up?" Andrew asked.

Angel shrugged. "I don't know." She chewed on her index fingernail and paced. "Maybe because there is some thread of conscience in her. Maybe because you were with Sophia and she still has feelings for you?" Angel shrugged. "We may never know her reasons."

"Wait a minute, so who killed Freddie, Officer Bernie and his partner?" Tony asked.

"Salvo did," Chase answered. "He tried to make it look like it was a gang killing by using a knife similar to the ones used to kill the Jane Doe in Tetterbaum's."

"The Snake knew right away that they weren't killed by the Brigatte Nero and Big Mike confirmed with Chito that the Cobras and Knights didn't kill them either," Angel said.

"Maybe Chito lied," Andrew posed.

Big Mike shook his head. "Chito would have told me if it was their handiwork."

"Whoever stabbed them was someone they knew, otherwise he wouldn't have gotten that close," the Snake explained.

"And they all three knew Salvo. Freddie from seeing him with Carl in New York, and Officer Bernie and his partner because they were working with the Brigatte Nero," Angel explained.

"Okay, assuming this is all correct, how did Anya escape that explosion at the hangar?" Andrew asked.

Chase grinned ear-to-ear like a kid on Christmas morning. "Pure brilliance," he said, bobbing his spikey head up and down.

"We're gonna need more information than just that, Ace," Tony Smirked.

Chase clicked on his keys and displayed a diagram of the hangar on the larger screen. He then hopped from his chair and rushed to the screen so he could point to it and reference exact locations. "There were two bombs, one strapped to Sophia and another one on a detonator switch," Chase explained. "Sophia was here, close to the hangar door." He pointed. "The other bomb was over here, in the far back corner." Chase went on to explain that the bombs had to be placed and timed perfectly to create a small tunnel of protection for Anya to make it out the side door. "Sophia's vest had to detonate first, causing an upward flow of heat and air pressure. The other bomb had to detonate immediately afterwards so that the upward flow from Sophia's bomb would create a momentary wall of protection from the forward momentum of the second blast." Chase bounced up and down. "It literally created a tunnel effect for less than a second, which was all the time she needed to get out the side door, unseen. It was absolutely brilliant."

"Where does this put us now?" Giovanni asked. "Are they still in Chicago?"

"According to Sal, the black van that left the hangar arrived at the Westin on Lower Wacker and Dearborne," Chase replied.

"That's right here," Angel said. "Why would they stay right here?"

"Because they have unfinished business," the Snake posed.

323

"Because they don't know we have an FBI connection that can track them?" Andrew suggested.

"Because they are taunting us to come after them," Giovanni pound his fist on the table. "So, we will walk into another death trap!" His face turned a darker shade of red and his eyes hardened. "I want them dead. Capisce?"

"Si," Tony, Andrew and the Snake answered in unison.

"Grandfather, you know you are ordering the death of Carl's grandson," Angel grimaced as the words left her lips. She knew Carl had been more than a trusted Compare to Giovanni. He was a life-long friend and the murdering of one's grandson was certain to put a damper on that friendship.

"Si." His face remained stern and no remorse shown on it. "I will handle Carl. We must rid ourselves of weakness and disloyalty regardless of what name it bears." Giovanni rose from his chair. "We meet again at 9:00am and I will hear your plan then." He left the meeting room.

CHAPTER 50

Chito, Trig, and the Knights leader, named Boomer arrived at the Towers right on time and were escorted to a small conference room on the third floor. They were patted down upon entering and were not happy about having their weapons confiscated. Boomer looked half black, half Mexican and had dreadlocks that hung almost to his waist. Chase, Big Mike and the Snake met them inside.

"This ain't how we roll," Boomer objected.

"Yeah, man, our guns are our tools of communication," Chito agreed.

"Well, you won't be communicating that way while the Boss Lady is present," Chase said.

Angel entered with two of Giovanni's bodyguards. She knew it was important to come in with a powerful presence and show no sign of weakness, which is exactly what she did. Dressed in black from head to toe, she took immediate command of the room. "Gentlemen," she spoke poignantly, "thank you for coming. We have a proposition for you."

"Proposition, my ass," Boomer spat. "You just want our help."

"Yeah, man, why should we help you?" Chito uttered.

The Snake, Chase and Big Mike instantly drew their guns, each taking aim at Chito and Boomer. "Because you have something to gain if you do and everything to lose if you don't," Angel explained, while sliding into a chair and folding her hands atop the table.

"What do we gain?" Trig asked.

"What Salvo promised you. One million dollars that you guys can split up any way you like," Angel answered.

"No deal, man, Salvo's a liar," Trig argued. "We ain't gonna see none of that dough."

"He is a liar, but I am not," Angel replied. She nodded her head toward Giovanni's bodyguard who handed her two large manila envelopes. She slid one envelope to Chito and the other to Boomer. "Go ahead and look inside. Each envelope contains five hundred thousand dollars in unmarked bills."

"Holy shit!" Boomer exclaimed, while Chito sat quiet with his eyes bulging from his head.

Angel nodded again and Giovanni's men took back the envelopes. "You do what I ask, you walk out of here with the money and our business dealings are done. You don't do what I ask and it gets complicated," Angel said.

"We don't want nothin' to do with no complications," Trig blurted. "I've seen it around here when it gets complicated and this brother ain't up for it."

"What do you want us to do?" Boomer asked.

Angel grinned at Chase. "Chase will go over all the details and answer any questions you have." Angel stood up and left the room.

"She's just using us," Chito blurted. "Sending us in like lambs to the slaughter."

"No," Big Mike replied. "Your job is easy. All you're doing is creating a distraction. We'll do the rest."

"What kind of a distraction?" Trig asked. "'Cuz if it's the kind where they're gonna be taking target practice at my black ass, I ain't interested."

"You don't have a choice, bro," Chase said.

"You got me into this mess, you can get me out," Trig said.

"I didn't get your crazy-ass into this," Chase rebutted. "You begged me for a chance to prove yourself, remember?"

"Well, you could've warned me. These people are crazy, man, really crazy." Trig's face contorted into a grimace that made Big Mike chuckle.

"There you go turning white again," Big Mike said.

"Shut up, man," Trig retorted. "I don't wanta die."

CHAPTER 51

The plan was simple, at least in theory. Sal from the FBI confirmed that Vladmir, Anya and Salvo were booked on a 5:00pm flight heading for Moscow. This meant they'd be leaving the hotel around 2:00pm and the drive to the airport would present Angel's men with the perfect opportunity for an ambush. Chase had printed schematics of the hotel lobby, the front entrance and the valet. Several police officers, wanting to avenge Officer Bernie's death, agreed to help Andrew under the guise of increasing security in the building due to gang related attacks nearby. The hotel manager was happy to have the increased security and each of the six officers moved into place with ear bud transmitters so they could communicate directly with Andrew. Two stood at the front entrance, two at the elevators and two more near the front desk.

When Vladmir telephoned the concierge to inform them to have their cars brought to the front, the plan was officially set in motion. The officers at the front desk notified Andrew of the phone call, wherein Andrew's men replaced the valet with one of their own and waited for the vehicles to appear. At that moment the Cobras and the Knights poured into the valet area, flashing their weapons, acting out of control and dangerous, which wasn't a stretch from reality. Their job was to cause a big scene, while the cops pretended to try and control them. All the while, the Venurini's took out the Brigatte Nero drivers, threw their bodies in the trunk of each car, and adorned their black jackets, hats and dark glasses.

Seemingly because of the disturbance, the officers quickly escorted Vlamir and Anya from the lobby to their black limousine, sliding a bug in Vladmir's jacket pocket. Salvo was then escorted to the second limousine and both limos pulled immediately from the curb, merging into traffic.

Angel, who was in the meeting room with Chase and Giovanni, neared the surveillance screen, where they watched the entire thing play out. "Now we wait," she said.

Angel slid her ear piece in so she could communicate with everyone in the field. "Andrew, thank your men for us and if they ever need a favor..." she began and he cut her off.

"I'll take care of it," he said.

"Big Mike, can you hear me?" Angel asked.

"Loud and clear, Boss Lady," he responded and Angel rolled her eyes and gawked at Chase. It was his fault people like Trig and Big Mike were calling her Boss Lady, a term Chase knew she didn't like.

"Tell Chito and Boomer to come to the Towers at 7:00pm for their money," she said to Big Mike and then turned to Chase. "Stop telling people to call me Boss Lady!"

"Roger that," Big Mike replied.

"If you want to be a part of this, you better high tail your ass to the chopper," Chase reminded Big Mike.

"On my way," he answered.

"Michelangela, how much money are you planning to pay these street thugs," Giovanni asked.

"Exactly the amount they were promised by Salvo," she said with a grin. "One million dollars."

"What!" Giovanni exclaimed, his face turning red and his eyes widening.

Angel grinned and Chase laughed out loud. "Sir, if you don't mind me saying, I think steam just flew out your ears. That was a crazy-ass expression," Chase chuckled.

"I do mind you saying it," Giovanni huffed, and then he turned his attention to Angel. "What is this nonsense about one million dollars?"

"Don't worry grandfather, it isn't our money," Angel assured him.

Chase gleefully chimed in. "Once I had Salvo's alias, I was able to hack into some of his accounts and transfer the money he promised the Cobras and Knights over so we could use it."

A slow grin overtook Giovanni's hardened face and he shook his finger at Chase. "You are a smart one," he said. "I am glad you are working for us and not against us."

"You and me both," Chase quipped. "I've seen the bad-ass stuff that happens to people who work against you."

Angel spoke into her headpiece. "Tony, are your men in position?"

"Locked and loaded, Babe," Tony responded.

"Snake, what about you?" Angel asked.

"Big Mike's here and we're taking the chopper up now and will be in position soon over Kennedy Expressway and Mannheim Road. As soon as I get a visual, I'll notify Tony," the Snake explained.

"Tony," Chase chimed in on his headpiece, "as soon as you hear from the Snake, maneuver the limos off course, heading south on Mannheim Road. This will get you off the main expressway and into a more open, less trafficked area."

"Got it, Ace," Tony responded.

Angel's heart was beating rapidly, as she stared at the surveillance screen, waiting for it all to go down and praying it would play out as easily in real life as it did on paper.

As soon as the Snake had visual, the limos appeared on the surveillance and Angel took a deep breath. Within seconds, Tony's team appeared in four black SUVs, two of which zoomed past the limousines and two which hung behind. The limousines slowed as Tony's vehicles came to a stop and turned sideways, blocking the road in front of them and behind them.

"You're going to lose the camera feed momentarily while I set the chopper down and drop Big Mike," the Snake piped in.

"Roger that," Chase answered.

Angel's ears perked, tuning into the bug that had been placed in Vladmir's pocket. Within moments she heard grumblings in the backseat of the car as Vladmir and Anya had obviously begun to wonder what was happening.

"What is going on?" Vladmir yelled in his thick Russian accent. "Why are we stopping?" Angel could hear pounding and assumed he must have been knocking on the divider glass, trying to get the driver's attention. He was obviously unaware that the driver was one of the Venturinis.

"I have a bad feeling," Anya said to Vladmir.

"She's beautiful AND smart," Chase quipped and Angel gave him an eye roll.

"Salvo is probably behind this," Vladmir seethed. "I knew he couldn't be trusted. He wants revenge for his father's death." Angel heard a scuffling sound.

"I guess this proves Miguel is dead," Chase said and Angel motioned for him to be quiet. She didn't want to miss a word that was said. Besides, she had already been pretty sure Miguel was dead.

331

"You shouldn't have killed his father!" Vladmir screamed at Anya.

"He killed MY father first!" She yelled back.

The next sound was the dull hum of the automatic windows being rolled down. "What are you doing?" Vladmir yelled to the driver, pounding on the Plexiglas partition. "You idiot! We are unprotected with the windows down. Roll them up!"

They could hear a repetitive clicking sound and assumed it was both Anya and Vladmir pushing the automatic window buttons, trying to put them up.

The Snake was back in the air and they could pick up surveillance from the cameras mounted on the outside of the helicopter. Angel watched as Big Mike approached the car from behind, staying low to the ground. With one swift motion, he rose and punched Vladmir in the face through the window. Vladmir was shocked just long enough for Big Mike to reach in, remove the gun from his grip, and drag him from the car.

Anya screamed, "No!" as the driver pulled her out the other side.

Big Mike pushed Vladmir to his knees. "Place your hands behind your head and lace your fingers," he instructed.

"Why? Are you going to arrest me?" Vladmir seethed.

"No," Big Mike said calmly. "I'm going to kill you."

"Maybe we can work something out," Vladmir said. "I am a man of great power and can offer you anything you want."

"No, you can't," Big Mike uttered.

"Yes, I can. I can give you money, weapons, power. Anything at all. Whatever you want," Vladmir begged.

"I want my father back," Big Mike said.

"Who is your father?"

"Aldo Maletta," Big Mike seethed and even from the far away surveillance, Angel swore she could see the color drain from Vladmir's face. "And then I want my mother back," Big Mike said and before Vladmir could respond, he added, "and then I want the Nelsons back." Vladmir never said another word. Big Mike fired a single shot through the back of his head and his body slumped forward in a heap.

Tony's voice came through the earpiece with an update. "Vladmir's dead and Anya is on her knees on the pavement, massacre style. Salvo should be sufficiently shaken at this point."

"We see her," Chase said. "Nothing like a woman on her knees."

"Roger that, Ace," Tony laughed.

Oh brother! Angel shook her head. "Can we focus here?" Angel's mind was whirling. She was experiencing a moral dilemma with killing Anya. After all, Anya had saved both the Snake and Sophia. True, she killed Miguel but that was an act of revenge because Salvo had killed her father. Having lost her own father, Angel could relate to the longing for retaliation.

"Are we taking out this trash or what?" Tony asked.

"Hold your position," Angel said and then turned to Giovanni. "We can take Salvo out now, or we can bring him in. What do you want to do?"

Giovanni's eyes shown the torment he must have felt in his soul. How was he going to tell his life-long friend what had happened? "Bring him in alive," Giovanni uttered. "Salvo will confess his sins to his grandfather."

"Bring Anya and Salvo in alive," Angel instructed Tony.

"Right on, Babe," Tony said.

"Anya?" Giovanni asked. "Why bring her in when you already know she is guilty of killing Miguel?"

"Because killing her isn't my call," Angel said. "Miguel is Carl's son. It will be his call."

Giovanni rose from the table. "You have done well Michelangela," he said. "Notify me the moment they arrive."

CHAPTER 52

Miguel's body, or what was left of it, was recovered from the bottom of the lake and taken to the morgue. As Angel had suspected, the whimpering sound she had heard coming from the guard shack at the end of pier four had been Miguel with his mouth taped, wearing a C4 vest with a trigger wire connected to the door handle.

Angel, Chase and Giovanni met with Carl privately in Giovanni's apartment and filled him in on all that had occurred. Tears dripped from Carl's eyes and it struck Angel as odd to see such a strong, powerful man break into sobs. It made her realize that no matter what position we hold in life, we can all be broken by love. Whether that love is familial or romantic, there is no escaping the heartache that comes from betrayal.

One of Giovanni's men knocked on the door. "Sir, Salvo and Anya have been escorted to the meeting room."

"Grazie," Giovanni answered and turned his attention back to Carl. "Would you like to speak with Salvo in private or do you want us to be there with you?"

Carl placed his hand on Giovanni's shoulder. "No, come, friend. I will require your support."

Angel didn't want to be in the room when Carl confronted Salvo. Even though Salvo had tried to kill her, she couldn't bear to see Giovanni have him killed in front of his own grandfather; assuming that was his plan. She didn't ask.

Salvatore entered the room first, on personal invitation by Giovanni as an elder to help discern what actions needed to be taken. Angel entered behind him, and then Carl and Giovanni. Salvo and Anya were each taped to a chair, with their arms behind their backs and duct tape covering their mouths. Giovanni ordered the tape to be removed from Salvo's mouth.

"What do you have to say for yourself?" Carl addressed Salvo.

"I have nothing to say to you, old man," Salvo spewed.

Angel watched as Salvatore's eyes grew dark and narrowed. "If I were you, I would take this opportunity to alter your tone and show respect to your father and the Capo di Tutti Capi," Salvatore advised.

"I don't respect them," Salvo said. "They have done nothing worthy of my respect."

Salvatore rose from his seat, pulled the gun from his jacket and laid it firmly on the table and then sat back down. Angel watched his every move, wondering if he was going to grab the gun at any moment and kill Salvo.

"Why have you done this?" Carl asked Salvo.

"We could have had everything!" Salvo spewed. "If you and my father would have stayed out of the way, I could have made millions and started our own family."

"We had our own family," Carl retorted, "and you destroyed it."

"No!" Salvo yelled. "You have chosen to be a lowly servant to him," Salvo pointed with his chin at Giovanni and spit toward him. "You were too much of a coward to become a Boss so you and my father lived in his shadows and lurked around with no one knowing your name, doing whatever

Giovanni ordered you to do and never getting credit for it."

"I did not need credit," Carl said. "My service and loyalty has been to my best friend and my own family, who has now betrayed me."

"You betrayed yourself old man," Salvo sneered.

Giovanni rose from his seat, removed his gun from his jacket pocket and placed it firmly on the table, exactly as Salvatore had done. Angel now realized this was a sign. It was an unspoken gesture, stating that they believed he should be killed but out of respect for Carl they weren't going to be the one to do it.

"No!" Carl raised his voice. "You have betrayed yourself."

"Too much of a coward to kill me?" Salvo taunted and Angel didn't need to guess what was coming next. In one fluid motion, Carl withdrew a .45 from a holster beneath his jacket and shot Anya straight through the forehead. "That's for killing my son," he said to Anya, as if she could still hear him.

Salvo didn't flinch. "Now, are we even, old man?" He seethed.

"No," Carl said with a slight quiver of emotion in his voice, and then raised his gun and shot Salvo between the eyes. "Now, we are even."

Angel could hear her heart pounding in her ears and she tried not to let the shock show on her face. Nobody said a word for a good few seconds. Then Carl holstered his gun and looked at Giovanni. "I am sorry for the mess on your floor."

Giovanni placed his hand on Carl's shoulder and escorted him toward the door. "Tile cleans up easily. I will have my men take care of it."

CHAPTER 53

Chito and Boomer left with their money and Angel made her way upstairs and out onto the balcony. It had been an emotional few days and her mind needed time to process everything that had happened. The good news was aside from Vincent Carlachi, Angel felt all the connections to the Russian Bratva and the Brigatte Nero had been exposed and eliminated. She was anxious to get back to life as normal, or as normal as it could ever be for a Mafia Boss.

"You really sent them away with one million dollars," Giovanni said, joining her outside.

"I gave them what they were promised." Angel shrugged. "And I think it will instill a certain loyalty toward us in their minds and ensure that I will have assistance should I ever need a favor from them."

"You really do have your father's smarts," Giovanni smiled. "My favorite part is that it wasn't our money."

"I'd have never given them a million dollars of our money," Angel acknowledged. "But Salvo deserved to lose it."

"Si," Giovanni nodded and Angel beheld a sense of sadness rush over him.

"How is Carl?" She asked.

"He is resting," Giovanni answered. "The doctor has given him a sedative. It will take time for him to come to terms with all he has lost. Miguel and Salvo were his only family. He is alone now."

"He has you and our family," Angel said.

"Si, that he does." Giovanni took a deep breath and exhaled slowly. "You have handled yourself well," he told her. "You orchestrated a trap for your enemies and followed through successfully. Your father would be proud."

"Actually, I think he'd be more proud if I could create peace," Angel uttered.

"Si," Giovanni acknowledged. "But you have already created peaceful relations between three of the five families, which is more success than your father had." Giovanni shook his head. "Never did I think I would live to see the day that the Maratinzanos, Andriachinis and Venturinis would be working together, but you have made it so."

Angel smiled. "You mean I've complicated things," she teased.

"Oh, my, yes!" Giovanni let out a chuckle. "How you have complicated things."

Angel leaned her elbows on the retaining wall and looked out over the city. "Sometimes change can be good," she said.

"Sometimes tradition is better," he rebutted.

"Round pegs don't fit in square holes," Angel remarked.

"But a square peg can be sanded down to fit nicely into a round hole," Giovanni quipped and gave her a wink.

Angel exhaled loudly. "Grandfather, about the spreadsheet..."

"Forget the spreadsheet," he interrupted. "For now."

Angel felt the smile spread all the way across her face. The pressure was off. She didn't have to marry someone she didn't love. "Grazie," she said and kissed him on the forehead.

"But, we will revisit the idea of an Under Boss and Compare for you in the next few months," he added.

"I'm fine with that," Angel agreed.

"Now, your men are waiting inside to be Made. If you don't come in soon I fear Chase will bounce right onto the ceiling with anticipation," he said and Angel laughed out loud. She could actually imagine it in her mind. "Besides, we need to rescue poor Salvatore from Olga's nonsense." Giovanni rolled his eyes. "Heaven help us."

"Is my mother there?"

"Si. She and Don Venturini are sitting on the sofa, looking as if they would like to be married but I cannot allow it," Giovanni said sharply. "A Venturini cannot marry a Maratinzano. The families cannot inter-wed. It is not customary. It is not tolerated!" His voice rose.

"She's a Buscetta," Angel said, looping her arm in his. "And a Buscetta can marry anyone she wants."

Giovanni made the sign of the cross over his body. "Può il dio aiutarlo," he mumbled.

"May God help us indeed," Angel translated and saw a gleam of pride in Giovanni's eye.

ABOUT THE AUTHOR

S.R.Claridge, nominated for the 2010 Molly Award, 2013 Pushcart Prize and awarded the 2011 Rocky Mountain Fiction Writers Pen Award, writes full-time and lives in Colorado. She loves autumn, moonlight and Grey Goose martinis with bleu cheese or jalapeno stuffed olives. She believes Friday nights are for indulging in Mexican food and margaritas and Sunday mornings warrant an extra-spicy Bloody Mary. Growing up in St. Louis, Missouri and earning her BA in Psychology from the University of Missouri, Columbia, S.R.Claridge is a mixture of mid-western family values and western wild nights. She loves Jesus, believes in the power of prayer, in the freedom of forgiveness and that life is a gift that should be enjoyed to the fullest. With a background in theatre, S.R.Claridge creates characters with dramatic flair and is known for her intense plot twists and engaging humor. S.R.Claridge would rather walk dangerously where there's a view than sit in idle safety and let life pass her by. Her spirited outlook comes shining through in her novels, as she takes readers to the edge of their seats with bone-chilling suspense.

AUTHOR ACCLAIM

"The Just Call Me Angel series is suspense at its best."
- RipeReviews

"A unique series from a one-of-a-kind author."
- APEX Reviews

"Riveting!"
- TrueBlueEbookReview

"One thrilling moment after another!"
- CanadaReviews

"A best-seller candidate indeed."
- BookWatchMagazine

BOOKS BY S.R.CLARIDGE

Tetterbaum's Truth *(book 1 in the Just Call Me Angel series)*
Traitors Among Us *(book 2 in the Just Call Me Angel series)*
Russian Uprising *(book 3 in the Just Call Me Angel series)*
Death Trap *(book 4 in the Just Call Me Angel series)*
Loose Ends (*book 5 in the Just Call Me Angel series)*
Divine Intervention *(book 6 in the Just Call Me Angel series)*
Petals of Blood *(short story; Pushcart Prize Nomination 2013)*
House of Lies (*Political cult suspense)*
No Easy Way *(debut novel; nominated for The Molly Award from the HODRW 2010)*
The Candy Shop *(Suspense Thriller)*

S.R.Claridge has also ghostwritten over ten novels.